PRAISE FOR THE WINNOWING DRAW

"With one of the most assured voices I've read in recent times, Tichy brings us to the old west - and well past the edge of hell - in *The Winnowing Draw*. An outstanding piece of literary work, echoing McCarthy, Zane Grey, and prime King, it's a harrowing, pitch-perfect amalgam of western and horror."

___ KEITH ROSSON, AUTHOR OF *FEVER HOUSE* AND *FOLK SONGS FOR TRAUMA SURGEONS*

"*The Winnowing Draw* invokes that queasy unsettling sensation I first felt after coming across the Tombstone Thunderbird vintage hoax photograph in a book of paranormal mysteries as a kid. While that photo hinted at a strange West, Tichy's novel promises a similarly occult frontier, though one plagued by violent horrors and malefic forces in a region where inescapable brutality and savagery mingle. His prose is as polished as a sand-scoured skillet. Sentences snagged between my teeth like dried meat. The dialogue is witty and robust, the characters fully realized beings. While the demythologization of the American West has been written about extensively, Tichy manages to infuse fresh bright blood into those dark withered arteries. *The Winnowing Draw* is a bleak trek across an unforgiving planet shadowed by a cosmic pall, and those readers willing to traverse its Manifest Destiny infected geography are in for a nightmarish journey."

___ CHRISTOPHER SLATSKY, AUTHOR OF *THE IMMEASURABLE CORPSE OF NATURE AND ALECTRYOMANCER AND OTHER WEIRD TALES*

"*The Winnowing Draw* is a remarkable entry into the Weird Western genre by a remarkable voice in dark literature. An elegiac and masterfully written exploration into the heart of righteous depravity and squalid hope, The Winnowing Draw is populated with vibrantly flawed and nuanced characters, sharply created in Tichy's contemplative and rich prose. *The Winnowing Draw* reads like a bloodsoaked travelogue of the cosmic horrors created by American exceptionalism."

____ PAULA ASHE, AUTHOR OF *WE ARE HERE TO HURT EACH OTHER*

"With *The Winnowing Draw*, Michael Tichy has scared Zane Grey's skeleton from the grave and made it attack Larry McMurtry's skeleton. This novel is that skeleton abomination atop the arcane foundation that Cormac McCarthy has built for us all. It upends and simultaneously carries on a tradition. It is a Western both moving, brutal, and poetic. There is a behanding scene that I cannot unsee in my mind's eye. An organizing image of the novel that refuses to release you. If you're a horror fan, read it. If you're a Western fan, this will create new hungers you didn't know you possessed!"

____ KYLE WINKLER, AUTHOR OF *GRASSHANDS AND THE NOTHING*

THAT IS

"*The Winnowing Draw* is Lovecraft by way of McCarthy. A story of regret and mistakes told in blood, dust and the unknown that casts shadows on the hearts of settlers."

____ O F CIERI, AUTHOR OF *LOCKDOWN LAUREATE* AND *BACKMASK*

THE WINNOWING DRAW

MICHAEL TICHY

Castaigne

publishing

CONTENTS

Eagle of the Rockies, bird of men that are masters,
Lifting the rabbit-blood of the myriads up into something splendid,
Leaving a few bones;
Opening great wings in the face of the sheep-faced ewe
Who is losing her lamb,
Drinking a little blood, and loosing another royalty unto the world.

Is that you, American Eagle?
-D. H. Lawrence

PART I

A PLAN IS JUST A FUTURE PAYABLE ON RECEIPT

1

ATROCITY IS A CONVERSATION WITH GOD

Autie watched the morning cool make a specter of his breath. He never missed the aching cold of Michigan winter, but these early mornings on the plain put a dull ache in his bones that recalled them. He remembered traipsing through knee high snow, sometimes even higher, so the lower limbs of the catalpa were lost in it. The ice encrusted hinges of the outhouse would fight him, and the snowpack leave him grateful he was skin and bones, so he only had to force the door a little to admit him. Then, exhausted at the battle to get there, he would sit and imagine his soul might leave his body before yesterday's supper exited his bowels. His breath was icicles then, and he thought that must be what the spirit looked like when it evacuated, and that hell must be cold -not hot- because cold hurt so much more.

He smiled to think of it now, of the innocence. His present self, having seen so many souls evacuate, knew there weren't nothing to it. No trumpets or vapors. A long rattling breath and the smell of shit. And sometimes not even that.

How long had it been now? Five years? No. Six years on the

raw edge of America. Her growth was a violent thing, the calcified thickening of bone that has been fractured, set, fractured, and set again. By any measure it must be a great success. These boys in front of him, the only measure that mattered.

The raiders were beanpole thin. Cheeks hollowed in a perpetual question mark of when or what they might eat next. The last year or so, it was all old men and young boys they skirmished, and long stretches of no action at all. It set Autie's mind to the next frontier, and his muscles ached with cramps, longing for the only thing that every really nourished them. He was born for war. A lot of men lost their religion in combat, couldn't reconcile what they saw with the words in the good book; for him, though, it was the war that resolved any doubt.

Autie steadied his horse, pushed his hat back on his head, and wiped his brow with the back of his hand. Yesterday's sweat and the condensation of the early morning had formed a miasma with the accumulated dust. The dawn was just then beginning to break over the far hills and cast everything in an eerie reddish glow, as though the gates of hell themselves were opening to him, and he only too ready to meet whatever grim boatman might guide him into that deeper darkness. His years of service had taught him there was no nadir to the desperation of man. Still, he longed for it, searched for it hungrily. A destination, the rocky bottom of the well where one might again find steady footing.

He looked to his men, them most loyal to him. Sullivan and Levi had been with him almost since the beginning, and having executed his most fevered and grotesque commands against the white men of the south, their loyalty was unquestionable. What's more, they had like him developed a taste for the work, so that they sometimes surprised him with their own deprivations against the men they captured.

These boys before him, for boys they were, maybe 14 or 15

years old; the leader of their band was at most 18. Stragglers. A few young bucks that peeled themselves from a dwindling herd when they decided they would rather take their chances against the Yankees than go willing into imprisonment.

There were a half dozen of them in all, standing quiet and nearly naked. Their skin a patina of dirt from the graves they had just dug, and the blood that dried and caked to their bodies. All of them were short an ear, and a few yet dripped blood from the stumps where phalanges had been sloppily removed. Souvenirs of an interrogation that yielded nothing of note, because the boys knew nothing of note. No, that wasn't entirely fair, was it? For it was noteworthy that none but the smallest among them had offered up so much as a whimper during the brute dismemberment, and for that, Autie found himself respecting them. He might have sent them east, where they would be picked apart and ground down slowly to nothing. Instead, he would deliver them himself unto the merciful arms of the Divine.

Their eyes were matte pools of resignation, and Autie thought perhaps he had misjudged them after all. It was not strength that quieted them through their torment, only surrender. He hated that look, truly there was nothing he hated more. Knew if it were him, he would burn with rage to the last. His world was a binary of predator and prey, and resignation was the domain of cattle, of victims.

Autie drew his saddle pistol and shot the oldest, the leader, in the head. A puff of blood hung in the air a long moment, a misty cloud that seemed to disperse only after the boy collapsed and lay still. Autie's horse shifted slightly. He sometimes wondered if she were proper gunbroke, or just deaf.

Levi and Sullivan drew their weapons and began shooting the others. They took their time working down the line. The younger boys only stood up taller when their leader was dispatched, and only flinched involuntarily at shots intended to be non-lethal, or not immediately so. Two were still squirming snakelike on the ground, gutshot, when the men finally turned their attention to the last. The smallest, he stared hard at Autie, like some animus yet moved in him and had been wakened by the crack of the pistol shots ripping through the quiet of dawn, ripping through his companions.

He dropped low to a crouch, and Autie half-expected him to turn on a heel and race away. Instead, he sprang toward the troop. There one moment and gone the next, he tucked into a forward roll that brought him under Autie's horse and came up between her hind legs. The men were so shocked that he was already ten yards away when they turned toward him, twenty yards when they adjusted their aim. Autie backed his horse, so she obstructed their view.

"Let that one go. If you shoot down all the fawns, in a few years there's naught left to hunt." He fired his pistol into the air, ran it dry, laughing and then howling his best coyote song. The others followed suit, and Autie smiled as the boy disappeared into the scrub.

The men began to work at the bodies, shifting, pulling them into the holes they had dug.

Autie left them to it, turned his horse and set back to the camp at a trot. He breathed deeply, feeling perfectly at home in the moment, felt an ease in his muscles. The air was sweet with moisture and the sharp taste of burnt powder.

Below him, currents of heat coiled and rippled in the soil, and deeper. He had felt it during the war, and it was stronger the further west he moved. This restlessness of the earth, he never spoke of. It was his, not a thing to be shared. If the men felt it, certainly one would have said something by now. No, it was the call of destiny. His fate to conquer, to pacify. Sometimes it was so strong - as that morning - that the steady thrum of it left him unsteady on his feet. But blood drunk were often little different from whiskey drunk.

This morning, he was grateful for the horse and her steady gait. He would tread carefully from her to his tent. By the time he rose later, it would have faded once again. The land had a thirst, and blood made her shiver and purr. He never tired of feeding her.

2

THE CRIME

I didn't push him. He slipped. I didn't mean to push him. I didn't push him. He slipped. I didn't mean to push him.

His guilt or innocence was a mantra. An endlessly flipping coin, two truths juggled in his mind like hot coals. They must remain airborne; neither seemed to fit nor absolve him. It was a prayer to be mumbled, to utter it aloud was too final. Instead, it turned and turned and turned in him, an equivocation he could tell himself until it was true.

At twelve, Cecil had already learned that truth was like the phantom silk of spiderwebs, transient and insubstantial. It itched at you that it was there, right on your skin, while remaining impossible to fully grasp.

He and Louis had been friends for years, an odd pairing given their disparity of social classes. Louis was monied, was being primed for a life of untold promise. Cecil meanwhile knew that his time in school had grown very short; his parents never stopped reminding him of it. Come summer, he would be leaving it all behind, to trade childish things for whatever gainful employment a boy of his age might secure.

It was a ticking clock beating in the marrow of him, the

knowledge made his time with Louis bittersweet, certain he was that their paths would diverge in the coming months. The kind of absolute ending that is inconceivable in youth. Things had been changing between them in other ways too. Over the last year, their playful wrestling had started to feel like something else, the arrhythmic crackling and popping of new fire that he was sure they both sensed, and was yet too tentative, too tender to speak aloud. Cecil felt an increasing urgency to their grappling and found his body wanting ever more of it.

That day, standing on the third floor of their secret place, a neighborhood building under construction, the grit between his feet and the girder crunching softly, Louis had told him of his parents' plans. He was no longer to socialize with his inferiors. It was unbecoming of the man they were shaping him into. His friend's voice, but not his words. Not his tone. The delivery was cold and impassive, could be easily confused with relief. It cut a hole in the center of Cecil, who felt his legs go numb and shaking, and his face grow so hot he imagined it might glow like the rivets pounded into the steel all around him. Gone cold and hardened now, dead.

Louis said he had protested. His eyes were downcast and tearing up. The building they stood in, nearly equidistant between their homes, then felt to Cecil as some guard tower meant to prevent the meeting of the two. He wanted nothing more than to be rid of it. He kicked at a support beam, and a jolt of pain echoed up his foot and leg. Looking up, the dark sky framing Louis' head was as merciless as anything he had ever seen, as bereft of hope as every possible future.

Louis sniffled, wiped at his nose. "It's not like I wanted this to happen." He looked at Cecil, a smile playing at the corners of his mouth. "They're sending me away to a boarding school out east." He looked down, again, sniffed, "I guess it's time to grow up." And there was that tone again. An icy edge returning to his voice. Of resignation and something else. The secret language of the haves, and Louis was learning it, leaning into the magic of it, its detachment.

Cecil had never felt inferior to Louis until that moment. Not really. He took hold of his friend's hand, in an effort to comfort him, to comfort himself. Then Louis broke free, yanked his hand away. His eyes were blue flame, the tears were gone.

"Don't touch me. It's your fault, all of it. The way you look at me. They want me away from you. I never liked you anyway. I guess it was just fun letting you follow me around. You think I want to spend the rest of my life with a penniless bore?" The tears streaked the fading sun on his cheeks. Even now he was beautiful, as the wet glistening was divorced from the eyes that birthed it.

Cecil grabbed his friend's collar, shook him. Loss and rage and all the things he never dared say – it all twisted and churned in him. His mind went to that secret place, the place outside of him where pain was remote and its edge dulled. Then it happened. Did he push him or did Louis slip from his grasp? He couldn't be sure in that moment or in the thousand moments that might follow. Like so many of their touches, its meaning lost in the fog of guilt, uncertainty. Everything or nothing. Which made him more guilty?

Cecil watched the shocked look come over Louis as his face grew smaller and smaller in descent. A puff of dust when his body broke upon the ground. Almost no sound of impact reached Cecil, just a shockwave that nearly crumpled him. Distant, his delicate head turned to the side, a black stain expectorated on the concrete like his last words were born and then died right there. Cecil stared a moment until the weight of it settled on him like a headstone. He was shut off into another world now. If only. But then a woman screamed, and the illusion was broken. A man crouched on the ground and touched his friend, turned his head and pointed. Cecil ran.

And finally, a truth that was anything but tenuous, a truth that was as solid as the concrete slab that held his friend's broken body: he would have to keep running. Run or die.

His feet knew every turn to get him home, every dark alley and bustling street to conceal his path, knew them as a child knows the dents and scratches of a well-loved toy. Each of them now took on a sinister shade. He expected every stranger to point a finger and cry out, expected at every blind turn to run face to face into a policeman. His heart jack-hammered in his chest, harder and harder, until he thought he couldn't take another breath, until finally, with burning lungs and feet pounded to ground glass, he slid into the back door of his tenement.

Cecil paused when he reached the door to the apartment. The hallway was nearly dark, with dust dancing softly in the single beam of light admitted through the boarded window opposite him. He leaned on rubbery legs and drew deep breaths as quietly and as slowly as he could manage. Slightly less exposed now that he was in the building, he didn't want to waste any time. Still, he couldn't afford to let his racing heart hurry him through what was next.

The creaking floorboards and the squeal of rusted hinges. These he knew like the scars on his skin. The two were of a piece – the means and the price of waking his Pa when he was sleeping off a drunk. Ma would still be at work, serving until the family she attended to retired of the evening. Pa worked nights and would be dozing.

Having recovered the better part of his wind, he gently nudged the door, enough to accommodate his deliberate slithering. Theirs was a basement apartment, and a faint scent of mildew clung to the air, itched his nostrils, and tickled his lungs so he had to pause to suppress a cough. He felt sure he wouldn't miss that smell, or the thick sputum he hacked up here on too many mornings. Or the relentless cold of winter and stifling heat of summer. Already his mind was running from the present, imagining what future might await him in the rugged, open places of his fantasies.

Pa lay on his back on the far side of the room, emitting a droning, regular snore. Cecil slowly made his way toward his own corner of the room and began filling a haversack with what scant possessions he thought might be of use – socks, an extra shirt, a water skin. He hoped that last night had been a good one at the card table, that his father might finally be good for something other than foul words and hard hands.

The old man continued his snoring. At this distance, his breath was a factory smokestack, pushing putrid rot and alcohol stink above even the scent of moldering floorboards. He wouldn't miss that smokestack either, or the engine that belched its wretchedness through it.

He tiptoed to the stove and the washbasin. A misstep and the wood beneath his foot squealed like a dying pig, the sound greatly magnified by his apprehension. Pa sputtered, turned on his side toward Cecil, who froze and held his breath until he feared he might pass out. Another snore, and Pa rolled back the other way. Cecil timed his breath to his father's, a bellows that fed a growing fire in his guts.

Reaching behind the coffee tin and the stew pot, on the shelf above the washbasin, he retrieved a tin box he wasn't supposed to know was there. Then he gathered his newer boots and wool coat and eased his way back out the door.

He was running out of time. Ma would be back any minute. If she caught him, that would be the end of it. Neither of the two would protect him, or let him go for that matter. He had never felt much more than a nuisance to them, an obligation. His mind was on Louis' parents too. People like that, they'd be calling on the police by now. If there was a reward, which there was certain ultimately to be, his own Ma and Pa would trip over one another to claim it.

Cecil eased the door close. He didn't dare press it home to latch it. Backing slowly away, he took three long and light steps before going into a full run again. He didn't stop until he had quit the building and joined the shadows of the alley one street over. He leaned heavy against cold brick and the shade sucked the warmth from him. Would he ever feel warm again?

He fell into a squat and snapped open the lid of the tin box. An assortment of bills and coins greeted him. Not as much as he had hoped, he counted forty-three dollars and change. His father's take from the previous night, his stake for the coming one. Folding the bills carefully, he put three dollars and the loose change in his pocket and retired the balance to the depths of his spare boots.

Pa's old pepper box revolver sat heavy in the box, loose ammunition tumbling around as he withdrew it. It was a six-barrel .32 caliber, the rifled barrels sawn down to next to nothing. This was the man's old hold out piece. Protection for if a game got hairy or someone tried to roll him on the way home. He had upgraded to a single action army a few months back, or this would have been beneath his pillow when Cecil had ransacked the room. There was a twinge of guilt that he was taking a piece of his father's security. The gun and the money would be felt, could put his parents in a bad way. Yet there was no denying he needed it more, would need it more.

Cecil picked a piece of newspaper off the alley floor, wrapped the loose bullets – sixteen in all – and placed them at the bottom of his haversack. The pistol went into the righthand pocket of his wool coat and was lost in the fullness of it. He shoved the empty tin box away and it skittered into the wall.

He slipped on the coat, swapped his shoes for the boots, and having nowhere to pack them, left the shoes to the alley where he hoped they might be of use to someone. He hugged the alley wall, creeping. The shadows stretching in the dusk were a small comfort. From now on he must forever be mindful of light and its thousand prying eyes.

He knew the terrain well, and plotted the most discreet course to the train station. He would make his way south and then west. First Missouri, and then to Kansas, where the Santa Fe and Oregon trails met. Let them try and follow him that far if they could. He would show them how clever he was.

From there, he would disappear into the frontier. The excitement he felt was at odds with his grief and his fear, an electric jolt that didn't ease the hurt, but offered a small hope of comfort. The exploits of Buffalo Bill and of the Texas Rangers, that he had read, had studied, over and over again, played in his head. A welcome distraction.

⸻

The ticketmaster was a pinch faced sort of man, all folds and creases. Thin lips and black marbles for eyes. He averted his gaze lest the man see through him, tightened his fists at his sides and released. Open and closed, open and closed, hoping to slow the pounding of his heart. But the man barely said a word to him as he made change and gave Cecil his ticket. He forced himself to a slow walk from the counter, and all his remaining fear was spent on sitting down in the train. The hard, wooden bench set an ache in his bones that was yet no match for their weariness and he fell into a restless sleep before departing the station.

He was jolted awake at the next stop, limbs akimbo and gasping for air, as he woke with a faint recollection of falling, and the impact. Then it was quickly lost. The sky was clear, and it seemed, staring into that starry night, that a million eyes stared back at him, their light penetrating, seeing what he sought to keep hid. Turning away, to the interior, the car was less than half filled.

There were no children, none younger than he. All of them who rode, men and women, sat threadbare and hollow. They were all hungry for something, but possessed of the knowledge that it would always pull away lest they grasp it. And like the train, forever moving forward and forever trapped on its course, their destination ordained as that of every soul since time's beginning.

He sat, wanting nothing more than a return to sleep, to just shut out the world for a moment, but the rest of the night, it wouldn't come. The train rattled as if to shake him loose, a feral beast, and he a pest it wanted rid of. He, specifically, who could no longer feel fully part of the world of men, having broken the most basic covenant it required. Or perhaps the world, in its violence, only now welcomed him into its bosom. There was no comfort in that thought.

By daylight, the landscape appeared desolate, while the train itself grew livelier, and all the more threatening for it. Cecil told himself it was too soon, but his mind wandered to wanted posters and gallows, and what a prize he might be to one of these strangers.

When he finally slept again, he dreamt again of falling, and of other worse fates. Nearly flinging himself from his seat, shuddering awake at the next stop, a phantom itch lingered on his neck. He poked and scratched at it before fully believing he wouldn't find a rope burn there.

He went on like that, sleeping restlessly, waking at each stop and often between stops. And there were so many stops. Each time he woke with a mix of resentment and gratitude. He was haunted by the glimpses he retained of his dreams, and he fought the heaviness that quickly returned to his eyelids.

3

THE GENTLEMAN

Charlie let the men scream until they run out of the air for it from pain and blood loss and both had passed out within a few minutes of the other. They had fallen forward, so their heads were lying near one another on the rock he had bound them to. Stark white and muscles gone to jelly, ankles still tied and spread eagled around the base of the stone, their arms bloodslick and loose, lacking hands to keep the rope from slipping.

They didn't seem to believe it, until the last, that he was really doing what he said he would. This wasn't his first, and it'd ceased to impress him what few reactions men had when faced with real peril -the kind that couldn't be turned from.

These two had stolen from a big banker out of New York. He and his wife had been on holiday. The men hadn't set out with them as the target. They were just a pair of rough dudes who saw a chance for some easy money. It happened on the trains all the time. A couple few guys sneak aboard, or get on at some small depot or other, clean out a car or two of what possessions the passengers bore on them, and then jumped off where their partners might wait for them with horses.

All they had taken was a watch, a pearl necklace, and a little loose cash. The necklace was an heirloom, passed down to women in the family for about 200 years already, or so the man had told Charlie. They always wanted to explain, these rich folk who hired him, needed to justify the cruelty they were paying him for.

The Forresters were livid when they reached out to him. The man especially. He wanted the pearls back, and the watch, and he wanted the men that took them punished. And if the items couldn't be found - and they couldn't - he wanted Charlie to extract something Biblical in its gravity. What that meant was left to his imagination. Them people never liked to exactly say, but much experience had taught that they were the kind of folk who liked to think they were getting their money's worth.

They started screaming long before the first chop. Charlie had hacked the wrists one at a time with his heavy Bowie, and the stag handle was dripping with blood when he was done. He had wiped the blade and returned it to its sheath, and it was like the knife didn't want him to let go of him, the way the gore stuck it tacky to his grip.

He had taken both of one man's hands first, so the other might look on helplessly and be more afraid when he got to him. He'd lost count of the men he'd done. The fear and the resignation of a broken animal were the only things that gave him a little thrill, so whenever possible, he took his time with this part. Location was everything, the only good thing about the frontier was all the space.

Charlie set a heavy skillet over the glowing ashes of the fire 'til it was too hot to touch bare handed. Using a thick glove he'd gotten off a blacksmith a ways back - just for this purpose - to hold the glowing metal and cauterize the bleeding stumps. The smell of blood was quickly overtaken by that of burning flesh. Of cooking meat, and he thought about the steak he would eat later, when all this was done.

When the screams had quieted, he sat back on the other side

of the dying fire. He retrieved a rag and some shine and a small brush from his saddlebag. Cleaning his knife first, he then turned to his shirtsleeves. Finally, his hands and his fingernails. Each of these he picked at first with the tip of his pen knife and then attacked with the brush, removed as much of the filth as he could manage. The shirt was going to need a professional to look after it, but he had lightened the worst of the stains.

The two were finally rousing as he strolled past them to his horse, returning his kit. They were still deathly pale, and their eyes were hardly slits, hair matted with sweat from the feverish pain.

"What you gon' do with us now?" The one on the left -the smaller one- spoke.

"Why, let you go of course. Your days of stealin' are done unless you're part lizard and can grow you some new hands." He stepped closer, stood over them.

The larger one tried to shrink away from him, but was still bound to the rock, so sort of folded in on himself.

"What, you don't believe me? The work I been paid for is done and I don't work for free."

"What are we supposed to do? You gonna leave us a horse or something. Town is near ten miles from here and a lot of it, mountain. Terrain we can't handle like this." He held up his stump such as the rope would let him. Blood still oozed thick and dark from the blackened appendage, but only a little.

"You're lucky I don't take your clothes, you men of will. Wasn't that what you told me when you thought I might join your little gang," He laughed. "You got enough will, I suppose it'll carry you home."

"Now, I'm going to cut loose your legs. With your hands missing, you'll have no problem wriggling your arms free. Just don't do it until you're sure I'm well gone. I won't kill you, but it wouldn't bother me none to put a bullet in you somewhere."

"You're a fucking monster," the bigger one had a soft voice for a man his size, ponderous.

"I'm a businessman," Charlie snapped. "You might have heard they call me the Gentleman, so don't make me get ungentlemanly with you."

Charlie sliced through their bindings with his smaller fighting blade, a little dagger he promptly returned to a sheath that ran horizontal on his belt. He stared at the two a few moments, then walked calmly to his big sorrel horse, mounted her and moved away at an easy trot. He listened closely. The men were talking but no sound of them wresting themselves free. He set his hat low. The sun was climbing slowly in the sky and his eyes had always been sensitive, a light blue. Good for night vision but terrible in the brightness of the plains.

As he made his way back to the main trail, he could feel it. He could always feel it out here. Something drawing him, beckoning him further west. He was contrarian by nature and so the feeling got under his skin. It always felt easier moving west and always more so under the shadow of violence. Like whatever it was that sought to compel him fed on the screams and the dread. He would take the first train east he laid eyes on. He would sleep in a hotel and he wouldn't sleep alone. Damn the bloodthirsty ground and whatever moved there. He was a businessman.

4

THE DRAW

It hadn't a name, came from a time before names. It had always been, could see its origins in the quivering miasma of the newborn universe. Nothing but heat. Energy, the divine will of limitless expansion. Was it not also the void expanded into? Its strength was a coiled thing, ever unraveling, penetrating. And yet somehow it was here, reduced to shadow and impulse.

Under the earth, a vermiculture unto itself, endlessly listening, seeing. The reshaping of the land, the beasts, seeing into the hidden places, the dark. The two-legged ones were most reachable, it found the voids in them, pale reflections of itself, easily bent. Their virtue was just a thin epidermis, their corruption deeper than bone.

All the stories, the shallow reasoning that drove them. Was it also like this? Perhaps it had never been among the stars but needed that divinity to be complete. Perhaps it had always been prisoner to the land and the water. It was a thousand stories coiling endlessly, and at the center a void. The absolute dark that invited the ambitions of the corrupt. And they were all of them corrupt and endlessly corruptible. And it was the land itself, the sweeping expanse of it, the ocean of sky that intoxicated, drunk up the eyes of all who beheld it.

A swirling, spiraling current that always moved west, drawing them deeper into its influence. It promised anonymity, found in each their secret shame and promised it might be virtue in this strange place. Momentum a self-perpetuating compulsion.

It had no need of sustenance, it had gone on, would go on eternally as far as it regarded time. Corruption was delicacy, the sweet nectar that ran red from every bludgeoned skull, every hole they put in one another. The little voids that glorified it, the suffering that made it swell and bloom, so it poured from the ground and up, up, up in proportion to what poured from them.

The ones that swarmed from the east, ever in greater numbers, may they never cease. Someday it might escape the pit completely, expand and reclaim the stars, the ultimate void.

5

THE COMMAND

The orders were from Sheridan himself, and if he was to be believed, from the president's mouth to his ear. He had come personally to Fort Lyon to deliver them, and his retinue would be a thing of secret mirth for Autie to reflect on for years to come.

It were no secret the man hated the west, hated frontier living. The kind of man who was habituated to soft couches and rich food and drink and traveled with an entire team dedicated to replicating this to the extent the trail would allow it. His buggy reminded Autie of a fine whorehouse he had once spent near a week in. Perfumed and soft, and outfitted with heavy velvet drapes that admitted nearly no light when drawn close.

A whole separate wagon followed, and functioned as a rolling kitchen. It kept the General in warm food and drink at all hours. Autie had never seen anything quite like it. Still, the man had been a merciless beast during the war, and Autie kept his humor to himself. Took coffee with the man in his rolling whorehouse and greeted him with the respect befitting his rank and accomplishment.

Autie didn't aspire to ever reach the level of smoky rooms

where men pulled the levers of war. Men who grew fat and soft while others did the bleeding. His were different goals. At West Point, he had read Aurelius, and the simplicity of stoicism found an easy home in him.

In war, he found in the struggle for life and death, the most pure expression of his philosophy. He'd distinguished himself with his ferocity and willingness to lead from the front. After the southern problem had been mostly dispensed with, they had given him a command on the frontier. He was aware of how the papers depicted him, that he was maybe even more popular than the president. The subject of cheap paperback novels read by children. It was the way of the world to make legends of extraordinary men, and this his only vanity as he saw it. But he knew the charm in such tales was in their distance from reality.

If the public knew the real mechanics of what they were doing out here, their approval and their awe would quickly turn sour. He liked to keep a biographer and a reporter or two around, but not too close to the action - tightly leashed enough that they saw what they were meant to see, heard what they were meant to hear.

"Armstrong. So good to see you."

"Sir," and he took the man's hand firmly and met his eyes. "You can call me Autie, just don't let the enlisted hear it," and he winked.

Sheridan had soft hands, held Autie's right in both of his like wrapping him in pillows. It sickened him, and he struggled to reconcile the man before him to the stories of his ferocity. How was this the man who razed Charleston? Who put daughters of the south to the blade and the boot. Executed women and children for little more than sharing a roof or a table with the enemy. Perhaps for him it was a trifle, a means to an end such as this.

Autie's greatest hope was that there would always be another frontier, another campaign for men like Sheridan to send him on, where the blood and the flame would reveal the truest, most noble version of himself.

The General shook vigorously, and too long, before finally unclasping, and taking up his coffee cup, bone china with roses. "Please, help yourself."

He watched the man pluck sugar cubes with a pair of silver tongs, one after another, and then pour cream from a small pitcher that matched the cups. Autie poured his own cup, added one sugar cube.

"Be careful, it's strong. Special technique of brewing I learned from a French ambassador."

Autie fought to keep the disdain from his face. The longer and further out from civilization he got, the more his mind and body rejected its formalities, its polite illusions.

Sheridan sipped from his cup. Small droplets clung to his neatly trimmed mustache, and his breath was sickly sweet, filling the close space when next he spoke.

"You're wondering what would bring me all the way to this god forsaken hell. Well, son. I have a job for you, that I think is perfectly suited to your talents. It's a secret thing. No newspapermen or biographers allowed. No reports to anyone but me, and that will be after. If you so much as write notes to keep it all straight, I ask that you do so in some kind of code not easily unscrambled." The man's tone was granite, severely contrasting his exterior.

"You have me intrigued, sir." He wondered if such a man could deliver the thing he wanted so desperately, that such a man could even see the treasure of a new frontier for what it was.

"Good. You're a natural killer, Autie. We're more alike than you know." He paused and Autie tensed at the comparison.

What I mean is, you see the way of things and make no apology for it. No reticence to bloody yourself or your men to get the job done. It's a precious rarity. What do you know of this?"

Sheridan produced a slim volume, slid it across the small table between them.

The book had been worried over. It was dog-eared and showed the wear of many hands. "Daemons and Leviathans of the American Continent. Is this a reader for children?"

"Far from it. We don't know much about where it came from originally. We suspect some descendent from the early expeditions. I'm sure you've heard the stories of things out on the frontier that defy reason. If they're making it to Washington, they must be positively dizzying out here."

"All kind of rumor circulates, sir. The mix of boredom and peril taxes a man's mind and his imagination spares him from the ravages of chaos. I put no stock in stories, less they come down from Him."

"I forget sometimes that you never made it to the deep south during the war, didn't see some of the things I did. You were already on your way out here when we were mopping up the last of it down there. Why do you think it took so long to stamp out the last of them, when their supply lines were crushed, their munitions all but gone?"

"I don't know, sir. I guess Americans make some fearsome insurgents."

"Bah," Sheridan waved him off. "We've been doing counter insurgency since before the ink dried on the Declaration of Independence. You could say the whole war machine was built for it. No. They found something very old down there, found a way to turn it to their service. I once saw a whole company of men frozen like statues. Just standing in formation on the march like time had stopped. And while they stood there, someone had come along and cut each of their throats, but it were just a red line across the front of each neck. I was standing there puzzling over it when whatever damnation was at work finally fell, and the lot of them dropped gurgling and grasping, blood jetting every which way until it pooled around them like a damned pond. We had to root out every one of them warlocks or whatever they were, burn them all to ash to end that war."

"Sir." Autie didn't know what else to say. Very little surprised him anymore and the sensation was unpleasant.

"I'm telling you," and he tapped the book as Autie began to flip through it, "more of what's in that volume has been verified than you would want to believe."

The pages were filled with drawings and descriptions. General locations, features. He landed on a page with a detailed sketch of a creature that looked half man, half frog. He stifled a laugh. Enough got out to bristle the General.

"I know you're a practical man. The business of killing demands it. It's why I want you on this. There will be no romance in it for you, no madness at the impossibility of it."

"What exactly do you want of me, sir?"

"Simple. All of it needs gone. Wipe every trace of every unconscionable thing in that book from the face of the earth. This continent has long escaped the attention of God. I truly believe that." And the man paused then, letting the weight of the moment settle.

"These creatures bred in the darkness of His disregard. It is His manifest will that we reclaim this continent for His glory. His will that we deliver it to a state of grace."

"How many people know about this?"

"Very few have the whole picture. You, me, the big man in Washington. Now, if you mean the book, we have done our level best to eliminate it. The press that published the one you hold no longer exists. Them that ran it are in a dark hole somewhere. Lots of cages to forget people in since the war. Other versions have started showing up, though. One offs, some copied by hand. And the lore is starting to creep into the public mind, showing up in those ridiculous nickel paperbacks. That could work for us if you do your job. Because if you do your job, the book becomes a work of fiction, a trifle… for children, as you said."

Perhaps the coffee was as strong as the General said, because Autie's heart was thrumming in his chest. It seemed his dream of another frontier, another campaign that would always await him was fated to come true. And this a path that asked only for the purest expression of his will, that demanded no reticence or restraint.

He looked at himself in his silver shaving mirror. "Colonel Armstrong 'Autie' Moorland." Sheridan promoted him from Captain, right past Major, to full bird Colonel. Not a brevet rank. This was not some temporary designation to give him the needed authority to continue his campaign were he to encounter some other officer who had need of he and his men. Anyway, he had the letter for that. Sheridan had penned it in front of him and placed his seal on it and woe to the man that disregarded it. No, the promotion was an inducement, a promise of other rewards yet to come. To be indebted to, so. He might never have to see Washington again.

He sipped coffee from a battered tin cup, the steam of it clung to his whiskers and tickled his nose. Walking up and down the line, making final inspections. It was a fine troop. A hundred cavalry, ten wagons loaded with weapons, ammunition, supplies, and trade goods. He expected to be on the range a while before resupply. Sheridan had brought him four of the new Hotchkiss guns, with hundreds of rounds of ammunition, preloaded into the long twenty round magazines. Two of the wagons towed field artillery pieces, an eight inch siege mortar and a twelve pound howitzer. He had done far more than was being asked of him, with far less.

Sullivan and Levi sat astride their horses a few paces behind him, stiffly attired in their new Captain's uniforms. He believed in pulling them who were loyal up with him and it didn't take much to convince Sheridan of the need of reliable officers for this campaign.

Autie would need scouts. Natives would be indispensable for tracking the beasts in that book, as well as any others that had been missed in its accounting. He hoped to find one or two in one of the makeshift prison camps, where it wouldn't take much to induce them to go with him. He would address the men on the specifics of their mission only after they were well clear of the fort, and even then, only to the extent necessary. Each had been chosen for their brutal efficiency, devotion to God and country, and willingness to obey orders without hesitation. The men were spread across the hillside on their horses, quiet. The morning was chill and moist, and condensation glittered on man and beast, and there was no more beautiful sight in all of His kingdom. The earth shifted below him, inviting him forward.

He mounted his horse and began a slow trot into the field. A drone of hoof beats followed, then the creaking of wagon wheels unmoored from their settlement. To onlookers, it'd be a strange sight. Autie's battle dress was a fringed buckskin shirt and the soft hat of a southern general, a trophy from the war. He kept the brim folded up on one side. His curly blonde hair bounced on his shoulders as he rode. He carried a Colt Single Action Army in a holster on his hip and a lever action Winchester rifle in a saddle scabbard. A big .44 caliber Walker Colt sat in a saddle holster just behind the horn. He had given up his cavalry saber after the war and taken up a lance, similar in manner to them he hunted. It seemed more practical from horseback. The one he carried, hoisted above his head to spur the men behind him, he had made special. A smith in Lawrence had forged the head. Nine inches of steel, razor sharp on both sides. The shaft was five feet of thin ash, a good combination of strength and enough flex to give a little without snapping. Just below the head, a length of leather cord trailed the scalp of a Comanche shirt wearer he had killed, named Ten Wolves, and a string of wrinkled bits of flesh - the ears of a number of other warriors. Gripping the rough wood, he felt invincible.

The entire party set off at an easy trot to the Santa Fe, with Autie riding at the front, high in the saddle. They would start out going east, where a guide might be secured. To the west were only hostiles.

6

MISSOURI, GATEWAY TO THE WEST

Crossing into Missouri was entering a new world, a place where all his paperback fantasies abutted the unfinished wood of reality, leaving his mind abraded and pricked with splinters. Everything at the St. Louis station was hastily built, with an unfinished quality, and the sixty miles to Franklin were a loud and rattling affair. The previous stretch was peaceful by comparison. At times, he found himself gripping the armrest beside him with such vigor as to whiten his knuckles, so afraid was he that they might fly from the track at any moment. It was a more salient worry then, than so many of his others, and he was grateful for it in that way. Still, he was relieved when he was finally free of the train a few hours later.

This was as far as Cecil was going to get by rail. There were sections of track extending like frayed rope in all directions, but no direct route remained to where he was trying to go. Franklin was the trailhead of the Santa Fe. Another hundred miles remained from here to Independence, where he could stay on the Santa Fe or divert to the Oregon. Forty-three miles after that, in Gardner, would be his last chance to choose. He was trading the speed of rail travel for the anonymity of the bustling multitudes.

Once he was on the trail, and the towns grew smaller and farther apart, he felt sure news would travel slowly enough that he could stay ahead of it.

In Franklin, the bloody seam of civilization was bound by flimsier thread, and the dusty chaos bore the stink of easy violence heavy as copper. In Columbus, many men went heeled - if discreetly so. Here the men ,and more than a few women, wore their pieces out in the open, either on gun belts or slung across their chest on lengths of rawhide cord, and with the casual regard a northerner might have for a hat or a pair of spectacles.

Most paid little heed to him. The few that seemed to take notice, he preferred hadn't. Here was a place of grim predation, where anything not held closely might be prized away. He found his hand going to his coat pocket quite often, fingertips brushing the pommel of his pepper box revolver and finding little solace in the gesture. He felt ill-equipped and undertrained for mixing with this lot.

If those crowding the streets were as green as he was, it didn't show. They carried a resolve in their eyes that he was surely lacking, and as such, signaling he might be easy prey.

Once he was free of the train station and its surrounds, the crowd thinned. Even with fewer people, he found himself often turning sideways to move through a group standing idle or to avoid collision with some pilgrim, whose bearing made clear his movement would not be slowed by the likes of Cecil.

The money he had would not see him the distance, and the only means to increase it would be found in some lowly saloon or other. For all his Pa's faults, he had passed on a fair amount of skill at cards to the boy. On days when he was too far in the bag to trust his instincts at the tables, they would stay up late into the night, playing hand after hand. Here it was a risky endeavor, though, as Cecil had little security and would need to avoid the more legitimate looking establishments, like as they were to attract the sort who might take greater interest in a boy traveling alone.

He found his way to a dingey rooming house, well away from the main street, and secured a room that reminded him of home in all the wrong ways. He was provided a dinner of biscuits and thin stew, only realizing as he sat down to eat just how long it had been since his last meal. The gnawing grip of his stomach sent him begging for seconds and his urgency sent him to the outhouse shortly after. Then, storing his meager belongings in his room, he made his way to the nearest saloon.

Tuckers, as the establishment was named, was a windowless affair, the wood raw and unpainted. The sign above the swinging doors was hand-painted in rough strokes, black on a cedar plank. The scent of tobacco smoke billowed out, was insufficient to cover the sweat and urine that lay under it.

He felt his face go red as, stepping to the entryway, the floor beneath his feet squeaked agonally, giving more than it should. For a moment, he feared his leg might pass right through to the ground. Instead, the wood only flexed and strained until he steadied himself against the wall. It drew countless eyes to him, and he froze momentarily before willing himself forward.

In Columbus, a boy of his age might be turned away by the barman, but the slumped and wrinkled mound of tortured flesh that regarded him from behind the oak slab only narrowed his eyes and continued cleaning the glass he held.

Beyond the waning light that held him through the aperture, the interior was lit by a mix of candles and lanterns, and the dim flickering cast a shadowed malignancy over those present.

"What'll you have, son?"

"I'm sorry." Cecil was still finding his bearings.

"I say, what'll you have? You can't just stand here and gawk. It's drink or go."

Cecil made his way the few steps to the bar. "Beer." He slid the man a dime.

The warm glass the man handed to him was filled more with foam than with liquid. The barman continued staring until he took a drink.

Most of the tables were just groups of two and three men, drinking whiskey, but there were two tables at the back that were fairly lively with game. Only one of the two had a free seat, and he took it without a word.

The dealer, a heavy-set man with a dirty top hat and thick gray mutton chops, raised his eyebrows and then raised a hand.

"Boy, this isn't a show. If you're looking for a trifle, wait your turn at the faro table over there."

Cecil broke eye contact with the man, looked to the others seated. There was a young man with blonde hair that hung to his shoulders like pale straw. He was clean-shaven and Cecil stared at the cleft of his chin a moment too long. The man looked at him through narrow, hazy eyes. Cecil quickly looked to the other side, where a woman stared at her cards. She wore a purple dress and a matching hat with a large white feather that stuck up from the side. Her face was full and friendly, and the nearby lantern's flame danced in her green eyes like the devil.

She offered up a whisper of a smile, "Give the kid a break, Philip. If he wants to watch, so what. Maybe his baby blues will give me some luck."

The dealer grunted. "Take more than that to help you, Cat. The game is five card stud, boy. The bring-in is fifty cents. House limit is twenty dollars. You want to run along and ask mommy to stake you?"

Cecil smiled, pulled his roll from his boot and fanned out the bulk of it. "Just deal me in, sir."

Hearing Philip addressed so, elicited a chuckle from the other two. The man stared sidelong at each in turn and nodded slightly to the boy. His top hat jostled askew at the gesture, but Cecil didn't dare laugh, much as his nerves begged for it.

He quickly fell into a rhythm with the game. As far as he could tell, there were no cheats at the table. Once, after a tough few hands, where he stared down the man to his left and ultimately wrestled a handsome pot from him, the man smiled and wiped his sweaty brow with the back of his hand.

"You've got grit boy. My name's Rook." And he shook Cecil's hand with a firm grip.

"Cecil," he gave the man's hand a squeeze and immediately felt stupid for giving his real name. He was momentarily dazed, buffeted by the win and by the focus of the game drawing his mind from its troubles.

"Cecil's buying us a round," Rook yelled, and the old barman appeared shortly with whiskey for the other three, and another beer for Cecil, this time with a thinner head and a proper glass mug.

The game remained friendly from that point. Cecil left the table late, richer than he had arrived but not by enough to elicit bad blood. He promised to return the next night to give them all a chance to win back their losses.

He shuffled across the dark street, back to his room, his head sloshing from the beer. He lay on the straw mat, hoping sleep would finally take him, but thoughts of what he was running from soon forced their way back in and it must have been nearly daylight when his mind finally came to rest.

He woke with a start, with a phantom sense of falling alive in his nerves, and his muscles tense. It was still the best sleep he'd had since leaving Ohio. He had missed breakfast, but the coffee tin was still warm on the stove, which still retained some heat from the morning cooking. He washed down hardened biscuits from the night before with the thickening dregs.

Cecil wrestled with his anxiety, thought he should move on. That he had handed out his real name the night before was a weight on his neck. He could spare one more night. Anyway, he would need to start earlier in the day if he wanted to make his way to Independence. Maybe he could find someone to travel with.

The general store near the train station turned out to be a great resource. He bought supplies for the first leg of his journey. Jerked beef, a proper canteen, a hat. He stared long at the new Stetsons, smooth and creamy white, and made of beaver. Cecil selected a more modest brown wool with a pinched crown and slightly angled five-inch brim. It should keep the sun off him well enough. He had never worn a hat his true size before, and with half his face shaded, he stood a little taller, felt like a grown man, if not a full fledged cowboy.

He told the shopkeep - a nervous man with a comfortable paunch - that he was John McNulty, out of Pennsylvania. That his Pa had run off and his Ma was sending him to family in Kansas, to follow later once her affairs were settled. He must have told the tale well, as he could see much sympathy in the man, who promised to try to find him a kindly family to travel with. He wouldn't let Cecil go until he promised to return the following morning, by which time he was sure he could help him.

Cecil felt a pang of guilt, which was quickly washed away with relief. At the very least, he needed to travel long enough with others to learn how to survive the trail. He had never so much as slept outdoors in a wild place before. He was poor, but city poor were a different set of perils.

That night, he returned to Tuckers. Cat wasn't there but Rook and Philip were, same as the night before. Where Cat had been, there was a well-dressed man with a southern accent. He had a head of thinning, black hair, slicked back with some fragrant oil. He had a thin mustache, waxed to fine points, and gold rimmed eyeglasses. His gray suit had no visible stains. He stared at Cecil for a long moment. When the others at the table seemed to recognize him, the man returned his eyes to his cards. Just one day in town and he already felt more acclimated than this one looked.

Danvers was the man's proffered name. He drank at least two rounds for every one that went to the rest of the table. His mood was erratic, at turns quiet and stewing, but as he lost more hands, he would sometimes curse loudly or stomp the floor. Each time he did so, it drew stares that made Cecil uneasy. He grew careless in his drink, and more than once, Cecil glanced over and caught his face down card, as he lifted it too far and too often. It was a healthy infusion of cash, and all three of them benefitted. Cecil and Rook fell into a rhythm with one another and began throwing a hand now and again just to keep Danvers on the hook.

It was growing very late, and after a harrowing run, which left Rook and Cecil each a full forty dollars richer, Danvers pushed back from the table, almost tipping his chair to the floor. He overcorrected and came down hard with his bootheels to the floor.

"You're all cheats. In cahoots with one another," He slurred, spittle dangling on his lip. "There isn't an honest man north of Arkansas, and you lot prove it." He was red-eyed, and the spit hung pendulous now, so Cecil had to look away lest he be caught smiling.

"Now you settle down. We run a clean game here," Philip stood and smoothed the front of his vest, brought his hand to rest at his hip, where a nickel-plated revolver glistened ominously.

"In cahoots…" Danvers mumbled. He threw his cards at Philip and then stared at Rook and then Cecil, stomping away to the protests of the floorboards.

Philip's calm demeanor immediately recovered, and he returned to his seat.

Rook stood up, fists clenched, his lips a thin line. He stood perfectly still a few moments, and then without a word, quit the building. Cecil watched him go, eyes following him all the way.

"Don't do it kid. Whatever you're thinking. Don't. Just sit with me and have another beer. Let the men settle the men's business."

Cecil told himself Rook was as close as he had to a friend here, and friends looked out for each other. Told himself that's why he got up and followed. The lovely cleft in the young man's chin, and the easy smile had nothing to do with it.

He moved quickly. In the dark, he just caught a glimpse of Rook rounding the corner across the street. Then he abandoned all discretion, closed the distance at a full run. Moving along the building, as he too rounded the corner in his pursuit he saw that Rook was already at the next intersection, headed into a blind alley.

By the time he gained the alley he could already hear the grunts and curses of men fighting, the scuffing of boots on the grit and the dirt. Agitated dust found its way to his nose and tongue, the taste and smell of danger. He saw a flash of a knife and one of the two rebounded off the planks of the nearby wall. Then there was a loud crack and the smell of smoke, both over-powering in the closed space. Retreating footsteps like the patter of raindrops on a windowpane faded and grew distant, dull in his ringing ears.

Cecil looked around, up and down the adjacent street and saw no sign of movement. He inched closer and could make out the shape of a man on the ground.

"Help," it was a sputtering thing, a lonely syllable bleeding out in the cool air.

Cecil crawled closer and a hand closed on his shirt. It pinched the skin of his chest, and he threw his weight backward. The grip held and the man rolled on top of him. Rook's grey eyes were wet and black in the near dark. His free hand still held the dagger that yet glinted, bereft now of any trace of menace.

Cecil felt Rook's grip ease on him, felt the warm strength of the man wet his knees and his palms. There was so much of it, and everywhere it touched him it cooled quickly. He shivered, tried to ease Rook to lean on the alley wall, but slipped in the mud and the slick, and the man landed flat on his back.

His mind racing, heart hammering, Cecil was in a panic. He could scarcely go to the authorities, even if he knew where to find them at this hour. Should he get Philip? Might he know what to do? He reached for Rook's hand, took it in his own. The man broke free, raised his head just a little.

"Mama? Help," the sound was softer now, gurgling, and Cecil could see blood at the corners of Rook's mouth. Then he laid his head back down and was still.

A cool, numbing feeling came over Cecil. He withdrew into himself and yet it seemed he watched from somewhere remote, a few paces behind and above. He watched himself go through Rook's pockets, watched as he found the sheath for his boot knife, watched as he shoved a great wad of bills into his own pocket and slid the knife into his own boot. Did Rook move just a little as Cecil brushed his cheek and pushed his eyelids closed? Was that rattle of teeth in a wooden cup the sound of a fading breath as he turned and departed the alley? These were the questions for his sleeping mind. A growing pack of wild dogs that must hunt him the rest of his days, its company growing, it seemed, with his every decision.

The sounds of the alley echoed in his head as the blood on his hands and knees dried and crusted. Staggering back to his room, he washed up as well as he could with his tiny basin. When he lay down, exhaustion delivered him to a quiet and dreamless sleep. The next morning arrived softly, without the suffocating terror that had been violently ripping him awake, and he had renewed hope that there might yet be a respite from his haunting, maybe even a deliverance. But at what cost?

Picking through the wad of cash he had secured from Rook

brought renewed upset. His empty belly growled and gnawed acidic as he laid out the red-flecked bills. In total, he was now in possession of nearly two hundred dollars, a princely sum, and combining his own haul with what he had acquired from him who no longer had use of it, diluted the dread somewhat. The blood money could scarcely be distinguished from the other, barring close scrutiny.

Gathering his belongings, he made his way back to the mercantile, and the nervous man was as good as his word. To his surprise, the man gave him a tin cup of hot coffee and some buttered bread, while he waited for the charitable strangers to arrive.

Timothy and Lucy were a comely couple from Pennsylvania. He wore a pressed shirt and a brown bowler. Leather suspenders and union blue pants. Between the pants and the limp in his right leg, Cecil reckoned he was a veteran. He had an easy smile but left most of the talking to Lucy. For her part, she was verbose enough for two.

"Such a handsome young man. Paul told us all about your troubles. Timothy and I are headed out today and would be glad of the company." Lucy smiled broadly. She had big green eyes and curly brown locks that framed her face and ran well past her shoulders. She wore a white prairie dress and cut a slim figure.

"I'm ever grateful of the charity."

"Tis nothing. Good Christian folk must look out for each other, the more so the further we get from the civilized world. You simply must tell me more about whence you come from. Paul said you too were from Pennsylvania."

Cecil froze. He'd never actually been in the state and in the moment could not so much as summon the name of a city or town there. Philadelphia rested just beyond the tip of his tongue, scared mute as he was to have this simplest of lies so easily undone.

"Give the boy a break, mother." Timothy slapped him on the shoulder. "Can't you see you got him scared as a jackrabbit."

"I'm so sorry. My tongue does run off faster than my head can catch it. I'm sure it's been a journey for you already and after such injury. A boy losing his father." Lucy shook her head and clucked her tongue. "Such a shame."

With that, they led him to their wagon, with two stout, black workhorses that were virtually identical. Timothy took the reins and motioned Cecil onto the bench beside him. Lucy sat in the box, under the awning, and they made their way down the dusty street, with the sun just creeping up behind them. The terrain was as inscrutable in the early haze as the future, broad and brimming with hostilities one could scarcely forecast. Comfort just the punctuation that separated events.

7

THE CONTRACT

The squirt didn't seem worth the trouble. It wasn't that he had any great reservation about killing a young 'un. Killing was killing. At this stage the only ones that troubled him were the women who yet had some miles in them. It were a wasteful thing. But if the money was right, well, there were always other women to be had.

The kid was a wisp of a thing, nearly spectral in the faded photo. It was a family picture, the only one they had. He was prepared for the boy's parents to press, and he was ready to offer a tidy sum if it come to it. The boy's father was clearly a card-sharp and he expected that alone to drive the price, but the man seemed to have little spirit to him. Charlie had that effect on people. A quail can pretend to be a lion until the hawk comes to call.

Not that Charlie was a large man. He didn't even carry weapons openly in the city. What he had was an unflinching quality, and further, them who had killed as much as he had bore the stink of it. It was a cloud that drifted along behind him, a train of spirits bound to him as they were bound to forever suffer. A bullet was a leaden weight that kept them trapped in perpetual remembrance of the pain and the shock of it, or so the spiritualist had told him before he strangled her with her own silks.

He didn't particularly like the Branaghs, didn't sympathize with the loss of their son, who would no doubt have grown to be a petty little grubbing shit like his old man. The first lesson he had learned about the wealthy was to keep everything on paper and never give an inch in a negotiation. He had expected them that had money to be free with it, as any he had known come into it seemed to immediately turn spendthrift. It was the opposite. It seemed the more they had, the more them that had it would clutch to it for dear life. Worse than that, they were crazy with it. A man might spend three times what he owed just to avoid paying to him he owed it to. Using whatever means, legal channels and less savory ones, because what they valued most of all was reputation for not being taken. Maybe it was the only thrill left to them for whom common law and morality held no sway.

Charlie was a quick study, had only been cheated the one time. The one who refused to pay him his due just up and vanished. That was the only kick his reputation needed. They all paid now. He thought it might cost him the clientele when he done it, but there was no loyalty among the rich, and they valued his services, and his discretion. There were a lot of killers out there, but precious few who could keep their mouths shut about it.

The Branaghs had lost their boy and they were sure this little Cecil was to blame. Said they had witnesses. The mother was especially keen on convincing Charlie. He told the woman he wasn't the law, supposed she still had a bit of a conscience. The father was more matter of fact. The men usually were. In those old families, it was them knew where all the bodies were buried, and there were always bodies when big money was involved.

Charlie carefully folded the photo, first the boy's mother, then the father, so the sides were rolled back and only the boy remained. He didn't want to look at the parents. They had taken a five-dollar gold coin for the picture and flat out asked if there was a reward if they were able to help. They thought he might get lonely and send a letter or something. It was unnatural. Like watching a dog feed on its pups. Charlie told them he wouldn't be needing any help, and excused himself before they might say something that would push Charlie. He didn't like violence where there was no money in it, but these two ghouls, if they spoke much longer, he could see himself sticking one of them just for the satisfaction.

Charlie's father had died when he was young, and his mother was a drunk who took everything he earned or stole until he got tired of it and left. Was still taking if he were being honest. Even she wouldn't have sold him out to some grim bounty hunter. People didn't surprise him much anymore, but they could still turn his stomach.

He knew where to start. The boy's pallet was scattered with western fantasies. Dog eared, tattered, he had probably read them all dozens of times. He would go south, and then west. With any luck, someone on the train or at the station might remember him. If not, there were only a few towns where he might have wound up. The boy would either be there, or Charlie would pick up the trail there.

Staring at his belongings, neatly packed and ready to go, it wasn't much. He lived on the go, and this kit and a little money in the bank was all he had to show for all the bodies and the miles. The rest was just a steady stream in a bottomless well. Mabel. His mother.

He was wearing his suit at the moment. Head to toe black, including his good boots and a flat brimmed cattleman beaver felt hat. He had trail clothes, should he need to ride. He wore a small .32 in a holster concealed under his jacket over his right buttock and the dagger he carried midline in the front - angled for a smooth draw. In the bag he had his Scoffield .45, wrapped with his big Bowie in his chestnut, calf leather gunbelt. His bulkiest piece was a collapsible spyglass of German provenance. It rested heavy in a padded walnut case. Other than that, it was a blanket, his toilet, and a few other sundries. Everything was imported or tailored. He believed in traveling light, but not cheap.

It was growing dark as he took the short walk to the depot, and there was a nip to the fall air that he would be glad to be rid of. Not that it wouldn't be cool in Missouri or Kansas, but he yet had some time before it would be uncomfortably so. The raisin of a man who sold him the ticket was of no help, nor were any other railroad employees he could find, but he decided to board the train for Missouri, anyway. He had come to trust his instinct for the hunt, it was no use questioning it now. He secured a sleeper and had a steak and a bottle of wine brought to him. The Branaghs had fronted him $500 for expenses, and if the chase took a week, he would do his best to spend every cent.

8

THE RIGHT MEN FOR THE JOB

Autie was charging his horse hard, trying to maintain his seat as he bounced and jostled on the rough terrain. It was harder with just one hand for the reins. In his other he held a white kerchief, which he waved as high as he could. It billowed and dragged in the air, flattened somewhat by his speed. He needed to catch these men and didn't want to alarm them. Didn't want to catch a large bore slug or get his horse shot from under him, and men such as these were prone to spook when they saw cavalry.

Levi had been scouting about ten miles ahead that morning when he caught sight of them. He did his best not to be seen and observed them only briefly before bringing news back to Autie. There were a lot of unknowns. They could have spotted Levi, probably had, despite his best efforts. They might already be long gone.

"Sir, I just don't think you should go out there alone." The man had sat slumped on his mount, weary from the ride and in no condition to accompany him, insisting nonetheless.

"You get a fresh horse and some chow and ride easy the rest of the day," he said.

Levi pleaded if not him, that Autie take Sullivan Jackson, his other captain.

"No, no. The men need at least one senior officer ready for a fight if fight comes." The man looked at him. His eyes walked right up to questioning his judgment, but it was a line he knew none of his troops would cross. He couldn't tell him why he needed to go alone, that there were things he wanted to keep even from them closest to him.

There were ten of them in the distance, all riding at a steady trot, with a half dozen pack mules trailing behind them. When they saw Autie, they slowed their pace and a hand went up. Then the lead man brought them to a stop. He made a circular gesture in the air and Autie thought he heard a high-pitched whistle. The man at the lead stayed seated, but three of the others dismounted and drew rifles from their saddle scabbards.

Stuffing the kerchief into his shirt, Autie slowed to a trot and proceeded gently the remaining fifty or so yards, both hands raised, palms out.

"I come to parlay," he shouted through a cupped hand, when he had closed half the distance. The other man didn't move, didn't give any sign that Autie shouldn't approach either.

As he got closer, he recognized the lead man and one of them with rifles, and a thrill rode his spine. "Perfect," he whispered to himself.

"Who the hell are you, come riding like a bat out of hell. I nearly had my man shoot you out of your saddle just for giving me a startle." Mortimer Crenshaw was the one who spoke. People called him Morte, or sometimes Muerto. He and the rifleman he gestured to - a man named Stagger Lee - were known scalp hunters. Autie didn't know the others, but these two didn't rate honorable company.

"Moorland," He nearly shouted. "Colonel Armstrong Moorland."

Two of those with rifles immediately lowered them. Stagger Lee kept his raised, not exactly on Autie, but not far off.

"Shit, I heared of you," Mortimer spit, "Last I hear, you waren't a Colonel, though. You know it's a dangerous thing to pretend."

"News travels slow in the territories," Autie smiled. "Coin travels faster, and I've got a fair amount of gold coin for him who has the right skills."

Mortimer waved his hand subtly, like shooing a fly, and Stagger Lee let his rifle drop at his side. The others took on a relaxed demeanor.

"Well, let's us parlay then." Mortimer gave his horse a little boot and Autie wheeled alongside him at a slow trot. There was a string of scalps dangling by a leather cord on the back of the man's saddle, and as he pulled close, it was hard to tell which smelled worse, them or the man.

Autie told him a little, as little as he could. He had torn the page from the book about the skunk apes that were said to populate the foothills to the south. He thought it would take some convincing, but Mortimer and Stagger Lee had been hunting in the area for some time. They had seen strange sign and heard stories.

"Now I know this is dangerous work, and I know you usually get five dollars for a scalp. I also know sometimes when you can't find an Indian you might pass off something else. And I'll have none of that."

"Are you questioning my honor, sir," and Mortimer sat tall in his saddle. His eyes went quiet and soulless. Autie floated his hand closer to his pistol, then noticed the big cap and ball gun that Mortimer kept in a saddle holster in front of him. He'd rarely seen one so large.

"Ha ha ha. You look fit to shit yerself. I'm funnin' you. Damn right. I've sold scalps of every denomination. Scruples don't buy much whiskey. Five dollars is five dollars."

"Well, I'm offering you twenty-five per for these scalps and I expect to get what I pay for."

"Mister, I'll scalp the good Lord hisself for twenty five dollars."

"Good. You can find me or one of mine at Fort Lyon. If I'm not there, I'll make arrangements. Good hunting."

"You don't like me much, do ye? I see how it troubles you to lower yourself to come calling here."

"We're cut from different cloth. Our paths might parallel and only rarely intersect." Autie efforted at a diplomatic tone. The man was becoming a nuisance.

"We're the same, you and I. I'm just doing the part of the work you can't stomach. Same gubmint writes both our checks."

"What I do, I do in service of peace," but Autie knew that wasn't entirely true, hadn't been for a long time.

"What you won't let yourself see, is your nobility of purpose, it's right here." Morte slapped his horses side, where the string of scalps dangled and bobbed lightly with each fall of a hoof. "America is a great machine, maybe the greatest ever built to separate wheat from chaff. Them that can fall easily, hell, it's our duty to make it so. It's the pruning of a thing to make it grow right. In the end, we'll be the greatest empire the world has seen. I'm sure you're well-read enough to know what that means."

"Why don't you explain it to me like I'm not." Autie didn't figure the man for having read anything more profound than the name stenciled above a saloon.

"All the great ones were built of bone and sinew, rivers of blood. It takes a special sort. Without mercy, without the soft ways. Those are the old ways, the ways that failed. They didn't do the work up front to refine them.

This place is a paradise. Hell come to earth. A man got to stand in hell to see heaven. We need to be hard to earn her. Without compromise. Seed the ground with blood enough to grow a thing that will stir God himself, make him take notice."

Autie looked at the man. He had spoke with conviction. They might be more alike than he cared to think too long on. That he had more in common with this man than with Sheridan was a bitter thought.

They rode back to the larger group in silence. Stagger Lee was passing around a bottle and tipped it toward the two of them.

"Your men are up to this?"

"Them that aren't won't be around to share the receipts." Mortimer smiled a black toothed smile.

That smile and the whole exchange was a cactus thorn in his saddle on the ride back. The job was too big and too broad for his troop. They could criss-cross the country for a decade and not get it done. And men like these were the only ones to delegate to. Men who mostly kept to themselves and who, if they did talk, no one important would listen or care. Still, he might have to wipe them all out when the job was done. It might be the simpler thing. Certainly the cheapest.

9

THE WAY TO INDEPENDENCE

If Franklin were the wolf's maw, the road out of it was the throat. An interstitial space between one danger and the next. Here was a restrained bustle, forced to a semblance of order by the bottleneck through which it flowed. The wagons and ponies crawled forth in an unbroken line as far as Cecil could see. Once fully broken from the shackles of the town, though, it became an uneasy herd, with teams attempting to pass wherever the belly of the trodden path permitted such maneuver. Spirits ran high. Young men ran their horses up and down the line, whooping and carrying on, their laughter like a patter of rain on a tin roof. The energy was manic, and Cecil could feel the pounding of the rutted earth through the wheels and bench and all the way into his chest. His urgency was of a different quality, but not so unlike the rest of them for him to stand out.

This was the very beginning of the Santa Fe. All were fairly rested and well-provisioned, and Cecil thought they all must imagine it could be so spirited the entire way, that they might ride a wind of good intentions all the way to New Mexico or Oregon, like some hawk coasting high along the thermals.

Things he had read, and heard whispered at the card table,

gave Cecil doubts that the going would long be easy. Some rumors carried on the aether of whiskey breath might even have given him pause if there were other options left to him. But it was already apparent that the most outlandish bits, culled from the remnants of nickel paperbacks he found stained and tattered at times on the street, or more rarely, given to him by his Pa after a particularly good night of gambling, were those stories of heroics and of paradise at the end of a long drive. The stories of wild things, of tooth and claw, of carnivorous leviathans that stalked the tall grass of the prairie, might in fact be closer to the truth, to the way of men at least. In the end, the shadow of the hangman's rope was most viscerally real and the most potent motivator.

The land was itself a hard and merciless thing, and would surely begin its slow attrition soon after they departed Gardner, where the Oregon and Santa Fe came close to one another for the last time. Perhaps sooner than that. After Gardner, they would pass from the land of men to the land of the savage, sprawling frontier, where proper towns gave way to the occasional outpost, and charity might be hard to come by. Scarcity having run it off, having cleaved already them that held too close to kindness.

He pushed these thoughts out of his mind. Resolved himself to enjoy this stretch, enjoy the thing he had dreamed of but never thought he would see. To enjoy the fantasy until reality swallowed it up. All he had to do was to let charitable strangers believe he was someone else, the child they needed him to be.

Shortly, Lucy moved deeper into the wagon and curled up on a cushion. Timothy kept glancing back and when he was sure she was asleep, took up his hat by the brim and gave it a little circle to get the attention of one of the young men, who had now settled into a steady trade alongside the train.

The boy was red faced and smiling, and his hat kited behind him on a cord that disappeared under his chin. He traded Timothy a bottle of whiskey for a silver dollar that shone like it must have been minted the week before, the way it danced flickering bright in the air, spinning and sparkling the whole tumbling way. The young man caught it and slipped it into his shirt pocket, trotted down the line without another word.

Timothy took one more guilty glance toward Lucy, then handed the reins to Cecil and went to work on the bottle. He pulled the cork with his teeth and spat it on the dusty road, took a great swig of the amber liquor. The man's movement betrayed much experience, and he didn't so much as wince from his greedy gulp.

Cecil had told himself he would never touch strong drink. He couldn't stand the smell of it, reminding him as it did of his Pa, and in her worse days, his Ma. The smell fired off nerves in the scars on his backside, set his mind to times he had hidden out away from home until well into the night. Then, some pebble set loose to rolling under the bench startled him, brought him back, and the sound was so like Rook's throaty end from the night before, that he felt breathless and cold even in the relentless sunlight.

He took the bottle from Timothy and drew deeply. It burned his throat and his gut tensed to reject it, but he took a slow breath and steadied himself. It wasn't as bad as he had thought it would be. It was a different kind of warmth that began to permeate him, and soon he felt unmoored. Like a wheel freshly broken loose from the mud. A kind of freedom where the specters that flitted through his mind could not quite reach him, or could yet only brush him with their cold fingertips instead of grasping and pulling him to their deeper darkness. It was nothing like beer. Soon, he and Timothy were laughing, he couldn't recall about what.

Another hour or two down the trail, Timothy had dozed and rested heavy against Cecil's shoulder. Cecil had never driven a wagon before. It seemed there weren't much to it, as the horses simply followed the road and the wagon in front of them. He feared he might doze himself, and set to counting the thin and pathetic little trees he passed, just to give his mind something to work on. When still his lids felt heavy, he set his mind to Santa Fe and what might await him there. Pushing his hat back on his head, he let the sun warm his cheeks

He had settled into a numb rhythm, nestled in the refuge of the mundane, when there arose a commotion behind him, hollering, whooping, and the rapid and heavy beat of hooves. One of the young men from earlier sped past, a rope pulled taut on his saddle horn like a piano wire, dragging a bundle that bounced along the rutted road. Suddenly, it emitted a howl, high and tormented, the likes of which Cecil had never heard. The man wheeled his horse and the thing rolled up beside him. It was a dog of some kind. Probably a coyote. Cecil had never seen one but it - what was left of it - matched the general description. The fur was earth toned where it wasn't bloodied. Having tumbled to a stop, it raised its head and let out another howl, this time so close that it echoed through Cecil's bones and drug a chill wind behind it. Its front legs were broke, and bone jutted white and bloody from its dusty fur.

Cecil barely got his head past the bench before vomiting over the side. The liquor burned his throat and his nostrils on the way up. His movement woke Timothy, who shook the sleep from his head and reached lamely for the bottle.

The young man on the horse wheeled again and took off down the line. There was a little yelp and then the coyote made no more sound. Cecil could hear some shouting and cheering whenever the beast hit a rock or some other protrusion that sent its broken body the height of the horse's haunches, or even higher, before the rope went taut again and hurtled it earthward.

Timothy handed him the bottle and Cecil drew from it again. It drew the hurt from him, like it was rinsing the ichor from inside his skin and, soft and sloughing, the pain ran to ground where it was trampled and dispersed by the endless marching hooves behind them. He thought that maybe this trail could crush it all to dust, all his bitter memories and hurts, and leave only the hardest remnants of him intact. And what a relief that would be.

It was nearly a hundred miles to Independence. Everything took longer than he calculated it should. It took them just over a week to get there. In that time, Cecil watched closely and learned the basics of surviving on the trail.

Timothy taught him how to build a fire, how to start it with flint and steel but also how to build for different purposes - smaller cooking fires for the daytime and longer burning ones for the night. The land was mostly flat, but there was enough scrub and brush and small trees to supply them. He learned that dead wood burned much easier and much better than green wood, and how to gather and bundle grass to get the larger material to catch.

Lucy taught him a little cooking. How to make biscuits with flour and water and lard.

They took turns resting under the canopy, he and Lucy. Timothy for his part wouldn't leave the bench in the daytime.

Mostly he learned the monotony of trail life. There were little hints of towns between Franklin and Independence. Few people slowed or stopped at these. That urgency held fast at the beginning, them that rode had no doubt spent months or years in the planning and wouldn't wait a moment longer than they must. Mostly the stops weren't worth the trouble, there were few available goods, and the prices were much inflated.

The boredom gnawed at him. If he let his thoughts run, they seldom found sweet sustenance, and rather sought out the most bitter fruit of his experience to suck and gnaw upon. In these moments, he wished Timothy would buy another whiskey bottle. He was still shy to seek one out himself, unsure what recrimination he might face for doing so. He was, after all, just a child to these two, and their charity might depend on them continuing to see him as such.

In Independence, they went their separate ways. Timothy,

with a quiet handshake, turned his attentions to the wagon. Lucy gave him a tight and tearful hug, and Cecil could feel the provocation to tears himself. He pushed it away, pushed it down. She wished him good luck. These two would be taking up the Oregon, and his story had him pushing further into Missouri and then to Kansas.

10

THE DRAW

Its form, when it takes form, is of black smoke and white eyes. Endless. Eyes upon eyes. Its teeth are of that other world and it has no need of them here. Its teeth are not of mineral because it bites at something deeper, and older. But there is always a need for eyes.

Even corporeal, its boundaries are thin, insubstantial. The greatest fiction of the fleshy things is that the veil of dermis that bounds their fluids has some greater significance. The first lesson of eternity is that everything touches everything else, and nothing exists unto itself alone

Few have seen it. Only a few have looked and those that have can remember little. It is the absence they will recall, like a puzzle piece cut from the world. The mind has no referent for it. The absence, the gap in their understanding, will haunt them like a phantom limb, like a cornerstone yanked from a crumbling edifice.

There are those that call to it, the desperate ones. Creatures clutching spindly roots and scrabbling for a foothold on the edge of some chasm. The topography of this ancient place is heaven and hell in one. It must be so.

The boy is the scrabbling sort. His desperate pleas are the filaments not yet woven into thought, let alone words. He might never find them, but those germs are as clear to it as petroglyphs.

It watches the boy sleep, his dreams playing out in twitches and moans, and it knows the boy is on the path. It doesn't own him yet, but soon. Its way is the way of liberation – from terror, from conscience – and aren't these of a piece to these lumps of meat and bone. The boy belongs to it because it can offer him escape from himself.

Eternal is its own kind of patient. Patience that no longer distinguishes what is from what was from what shall be. The river doesn't know the rough rock from the smooth. All are smooth eventually. Events. They themselves are but a scrim of dust obscuring the glass.

11

MABEL

"To what do I owe the pleasure?" Mabel caught him off guard, as always, emerging quietly from the shadow of her doorway. The ghost of who he once was, of all his secret shame, she moved like a spirit, her footfalls like soft kisses. She kept the door open near all the time, no matter how often he warned her of what might wander in. There were fresher ghosts known to him, after all, and some of them had kin.

"Here on business, if I'm being honest, but I knew your witching ways would sense me passing through and I'd never hear the end of it if I didn't stop by." Charlie stood in the dust, hat in hand, squinting in the fading sun that sagged just over his mother's roof top, spreading its fading red behind it like soft butter.

"Your skin's too fair to be standin' there with no hat on. You've been getting too much sun as it is. Your hair's hardly got color no more. Almost didn't recognize you." She stepped closer to the light. The shade exaggerated the lines on her face, even as it softened them. She was old and looked to have got too much sun herself, too much of a lot of things. Her eyes were still bright with youthful energy, though; they had always been. Had a light

58

in them Charlie never saw in the mirror, he wondered if he ever had such light or if it was the domain of them who feel more than they think.

"I don't know why I paid for a door you ain't never used, or a house you're letting go to shit."

"Oh, hush. I'm a little behind on the chores is all. I get distracted."

Just then a heavyset man shuffled past her, shrugging into a loose suspender. When he saw Charlie, he pulled his hat down and nodded to him, didn't say a word. Charlie tensed, but Mabel cut him off before he could so much as speak. The man quickened his pace, bootheels crunching the hardpack.

"Don't you ever." She lay her hand on his shoulder, gave it a couple of squeezes, and the smell of lavender coming off her settled him a bit. "If you're too busy to ever spare me more than a few minutes, don't you go chasing off them that dote on me. Now come on in."

Charlie willed himself to relax. He wanted to lay a beating on the cowpuncher. The man trailed a scent of musky sweat and whiskey like a confession. He shook his head and followed his mother into her cottage.

"Now have yourself a seat and let your mama fix you something. You're skin and bones. Too many miles between meals I reckon."

Charlie passed a red upholstered chair. It was weathered in the seat and the legs were faded. Mabel liked to sit outside sometimes and didn't much care about getting things out of the rain. He couldn't figure how she had so little care for the value of things. Their life when he was coming up seemed to have the opposite effect on her it did him. He sat at the small kitchen table, grateful she hadn't used that chair for firewood or some such.

"What's that smell? It's even worse here than in the other room." He knew what it was and regretted asking. He'd smelled the same scent every time Mabel had left him sitting outside while she entertained. He never noticed it in his own rutting, and it spoke to the company she kept.

"Charlie, you know how it is. Some men's passion don't fit in just one little room in a house. Or maybe you don't. You've never struck me as the passionate sort."

"You scared it out of me, Mabel. Anyway, you got enough passion for the whole family. Don't know where I'd fit it. The only thing passion ever got me is a night sleeping on the ground with the scorpions and rattlesnakes. Seems to be taking a toll on you finally, too." He smiled and leaned back in the chair.

"You can wipe that smirk right off your face before I slap it off." Her back was to him, she was fiddling with the stove, but somehow she knew. She always knew.

"And it wouldn't kill you to call me Mama."

"Mabel suits you better."

"Now, you want me to get this place more livable, you might loosen them purse strings a little."

He sent her over half of what he made, but knew she spent it faster than he could make it. On whiskey, and probably throwing it away on useless drunks and drifters. Anyone with a stiff pecker and a sad story or a bit of blarney.

"I send you more money and it's like as not to kill you. How much whiskey can one woman drink?"

"A boy should take care of his mother." She sighed and seemed to collapse on herself a little and in spite of everything, in spite of how he knew he should feel about her, her grip was the only thing left could squeeze his heart 'til it near burst.

"This job's a big one, Mama, maybe after I can come round and fix up the place a little, myself."

"Big promises. We'll see." She turned from the stove and set a pan of biscuits on the table, then poured him a cup of coffee. "I got some fresh preserves for the biscuits. One of my friends brought them over yesterday."

"Guess they're good for something after all." Charlie took a big bite. He always ate the first one plain. He felt the steam tickle his mustache, and the taste was like really coming home. Coming home to a place that never existed: a place of comfort.

He took a sip of coffee and it brought him right back. The bitter tang cut through everything. It was all he could taste, tickled his throat.

"What the hell is this?" But it was already growing on him.

"Don't it beat all? Like a right smart slap on the ass of a morning." She jiggled and looked over her shoulder at him, winked. Turning from the stove, she presented the coffee pot. It was tarnished copper with a little nub atop it. She undid the lid so he could see inside. The coffee was all bunched up in some kind of basket.

"It's called a percolator. Newest thing."

He wondered at the cost, took a big gulp that chased thought out of his mind. The bite of it was invigorating, she was right about that much.

"Well, I have to admit the luxury of not spitting grounds is fairly nice." He took another gulp. It reminded him of some of the better restaurant coffee. Almost.

"Sometimes I put a little dram in it. It's a real hoot. What kind of business brought you here, anyway?"

"Just a boy. He done some things he oughtn't and then run off. Boys never run east, or south. There's no romance in it. I figure he's headed to the Oregon or the Santa Fe, and either way he's gonna start here."

"So why aren't you out there then, hunting him? Not that I don't love seeing you."

"Well, them rich folks don't appreciate anything comes too easy. Gotta give the kid a running start. Take my time so they feel like they got a real villain on their hands, feel like they're getting their money's worth."

"That's my boy. So clever. No doubt running up the bill too. No better kind of fool than a fool with money."

"Ain't that the truth." He smiled momentarily, but it faded when he thought who the fool was in Mabel's life. Then his mother rubbed his shoulder, and he let loose just a minute his grip on the past, on their history, and let her be the mother he wanted, if only for a minute.

12

WILL O' THE WISP

There were many barren miles following the parlay with the outlaws, flat land and prairie grass that did little to pull at Autie's attention. The steady rocking of his ass in the saddle was as a lullaby, and these quiet moments -these calls to rest- were the hardest for him, only ever elicited a reflexive apprehension. Action was forever a balm, and in its absence his mind turned his every decision like a puzzle box, starting with the most recent, and possibly most impulsive. Could he really trust these men to do the work? Without doubt, the job was too great for the entire army, much less the fraction of it under his command. He chased his doubts away with faith, that his destiny had always been to conquer. He sat up straighter then, and it seemed even the breeze took on a stronger gusting from the rear, as though the elements themselves found favor in him.

The sun was halfway between apex and horizon when the land finally showed some character. The flatness gave way to gentle hills, and coming over the rise of one of these the troop fell upon a little wood. As they drew closer, the band of trees took on an L shape. Autie ordered the men to make camp in the elbow. The trees were the squat affairs common to the region but were clustered such that they made a serviceable windbreak to the south and to the west.

They set perimeter with the wagons, and soon a number of fires were lit. The smell of roasting meat quickly ran off thoughts of much else. Autie took a cup of coffee and retired to his tent. One of the men would bring him a plate. His stomach growled at the thought, and he removed his boots and stretched out on his roll.

They should make Red Sky camp the next day. There was a woman, survivor of the war on the plains who he had heard whispers about. She knew all the old stories of the land, might know things that would make the work more manageable.

An enlisted man interrupted his reverie. Someone had got a deer during the ride that day and they had made a thick stew with potatoes and onions. A chunk of corn bread the size of his fist rested on the edge of the tin plate.

"What's your name, son." He looked like little more than a boy, rosy cheeked and without so much as the shadow of a beard. His dark hair had a natural curl and ended just above the shoulder. He was one of Sullivan's picks for the expedition.

"Private Carlson, sir." The boy stood straight as an oak stave and saluted him.

"At ease, soldier. Thank ye for the plate. Give the cook my compliments." He ate slowly and the boy stood for the duration. Not watching him but glancing with fair frequency.

"You look like you want to ask me something, son, so have at it."

"Well, sir," and he paused, hunting for the right words, "I was just wondering what all we're supposed to be doing. It seems like we're moving away from Indian country. From ones that ain't been rounded up, anyway."

Autie smiled. "We're set to hunting something else, kind of

the new Indians. It will become clearer as we get along. For now, just keep your eyes and ears open. Ain't none of this country safe. Believe that."

Autie handed back the plate minus the corn bread and relieved the boy. He was considering how to explain things to the men, especially them that were too young to have seen war. A man who has lived through war has a certain credulity for the strange that other men lack.

The light of the camp was dimming when Levi came to call.

"Come on in."

Levi stepped under the flap of the tent.

"You look good, my friend, those Captain bars suit you."

"Thank you sir. Um. We've got an issue. Somethin' is stirring out in them woods."

"Well, let's us see."

The two of them stepped out and the source of the upset was immediately apparent. Lights danced between the trees. They appeared fairly far out, the way the wood obscured them at times. Yet they were bright, and an unnatural sort of green, like sunlight through a gemstone. The longer he stared, the more Autie wanted to know of them. He caught himself taking a step toward the wood, blinked hard and shook his head. It was like breaking from a spell.

"Well, what the hell is it?"

"We just don't know, sir. It started right around full dark. We count five of them. They look to get closer and then move back out."

"Indians?"

"That's what we thought at first, but the light don't flicker like a torch. Not to mention the color." Levi wasn't usually a man of emotional displays; the hesitance and the subtle frown playing at the corners of his mouth now meant he was troubled.

"Some of the men swear they hear music out there, others are stumbling around like they're drunk."

"Well, what do you think it is, then?"

"I hate to even say. Some of the men, the older fellas, are talking about witches. They're afraid they might sneak into the camp and turn them into something, lizards maybe. They say witches been known to truck in such powers."

Autie laughed, thin and half-hearted. The world was apparently full of things he had only the faintest idea of. Witches seemed preposterous, but he couldn't really know, could he?

"Put together a party of ten. Send them out to snuff out whatever is moving out there."

"Yes, sir." Levi appeared satisfied. Autie thought they might not find anything at all, but it would help the men rest knowing something was being done.

He lay down and fell quickly to sleep. In his dreams, he floated toward something beautiful and warm, a thing the mind of words and ideas could not reckon, and in the dream its radiant glory snuffed out his eyes like sputtering candles, and when he woke to the screaming, his cheeks were still warm with tears.

It was pitch dark, and the screams that yanked him out of that deep sleep set his heart to pounding, every muscle tense before he even sat up.

Pulling on his boots and pants, grabbing his pistol, he was out of the tent in under a minute.

He found Levi and Sullivan huddled close by one of the wagons, whispering and staring into the wood. There was a general din of men getting dressed and readying for a fight.

"Guess we won't be getting any more sleep tonight. What's going on here?"

If the two were surprised by his arrival, neither showed it.

Levi spoke softly, his eyes fixed on the shadowy wood. "I

sent a party, just like you said, sir. I thought they were meetin' with some success, such that the lights were dimming, or retreating at least. I expected they would be back shortly, and then we heard the first scream. They've been carrying on like that for near half an hour now. Sullivan and me are debating the finer points of sending some more in after them."

Autie scanned the sky, then the woods. "It's darker than pitch in those woods now. I don't even see the lights no more. A man could be so close you could smell his breath and you wouldn't see him. No. It'll be first light in a few hours. We'll move in then, in force. I don't suspect anyone is getting any more sleep, so let's get the fires built up and get some coffee and some food going and have the men ready themselves for patrol."

At first light, Autie led the way into the wood. Lance in one hand and pistol held in high ready in the other. A mist hung to the trees and a subtle sweetness of rot filled his nostrils. He was glad he was walking point when he found the first body. Two realizations struck him at once, and he could scarcely ascertain which was the more disquieting. First: the body was the boy who brought his dinner that night. He recognized the unblemished boots and uniform. Second: he was missing his head.

As they traipsed further into the wood, the ground grew softer and the limbs of adjacent trees criss-crossed and bit at cheeks and hands, anything exposed. It was hard going. They came upon eight more bodies just like the first. There was surprisingly little blood, possibly owing to the softness of the moist ground. It was strange. They never found the tenth body, and the woods terminated abruptly in the cleft of a hill. The depression was a swampy affair, with ankle deep, fetid water that stunk of the same general rot of the wood, but much stronger, and with a sharp undertone of copper. Small caves disappeared into the hill just above water level.

Autie gathered his captains, and they huddled close. The men stood nearby, shuffling audibly in the crust of leaves and twigs. They needed something sensible in the madness of the morning.

"We could get them or lose them right here."

"Sir?" Sullivan was almost as uneasy as the general troop.

"The things we have to do, it's only going to get more mystifying, I'm afraid. We need to show them we can triumph. We need a grand gesture."

"We got no enemy to kill here, sir. If they've gone in them caves, they must be no bigger than whistle pigs. No way to go after them that I can see."

"We dynamite the caves and burn the woods. Bury the men. We leave this place no more than an ashy smudge on the landscape. Use what dynamite we have. We'll get more at Red Sky. We need spectacle."

"Yes, sir." Sullivan seemed reassured then, and Autie knew his captains would settle the men.

It was a grand spectacle. They set the dynamite with long fuses and still, having retreated behind their wagons, were pelted with mud and rock that fell from the sky in a great smoking arc. The sound of the blast shook their teeth in their heads, set ears ringing. Next, they gathered dried grasses and built a long mound of them on the near side of the wood. The fire they lit there took quite well and was soon moving through the trees with alacrity.

They stood for a while, watching the fire take a firm hold of the woods. The smoke was thick and acrid, so it burned the eyes, and all of them backed away a fair distance except Autie, who was aware of the dramatic figure he cast in the glow and the smoke. Soon, the entire wood had caught, and what wildlife lived in that wood stood little chance. A cacophony of animal cries rose above the general din of popping and crackling greenwood. Some of the sounds were from no beast Autie had ever heard.

He watched the men close, and if any felt a pang of

sympathy or regret, he didn't show it. These men were hard, and would do what needed done. The smoke obscured the sky behind them once they set out, and Autie could feel the calm that settled on the troop like a spring rain, the balm of certainty, of dominance.

13

NO PLACE FOR HEROICS

Cecil became a killer for the second time in as many weeks in late September of 1883. He was already losing track of the specific date, but knew his birthday was close, if not passed. Knew also that birthdays would no longer be a marker of any significance, other than each from here on out a measure of how long he might outrun the odds, or justice, whether there was any difference between the two. He thought maybe this was what it meant to be a grown man, that childhood was an accumulation of stories and affections and adulthood a slow shedding of them, with whatever means were available.

It was, in fact, his 13th birthday that found him hiding out in the cheapest room in Independence, Missouri, watching his savings winnow away, evaporating as the pooling rainwater that cast his grim reflection back at him when he ventured out on the muddy streets. The gaming was not so easy here, or he had lost his luck. More likely, the men and women were better cheats here. There was also the whiskey. Having found relief in it, he could scarcely resist it when available, and it dulled his acumen the same way it dulled the knife of memory.

Santa Fe or Oregon. Independence was the last big town

before he had to choose. He had about two days ride to Gardner, Kansas, where the two trails diverged for the last time, but Gardner was already a toe into the wild, so he'd been told. Each trail had its season, and the fall was especially perilous to undertake the Oregon and only slightly more favorable for the Santa Fe. He had hoped the fear of the law bearing down on him might nudge him past the fear of the unforgiving frontier, but humanity shuffled constantly through this town like a weathered deck of cards, and no one seemed to know anyone, or even look close at anyone other than to barter or fight.

He was cataloguing his provisions when he heard the scream. Not the first he had heard in the nearby rooms. There was a steady trade in human flesh here, and he accepted that he didn't know the language or customs of it. This scream was of a different character, high and desperate; a sound that could scarcely have come from a willing partner.

He had met Trixie the day before. Returning with the last of his supplies, what he was told he would need to start the next phase of the journey. She was standing in the hall just outside his room, and he nearly ran into her, so lost he was in the internal debate over his next move.

"Whoa there, cowboy," she had said, and laughing, took a step back from him.

He was grateful for the peppermint stick that dangled from his lips, and his full hands, that spared him the burden of a quick reply. Her eyes captured his before he could shuffle past.

"You got anymore candy?"

He mumbled "no," and shifted his package to his left-hand side, moved closer to his door.

She was faster, blocked his way.

"I'm Trixie. Friends call me Trix. If I had any friends." Her features slacked a little after the last part, Cecil wondered if it was deliberate, a play for sympathy.

She reached for what he thought was a handshake, then lightning quick, plucked the peppermint from his mouth and thrust it into hers. His teeth clacked together on the nothing.

"Thanks," and she was already turning, so her checkered dress spun a little, and flitting, half skipping down the hall.

"Cecil, nice to meet…" his words fell dumbly into the soft pattering of her retreat. She turned and winked at him before disappearing into her room.

She looked younger than he, and dressed younger still. Her dress was of the kind a child might wear to church. Frilly at the edges, modest; it was yellowing and dirt-stained on the bottom hem. The surface could never be trusted in this place. She was apparently alone, as he was. He pushed from his mind thoughts of what she might be conducting in her small and dingey room.

When he heard the scream, his thoughts immediately jumped to her, of her helplessness among the hard men that packed the foul-smelling streets and saloons, and these very rooms. Then a flash of thought about what he had done, what had brought him here. A need to demonstrate that he was not of a piece with those who poured in and out of this town, these rooms.

Retrieving the pistol from his coat, he eased his shoulder to the door, opened it just enough to glance down the hallway. His mind was bent to redemption and heroics, to restoring some sense of virtue of who he imagined he was, or leastwise could be.

The hall smelled of sweat and urine and the sawdust liberally applied to cover the worst of it. A second scream rang out, and he was sure now it came from Trixie's room.

He shoved the pistol into his waist and charged. The sound of his footfalls was thunder in his ears, trees falling under the axe, and his heart was a tight fist against his ribcage.

Expecting resistance, and heart pumping fear and anger, he

shouldered too hard into Trixie's door. Unlocked, it gave easily, and his enthusiasm sent him sprawling inside, nearly pitching to the floor.

Sitting in the far corner, her face a torment of flickering shadow cast by the weak lantern beside her, she was half buried in a pile of blankets she clawed at and pulled to her knees. In her other hand, she held the tattered remnants of her dress. The whites of her eyes were china plates that seemed to take up half her face. The other half a smear of blood rendered black in shadow, and dripping its darkness onto her chin and chest.

The man was tall and lean. Grey streaks stood out in his dark mane, and his beard was a thin scrub. Naked to the waist, even in the dim light it was apparent his tanned skin was deeply scarred. Great pink lines stood out in relief on his chest and right arm. Cecil froze, realized what got him here did him no good with being here. Good intentions do not a skillset make.

"Who's this?" the man slurred. "Your partner? You two think you can roll me? I aim to get what I paid for and then some you little bitch."

His mind a blizzard, Cecil forgot about the pistol. He was a great raging blank. Every thought was of doing something, anything. He took a step toward the man.

"This some kind of joke?" The man took Cecil's shirt in one massive hand, pulled him close and then slapped him hard across the head and right ear with his other hand.

It happened so fast, it felt like he had been struck with a wooden plank. His ear popped just before the other side of his head rebounded off the wall. He collapsed backward, falling into and slamming the door closed behind him He came to one knee, vision full of black spots and a whooshing in his ears, nauseous. The man looked at him a moment, his laugh was cold and mirthless.

"Fine, you can watch, youngster. Maybe learn a thing or two."

He went to work on his pants, half unbuttoning them and pulling them over his hips.

Trixie pulled her knees in tightly, like she might recede into the safety of the wall behind her. Her eyes darted between Cecil and the brute, but she made no sound.

The man approached her on hands and knees like a feral beast closing on its prey. Then he lunged, grabbed one of her ankles, yanked her flat from the wall with a thud.

Cecil's heart slowed its pounding. An icicle stabbed his gut and then glazed his insides with numbing frost. He felt the sweat cool on his skin like snowmelt. Finally, even his thoughts stopped their relentless clawing.

The calm was a soothing embrace, like in the alley with Rook, but now his body was even more remote. His hand didn't tremble as he retrieved his pepperbox pistol, slowly, quietly. He inched his way across the narrow distance separating him from the man. When he pressed the barrels into the center of the man's back, the man didn't notice. So intent was he on his predation, that he had tuned all else out.

Cecil squeezed the trigger.

Bang.

The sound roused him, muffled though it was by the pistol pressing into the man's flesh. Cecil fell back into a low squat, and watched the life rush out of the man, first a crimson flower that grew from his back as he pitched forward, and then a spreading pool that grew around him.

He grunted, dug his hands into the blankets. Gripping, releasing, gripping again. Finally, they went soft.

Cecil sat, stunned. His mind flashed to all the nickel books he read. Stinking of alley rot and missing pages. All those stories of marshalls and rustlers, frontiersmen and Natives. The heroes said the first one was the hardest, it gets easier after. But the first, whether an accident or no – the further from it the less sure he was, like some receding mirage – had been obscured by adrenaline. Fear and running. The thing itself was like a blank, a void made real by the before and after.

No, the second was the hardest, because there was no denying he was a killer now. It was as burned into his identity as the scars that covered the lifeless body before him. He thought he would restore something here, but none of his decisions ever yielded the desired result. He already missed the numb resolve from just a moment before. Why couldn't he live in that state?

The thing itself had been easy, hadn't it? Too easy. Like the trails leading west, each traverse a reinforcement. Violence, a brush beaten path that once you find it, it must be easier to stay the course than to forge another. Knowing he had this steel in him, this smooth, cool center like the rifled barrels of his pistol, the pieces fitting together for but one possible use. But the pieces of him didn't fit together. They abutted and clashed in unending conflict.

All of this a flash, like lightning, so bright it casts shadows of itself on all you see for a time after. A sting in his cheek brought him back.

Trixie? Not Trixie? She stood before him dressed as a boy. Trousers, suspenders, a heavy woolen shirt that hung loose on her. She slapped him a second time.

"Wake up. We have to go. People ignore a lot of things here. A gunshot isn't one of them. Everyone wants to see the story behind a gunshot."

Cecil shook his head, watched her methodically go through the dead man's pockets. She held up a wad of bills, leafed through them and shoved them in her pants pocket. Held up a watch, dropped it in a grain sack stuffed with her other possessions. Some papers she held up a moment and tossed aside.

"Don't look at me like that. You're the one who shot him."

"To save you, yes I did."

She laughed a cawing laugh, eyes flicked toward him. A carrion bird. "I could have handled him. I've handled lots worse.

Some of them, they just need to hurt you a little, can't get their peckers hard until they see some blood."

Cecil felt sick, felt the warmth drain from his face.

"It's ok." She smiled. "What you did was kind of sweet. Now, let's get your things and get out."

Cecil let himself be led, pausing only to pick up the wad of papers Trixie had discarded, giving them only the briefest glance before shoving them in his pocket.

She pushed him out the door. The hall was darker than before. He was still getting his bearings when she pulled him into his own room, easing the door closed behind them.

"You really need to snap out of this, or neither one of us is getting out of here."

Most of his belongings were carefully packed from his last round of meticulous organizing. There were a few loose items on the floor. She gathered a small pocketknife and some change, and shoved them in her bag, as he took up his satchel and haversack.

"Ok. Ok. Where do we go now?" He was waking to the reality of the situation, which was grim. Suddenly, he didn't feel as anonymous in this town.

"I've got a place we can at least sleep out the night and think over things." She showed no sign of being scared -no hitch in her voice or trembling hand- only a clipped tone that spoke of annoyance and impatience with him.

A few people had congregated at the other end of the hall when they exited. They were talking among themselves and gave the youngsters little notice. Cecil stepped lightly, to sneak the opposite way from the crowd.

"What are you doing," It was less a question and more a frustrated command. She shoved him, and they made their way around the corner and down the stairs to the exit.

She pulled him into the nearby alley.

"Unless you want to look guilty, stop looking guilty. People see us and they see a couple of kids. The only way to draw attention is to keep trying not to. Now follow me."

She led him down a series of paths that wound between the town's many structures, crossing a few streets, while mostly sticking to the shadows. She walked normally, as on a nighttime stroll. Like it was the most natural thing in the world.

Lantern light made flickering shadows everywhere, and the standing water stared up at him black and empty, occasionally catching his reflection like the ghoul that haunted his steps.

They finally made their way to a barn that abutted the rail station. In a narrow gap between the structures was a pile of packing crates, covered in a canvas tarp.

"Under here," and she pulled up a flap in the tarp to reveal a void between two crates. She crawled through and beckoned he do the same.

Emerging on the other side, there was a void concealed by the tarp. A candle flickered on a makeshift table, and a pile of blankets shifted and snored.

Trixie crawled over and placed her hand on the covered form, shifted it gently.

"Ungghh." An arm came from beneath, brushed at her.

Trixie pulled at the blanket and the man beneath finally revealed himself.

His face was chiseled rock, his hair jet black and long. He said something to Trixie in a language that Cecil had never heard.

She motioned to Cecil and said something back in the same tongue, but struggled with it, pausing and looking down every few words. They went back and forth like that a few minutes and the man seemed agitated, then dismissed her with a wave and rolled over in his blankets.

"He says we can stay, at least for the night."

"Who is he?"

"Just an old friend. The only one left. He's from all the way in Florida. He's a bit on the run too."

"Wait, what do you mean, too?"

"Well, you were running from something even before tonight. Your eyes give you away, like some cornered animal. You're lucky I'm the only one who gave you a second look."

"What do we do now?"

"I don't know. You're the hero. You came to rescue me. What was your plan?"

"Did I look like I had a plan?"

"Oh, that's just great. Well, for now, let's get some sleep. You have some serious thinking to do tomorrow. Because we're partners now, and you need to get me out of harm's way, partner."

Just like that, she retrieved a serape from her bag, and kicking off her boots, lay down in the corner, and closed her eyes.

Cecil's mind was racing again. What could she expect from him? He moved closer to the flickering candle, retrieved the papers he had pocketed from the dead man.

Unfolding them, flattening them out, slowly reading. His heart froze in his chest. The scraps of paper Trixie had thrown away were the most valuable thing they could have found. Cecil's hands shook and he willed himself to steady them, read through the document three more times. It was a contract as best he could tell, granting one third interest in some mercantile in California. The paper gave him a destination, and the feeling that he might be moving toward something instead of just away was the first pleasant thing he had felt in days. It might be worthless, but it was hook enough to hang a withering hope upon.

After a nearly sleepless night -there were more restless than restful ones- Trixie stirred. There were several false starts, when it appeared she might rouse fully, and then she would yawn, or mutter something unintelligible, and then again roll away from him to her corner. Sunlight was revealing every gap in the canvas, and between wooden slats in the crates, and by the time she surrendered to its incursions, it had become uncomfortably warm for Cecil.

Her friend had dressed quietly and departed at dawn, without saying a word to him. He had been efficient in his movements, remarkably so when it became apparent how much out of proportion he was to the space. Cecil estimated him to be over six feet, and broad at the shoulders. He was lean, in a muscular way, and his face, though expressionless, bore the marks of age, or of miles.

"So, what's the plan? You look like you didn't sleep so you must have concocted a real whopper." Her transition to wakefulness complete, Trixie was back to her enthusiastic self. So far, she only had two modes, and could vacillate between them with alarming quickness.

Cecil rubbed his eyes. The space was increasingly uncomfortable, and he could feel sweat starting to bead at his forehead and the middle of his back. "I guess we need to get out of here. The Santa Fe."

She frowned, raised her eyes, then her hands. "I've got to say I'm a bit disappointed in you Cecil. That isn't much more of a plan than we had when I went to bed. A little short on specifics, don't you think."

"Listen, I'm new to this. I reckon a lot newer than you, anyway." He stammered. He hated when he did it, always the worst of times. "I've been gathering what supplies people say you need. I've got a canteen and water skins, a cooking pot and such, some basic dry goods. What else do we need?"

She rolled her eyes.

"I'd say four hooves is a good place to start, unless you're planning on walking to Santa Fe. They're probably looking for me or I'd go myself. Who knows what kind of mangy beast you'll bring back here. You go to the livery. It's not far. Other side of the train station and over one street. I'll chance a trip to the mercantile to get what sundries I need. I've done a little trail riding, so I've a pretty good idea. Come back here when you're done, and we'll get sorted and go."

Cecil was relieved to have something to do, to be dismissed from this cave that was rapidly becoming an oven, but was in no small amount terrified of the job he'd been given. It was an important task to be granted to one such as he, with no experience in dealing in horseflesh. The work horses pulling wagons and trolleys in Columbus, and more recently those on the trail, all looked the same to him. What qualities indicated a good or bad horse? In the paperbacks, it was all adjectives. Spirited, lean, stout. Nothing in the way of guidance for what might inform such qualities.

"Tell Greeley that Trix sent you. He'll know not to cheat you at least."

14

THE WHIFF OF THE PREY

The young couple had made excellent time. Too good to make any rational sense. The landscape of the wild places expanded and contracted like a living thing. They were well into Nebraska, nearly to Wyoming when he finally caught up with them. The trail -its terrain and its cold- had put him in a foul mood, a general state of annoyance that had settled on him for many days. Charlie rode with his hat pulled down and the collar of his jacket up; the wind off the prairie bit mercilessly at any exposed skin.

On hoof since Franklin, where the crowded poor and the stench of cow shit had irked him. The stink followed wherever the people poured out of that town, such that even the open prairie could not completely wrest it from them. By sheer luck he had retreated to an out of the way saloon before he left there, where the sole subject of conversation was a dead card player and the boy who had disappeared with him. From there, he found the rooming house and the mercantile.

The shopkeep had been in no hurry to divulge any information, seemed less so the more Charlie intimated he might represent the law.

"Go get the sheriff, I'll tell him the same thing I told you. A thousand people a week come through here at least, you can't expect me to remember some brat." The man spoke with a dismissive tone. Charlie was still attired in his suit, thought maybe that gave the wrong impression. Most folks who called him Gentleman Charlie, did so with a sort of guarded irony. Them who didn't know him -by looks or by reputation- sometimes erred. Maybe some, like the shopkeep, spent too much time looking at faces, so they were grown immune to the clues those features contained. Like a nose that had clearly been broke more than once.

Charlie pulled the .32 from the small of his back and smashed the man across the face. He had moved so fast the fella didn't know what hit him, and nearly toppled. Charlie credited him with a stern constitution for staying afoot. Much bigger men had gone down more easily.

The shopkeep spit fragments of two or three teeth, and blood ran from his split lip down his chin in a ragged cord. He raised a hand defensively and lowered his head. After that, he told Charlie everything, such as it was. He had little to offer other than a description of the couple and their wagon, that they were headed to Independence, and then the Oregon. It was enough.

"You could have saved yourself a lot of trouble. You don't know enough to give up so much to protect it." He set five dollars on the counter. "For the dentist."

The man smiled a weak smile, a bloody caricature. He shrugged, collected the money as he kept one eye on Charlie until the door closed behind him.

It was early on the sixth day riding the trail when he first caught sight of them. Had he been more impetuous, he would have closed the distance then and there. No. It was broad daylight, and his work was best done of an evening, and the better with fresh eyes.

He had been riding hard with little in the way of breaks and both he and his animal were much in need of a rest. Spying a patch of dense green a mile or so distant, he turned from the path and in a brief spell came upon a sort of oasis, where a trickle of a stream stretched into a restless pool beside an alcove of trees.

He let the mare drink to her satisfaction and then left her to wild graze on the nearby shrubs and grasses; the sounds of her maceration and of the water was soothing and pleasant. Scarcely had he cupped some of the cool water to his mouth and splashed some on his face, when he felt a desperate need of sleep, and wrapping up in his wool blanket, he dozed.

When he woke, the sun was almost directly overhead. It had been four hours at least. The animal slept where he had left her. Plenty of time, he thought.

Removing a rolled goatskin, he laid it out on the grass. Brushes, shaving kit, mirror. All polished silver, gleaming bright and clean. First, he stripped, washed his shirt in the river, using the smaller brush to scrub out a few light stains. He laid it on a nearby rock in the sun to dry. The larger brush, he used to clean his pants and jacket and hung these from a treebranch. Then, he retreated to the water, squatting in the pool to fully immerse. The chill set his teeth chattering something fierce. He bathed and shaved and then submerged his head over and over, shaking it under the water and then bursting out, throwing water everywhere like a wet dog. He trimmed his mustache carefully with a small pair of scissors and then waxed it, so the ends feathered and rose in gentle arcs.

It was a daily ritual for him, and in his haste he had denied it the last several days. It ate at him, that others who saw him in a flash, speeding by them on his horse, might judge him no better than common riff-raff, a lonely homesteader or fool thinking to make his fortune panning gold dust.

He hated that the trail made it so difficult to maintain a proper appearance. The grit and the filth and the sweat were like unto the past that always threatened to undo our best efforts. Civilization was an act of will. Vigilance -constant vigilance- the price. Chaos, the weakness of men, was ever patient, waited only for an open door, a loose shingle, that it might work free like a dead tooth. Every pathetic settlement on the frontier was just that shack he grew up in with a fresh coat of paint. Iteration after iteration.

Charlie stayed clear of the trail but well in sight of it for the next few hours. It was good riding and there was game aplenty in the scrub. Every few minutes, a hare would spring out from under a bush and dart away, or a snake would slither nearby. He drew his Scoffield and rested it across the saddlehorn, waited.

Not two minutes later, a fat rabbit came springing out of the weeds. He gave it a few seconds, even guiding the mare away from it to make space. Then he raised his pistol and fired. The creature tumbled like a deflated ball, rolling and sliding to a rest. He dismounted, lashed it to the saddle and then continued.

Repeating the process two more times, he got one more hare. The second went much as the first had. He missed the third, but was untroubled by it. Very few men could have made the shots he had. The trail was good for one thing at least: this practice.

He caught up to the couple in the midafternoon and matched the pace of the wagon about 200 yards behind it. It was slow going from there, and he spent the rest of the day watching. There was no sign of the boy, and he hoped he might be asleep beneath the canopy. At one point they stopped, and the man and woman took turns making water. When there was still no sign of the boy, Charlie began to worry. If the shopkeep had lied to him, it would be bad for the man.

At a slow trot, there was little to do but watch. The trail was not so densely populated this far along, and no one passed him. Despite the cool air, his head grew quite warm under his hat, and he had to regularly mop sweat from his brow. The sun was bright, even late into the day, and strained his eyes so that his head began to hurt. That and the boredom fueled his nerves, and every bump, every sweaty part of him magnified his irritation.

There was little to learn from his observations, other than that the woman spent a fair amount of time under the cover and left the man to steer the course. He was growing tired, growing to despise them. All these fattened calves hurrying their way to slaughter. The soil had a pulse out here, stronger the further out he went. He wondered why so few could feel it. Perhaps they did, and in their ignorance mistook dread for excitement.

As the sun was setting, they finally stopped to make camp. Charlie closed a bit of distance, hobbled his horse to a stout bush about a hundred yards behind and half that distance off trail. He retrieved his jacket from his saddlebags, gave it a quick once over with the brush, then made his way on foot to the others' campsite.

The first thing he noticed was the voices. Two adults and no hint of a boy. His concern was building but still not definitive. He stepped into the light of the fire, leading with the two hares, which he held by their ears in his left hand.

He glanced in the wagon as he passed. No sign of the boy, just the trail provisions and the meager possessions of homesteaders. He had nothing against anyone trying to make their fortune; his contempt was for the careless, the ignorant, and the ill-prepared. Most of these homesteaders were fools who were crowning a lifetime of small errors in judgment with one very large one, and for many, the last one.

"Hallo there," the man greeted him immediately. He looked older than Charlie had expected from the shopkeep's description, his full beard more gray than brown.

"The fire's warm and we just put coffee on if you want to join us. What have you got there?"

Charlie stepped fully into the light. The horse nearest him

made to move away and he stroked its muzzle. It calmed, but continued eyeing him suspiciously.

"I'm camped a ways yonder and saw the fire, thought you might like some company and to share in my bounty" He tossed the rabbits to the ground, where they landed with a solid thump. "Is it just the two of you?" The woman was tending to the coffee pot, finding a position for it at the edge of the flames.

"Yessir. And you, are you riding the trail alone? You seem weary. It's a rough road without company." The man smiled broadly. Charlie suspected he might be drunk.

He worked his way around the fire, shook the man's hand. "It's a lonely task I've been set to, I'm afraid," and he affected a lowly scowl. "Heartbreaking, in fact."

The man shook his hand vigorously.

"I'm Timothy by the way. Lucy, why don't you see to them fine rabbits this man brought us."

Lucy set to dressing the animals. She smiled at Charlie but didn't say a word to Timothy.

"Forgive my husband, his manners vanish like smoke in the wind when he tips the bottle."

"Pleased to make your acquaintance, ma'am," and he touched his hat. "My name's Charlie. The trail can wear down a man, and I'm the intruder here."

He gave Timothy a wink and a nod.

She motioned for him to have a seat and he eased onto a log near the fire.

"Well, let's warm you up and let you rest your weary bones. Maybe the burden will be less on a full stomach." Timothy gave Lucy a stern look but said nothing to her. Charlie had seen the look before. She would pay for her remark later, probably moreso the more whiskey he had to drink.

Leaning forward with a calculated slouch, to put them at ease, he began his interrogation softly. Where were they going?

What were they hoping to find? Let them fill the quiet and say more than they might intend.

Timothy cluttered the still and smoky air with all the usual homesteader fantasies. There was land for the taking, fertile and beautiful, and he would farm and slowly build a herd in Colorado or maybe further west. By the time Lucy brought Charlie a plate of stew he was grateful to have something to look at other than the man's face. Timothy's doe-eyed stupidity was beginning to excruciate.

They ate in silence, and Lucy brought him a steaming tin cup after. The smell of coffee was spiriting.

The man poured from a flask into his own cup, offered it to Charlie. He took just a little nip, to be polite. Whiskey didn't hold much appeal for him. It blunted vigilance and softened resolve.

"So, if you don't mind me askin', what troubles you?"

"Well," Charlie took a deep breath, sighed. "Well, you see, I'm on the trail of my son. A shopkeep in Kansas said he left there with some folks like yourselves. The boy has run away before, but never made it so far. His mother is worried sick for him. I just don't know what we're going to do." He sipped his coffee slowly, shut his eyes and shook his head, every inch of him the aggrieved father.

Lucy stiffened, then shuffled quickly to the wagon and busied herself there. A general clatter of pans could soon be heard.

The man got up slowly. He had a hitch in his step. Charlie guessed he was missing part of his leg. He was the right age for it.

"Well, you can see there's no boy here. The missus and I have been trying, but no luck so far. What did you say your name was, again, your family name, I mean?"

"Burroughs, Charlie Burroughs. The boy is thirteen. His

name is Cecil but he might be saying otherwise. Thin. Brown hair. Clever boy. Smart as a whip."

"Why you think he come to run off?" The man was pacing a little, favoring the stiff leg, feeding a few sticks into the fire.

"Forgive me for saying, but I get the impression you might know something about the boy." Charlie was growing impatient.

"Forgive me for saying, sir, but folks got lots of different reasons to run off. Sometimes it's better for them not to be found by them they run from." He was staring at Charlie now, attempting to size him up. Here was the other side of whiskey. Men like Timothy –Charlie had seen hundreds of them– they crowd saloons and act like fools. Then, like trains at the switching station, they change tracks, as though all their buffoonery doesn't undermine the pretense of toughness.

He maintained a level voice, let it crack a bit with the distant promise of tears. "The boy's always been of a delicate disposition. He don't take criticism too well. His mother and me, maybe we're hard on him from time to time but only to raise him up right."

"Well, mister, my daddy had some strange notions about how to raise a boy. And thirteen is practically a man. I reckon a boy deserves the benefit of the doubt, regardless. So why don't you stop your equivocating and tell me what you're really doing here."

"Ha, fair enough," Charlie rose, smiling, shedding the ruse. The man instantly took two awkward steps back.

"I'm with the Pinkertons." Charlie pulled a badge from his pocket. It was a well-made fake that had gotten him out of a few problems in the past. It worked best when someone didn't look too long at it though, so he quickly replaced it in his pocket. "The boy stole some items belonging to a couple on the train from Columbus. I'm on his trail to get the merchandise. I don't really care about the boy and neither do they. Just want to collect the property that was took."

"I do like to help the law where I can," it seemed the man was fighting off a smile forming on the edges of his mouth. "I surely wish I had information to give you."

Charlie closed the distance, splashed the dregs of his coffee in Timothy's face, then kicked his good leg out from under him.

Lucy let out a throaty gasp and ran toward her husband. Charlie intercepted her, grabbing her left arm at the elbow and flinging her earthward.

Timothy was working at regaining his footing. He was manually manipulating his right leg, fighting to get it under him so he could rise. He lunged at Charlie, trying to get between him and his wife.

Charlie put a foot to his chest and shoved Timothy backwards to the ground. Landing with a thud, his head rebounded off the log that had been his seat.

Pulling the small dagger from his waist, Charlie grabbed Lucy by the arm again and held the blade to her neck. A tiny bloom of red emerged at its tip.

"Now let's all calm right down." He could see a scream coalescing in her face, and there was little Charlie hated more than a shrieking woman. He pressed the dagger until a rivulet of blood ran down the blade, a slick of black in the flickering light. "Don't you make a goddamn sound." He shook her by the elbow and her fear resolved into a whimper.

"It could have been easy. Why is it always such work with you rubes. You don't know anything worth a shit, and yet you hold onto it like you do every pathetic trifle you truck across this goddamned country. Now, tell me where the boy is or watch your wife bleed out on the grass."

Timothy was crying. His hand was dripping blood where he had touched it to the back of his head. He stared helplessly at his wife.

"I'm sorry. Just let her go. We don't know anything. The boy was with us from Franklin to Independence. He said he was going on west to stay with family, that his mother was to follow, and his father was a drunk who run off. We was afraid you were his drunk Pa, out to hunt the boy down."

"Noble of you. Just look at the price of your nobility." Charlie wiped both sides of his blade on Lucy's sleeve, then sheathed his knife. She crumpled as soon as he released her, pressed one hand to her neck and the other to her mouth to muffle her sobs. He grabbed her wrist and yanked it as he stood up fully, then held it for leverage while he punched her twice in the jaw. She collapsed into a heap, unmoving.

Timothy was trying to stand again, and Charlie pulled a half-burned log from the fire. He struck the man's head in an explosion of ashes and cinders. Timothy went down hard, and was still. Tossing the club aside, Charlie retrieved another brand, one with an end deep in the fire pit. He set it to the canopy of the wagon, rolling it along the canvas until it was well lit, then tossed it inside. He pulled the bolt from the rigging and with a slap, sent the horses -harnesses and all- trotting into the dark. The glow grew bright behind him as he walked back to his camp.

15

FLOWERS FOR HAIR

Autie had plenty of time to consider his prospects on the way to Red Sky camp.

The road was beaten smooth and bereft of dangers, and he found as always, that with no conflict to occupy him, his mind stirred with endless unease. Smooth roads and ease of travel was the future, a future he had no place in, even as he was party to its creation. It set his stomach sour to consider. He might ride his band to the Pacific, the trail dust red behind them with the blood of glorious battle, but the writing was on the wall. If he lived long enough -and he had always known his life would be long- he would see the end of the frontier, of all frontiers. He was ill suited to the peaceful world. He also knew that much as the public celebrated his courage and his exploits, this too would end.

The carnivorous masses enjoyed the spilling of blood, but appetites are fleeting, and nothing so delicious as a fall from grace. When their need of him was done, it wouldn't take long for those who prospered in the tame he had created to find him that gave it to be nothing but a repugnant holdover from barbaric times, a reminder of what they all really were, the things they were ready to forget.

Sheridan knew his weakness for praise, knew him well enough that when he departed, he had taken Autie's biographer and the two journalists back east with him. Sure, Autie yet had his own journals, which he wrote in daily, obsessively. It was a poor substitute. He lacked the imagination of them that wrote about him.

Regardless, his job was his job, and his vanity demanded he always dedicate himself to its most aggressive completion. So, on to Red Sky camp in northwestern Missouri. Where some of the last holdouts from the campaign against the Sioux resided, under the watchful eye of an entire battalion. Here he would secure a scout.

Flowers for Hair was winyanktehua, born with the trappings of masculine biology, but a creature of spirit who transcended the clumsy distinctions of the flesh. She lived as a woman, had big medicine according to her people. More importantly, she was revered as a keeper of knowledge, a collector who knew the legends. And not only of her own people; she also had gathered stories from many other bands across the plains. He couldn't imagine anyone better suited to such a chore as he was now embarked upon.

When he entered her tent, it was a cozy affair. The walls inside were painted with scenes of vast prairies and buffalo hunts. The ground was covered almost entire in blankets, with cushions of grain sacks stuffed with prairie grass. Flowers bounded the interior walls and Autie, who had never before met her, was shocked by her appearance.

Flowers for Hair was so named, apparently, because she kept wildflowers woven so densely into her braids that hardly a stray hair could be seen. Like multicolored garlands, they hung across her chest. Light filtered through the open top of the structure, illuminating a face delicate boned, with high cheeks, a thin nose, and sleepy eyes that instantly trapped his own. Their sparkling amber mesmerized, or perhaps it was the air, which was thick with the scent of all the flowers. The way it stirred his guts was unwanted. She was an abomination, after all, to his faith, and she was the enemy. A thing to be reviled and the more so because his body spoke otherwise. He prided himself on his evenness of temper, and here he felt anything but even.

He came to an awkward seat on a cushion opposite her. His legs would not cross as hers did, and his knees splayed out, where he held onto them to stay upright.

She leaned toward him and handed him an earthenware cup. Steam rose from it and wafted bitter into his nostrils.

"It's tea, drink," and she took a sip from her own cup.

He smelled it and took a small sip himself; the heat numbed his tongue and it felt thick in his throat.

"I've come with a proposal."

"I know why you've come. Knew that you would for some time now. You do not come to propose. One does not ask of a prisoner, does he? He may command, demand, punish. So, you come to soften this, to use words that string pretty beads on the cords of a whip."

"I can offer you some compensation."

"What compensation do you have for me? Beads or blankets? I have none left to warm or to decorate. No, there is nothing more to give and none with the authority to give it."

"We might be able to resettle you on fairer land, farther from the army."

"Might. Might, maybe, perhaps. No. These are just the magic words with which you wash your conscience. I am Flowers for Hair. Oglala, of the Lakota. The Sioux as your people say it," and she spat on the ground, nearly hit his foot.

"I am of the Oyuhpe, the Soreback. My Tiwahe, my family name, is Maka. The Grandmother of All Things. My mother, her mother, and all of them that come before, back to the oldest, to the time of dreaming. We have studied, always, the ways of this land. Knowledge passed unbroken is like unto a god, it has a soul that stretches beyond the measuring of man. All of this, and I know that I am the last. And you. You do not wish to learn, to possess this treasure of mine. You wish only to hold it, to consume it."

Flowers for Hair didn't know that halfway around the world, men like Darwin were plucking the wild things from the world and pinning them to boards, replacing their insides with sawdust and packing them in crates. Didn't know that these men cared nothing for the living ways of things so long as they could examine their parts. She only knew the spirit of this man in front of her, and all the men like him.

Autie needed her cooperation. He could compel her to join him on the trail, sure, but could not prize from her head the knowledge he required. His anger was increasing, and it took great effort to shut out the impulses to violence. He had never been spoken to so, by any woman, let alone a Native.

And the worst part was that she was right, he had no real capacity to grant the things she wanted, only empty promises to entice. She was sly and that only heightened his contempt. He wished he hadn't left his lance with his horse. Could picture it glinting in the pillar of light at the center of the space. He had found it a great tool for compelling. Looking at her, her resolve, he knew it would be of little use here. She would not be intimidated. Even as it seemed she could read his mind, his thoughts of violence did not register on her face as even a hint of fear.

"I will help you. The wild lands may do what we who have lived on them failed to. It is an indulgence to kindle what will happen in time, what must happen."

"You want to watch me and mine undone by the beasts of the prairie and the mountains, is that it? Well, I fear you will be gravely disappointed."

"I have seen much but can't see the fruits of this. It is rare. I suppose it may be that I die on the trail with you. I only know that this thing you want to do is beyond the powers of men, and that your vanity is like unto the soft flesh behind the shoulder of the bison." She sipped her tea, stared at him.

Those sleepy eyes lulled him. The world shrank around them, dark. Again, he wished for his lance. Something to hold onto for strength.

"We have the favor of God, who has seen us make pitiful work of every savage thing on this continent."

"Your god, whose love finds its fullness in such violence. Do you ever fear he might find one more favorable, one more capable than you of providing him the blood he demands?"

"You don't understand our God."

"I think I understand him better than you, having witnessed the bounty of his favor. We may both understand him better before we leave each other's company. I hope so."

Autie finished his tea in one great gulp. The dregs lumped in his throat, and he had to swallow hard not to choke. He felt weak, gripped his knees tighter so as not to teeter.

"I need to make preparations," she said. "Return near sunset and I will be ready."

Just like that, he was being dismissed. His head spun as he stood. He staggered into the bright sun and felt in his legs the same numbness of his tongue. He thought he might fall for a moment, but then a warmth chased the numbness away. He felt soothed, a general ease as he hadn't felt in some time. His mind flashed to his childhood, a thunderstorm, curling with his mother under a heavy quilt, her hand at his back and her sweet breath on his neck.

When he looked up, the sky had broken into fine crystal, sun and cloud and the endless blue, all folded into one another. As he stared, it broke into shapes. He saw beasts that recalled the images in the book Sheridan had given him, like crude drawings writ large. He saw himself, lance in one hand and torch in the other, and waving it, he set the sky alight. He watched every abomination burned to oblivion, until finally he himself was lit. The fire did not burn him but only magnified his presence. And then it was all gone. All was as it had been. Wisps of cotton in the bright blue, and the sun blinding bright in the midst.

Blinking hard, shaking his head to wrest the images. Surely, they had been a spell. The heat was unforgiving, and he had not drunk enough water on the road, so distracted had he been in his thoughts. The images clung to him, though, and he felt even more committed to the task ahead, saw in it a destiny greater even than what had come before.

He walked toward his company with renewed strength in his legs, and an urgency. They must rest and eat. They would be riding through the night.

16

JUDAS AND TUCO AND THE WAY TO GARDNER

Arriving at Greeley's Stable and Livery, Cecil was surprised at the bustle. A heavyset man in a faded, beaver skin top hat was having an animated discussion with the man he supposed was the proprietor. Half a dozen others milled about nearby.

Hoping to kill some time and to get a sense of his options, Cecil made his way to the barn. He was surprised to find Trixie's friend mucking stalls. The older man gave him a slight nod and resumed his shoveling.

With ten spacious stalls to a side, the barn was large and airy. Each stall held one to two animals; he reckoned maybe thirty or so horses in all. The smell was overwhelming. He'd never been so confined with so much piss and shit. He did his best to take his time, walking from stall to stall and examining each animal, hoping to divine some clue that would help him when it come time to choose. Certain he would be cheated, he realized he didn't even know what a fair price would be. Suspected whatever it was, was more than the loose collection of bills and coins held in his sweaty fist in the pocket of his dungarees.

Walking the length of the stalls, he realized the most obvious distinguishing feature between animals was how lively they became as he neared them. Which was better, a more docile creature or one that stared white eyed at him and snorted? He guessed that those who jerked their necks and snapped their teeth were a bad fit at least. The last thing he needed was another traveling companion full of bite.

By the time he reached the end of his examination, the heady smell and his nerves had gotten the better of him, and he felt less prepared to make a choice than when he started.

He walked back to where the man was busy cleaning.

"Excuse me. I wonder if you might have any advice? I don't know how to pick a horse and how not to get swindled, to be honest."

The man looked at him. Shook his head, grunted, and returned to his labors.

Just then, a bespectacled man, with a frizzy gray horseshoe of hair around his head, entered the stable. He wore a vest with a gold watch chain, and a collared white shirt with the sleeves rolled over thick forearms.

"Are you here for business, or just to encumber my man?" He stared quizzically at Cecil, who momentarily froze.

Trixie's friend continued his mucking, quietly whistling a tune Cecil didn't know.

"Yes, sir," he finally managed. "I'm here for business, that is."

"Good, good, I'm Greeley, like on the sign. Didn't mean to unnerve you. The Natives are good for what they're good for, but you distract this one and I might never get him back to task." He extended his hand.

Cecil took it slowly. The grip was firm as they shook, and he felt he was already in a game he didn't fully understand.

"I'm looking for a cart and horse, something with a quieter demeanor."

"Well, it doesn't do for a working animal to be too quiet, does it? What are you looking to pay?"

"About fifty dollars. What can I get for that?"

"Son, you can't buy the cart for that much, let alone the beast to pull it. Where are you from to think horses come so cheaply?"

"North." He didn't want to give this man too much information. He didn't seem the type to withhold it from any who might ask, leastwise if they offered him the slightest inducement.

"Well, I don't know what kind of horse a man buys for $50 in the north, maybe one with a game leg, or maybe just a picture of one to hang in your parlor. Now if you'll excuse me, boy, I have serious customers to attend to."

"I'm a friend of Trixie." He blurted it, desperate, felt unmasked in the utterance. "Does that make any kind of difference?"

Greeley cast his eyes downward, licked his lips.

"Trixie, you say. Did she mention how we know one another?"

"No sir, she just said you were an honest man, a good man who might help us."

"So, the animal is for Trixie? You mean to set out?" Greeley rubbed his hands together. "Well, I would be remiss not to do everything possible to assure the girl a safe and rapid journey. No doubt she will be going far away from here. Still, the girl is too small to handle a full-grown horse, and by your ignorance of the horse trade, I'm guessing you're ill prepared to ride alone. The added burden of a passenger would be an invitation to a broken neck."

"I'm sure she will be grateful for any kindness, as am I." Cecil felt a tension in his stomach and the sweat on the back of his neck went icy. He guessed at what history Greeley and Trixie must share and his thoughts returned to the night before. He wanted to be far away from this man, and this town which was full of the most despicable people. This was the portal to the lawless west, and he wondered if it was worse the further one went, and what could be worse?

"Anyway, friend or no, I can't sell a horse for that money, but I recently came into possession of a pair of mules of spectacular lineage, just spectacular. The mare who bred them was of heavy stock and such a pleasant animal as you could ever hope to meet."

Greeley ushered him through the stable and out the other side. The two mules stood in the shade of the barn, facing one another, heads down and eating hay without the slightest urgency. The one facing them gave Cecil a glance and returned to its chewing. The other creature didn't so much as raise its head as they approached.

Greeley slapped the closest on the rump and it finally, slowly raised up and looked at him, still chewing. Bits of hay fell to the ground as it chewed and looked.

"See, calm as the Dead Sea. But look at how well muscled he is. Judas. Judas the Gray. A proper gentleman. And Tuco, his partner. They will take the two of you where you need to go. I'll throw in some saddlebags, blankets and bits, for just a few more dollars. Maybe seventy-five dollars even."

He settled for seventy dollars, which was the bulk of what Cecil had left. Between the gambling and the whiskey, his funds were grown perilously thin. He hoped the few remaining dollars might be enough to stake him in Gardner, and that he might have better luck there. He had no money left for liquor, so at least he might keep his wits for a time.

And so, Cecil found himself walking back to the hideaway, leading Judas by a soft leather pair of reins, Tuco trailing behind him, with nothing more than three dollars in pocket change left to him. Maybe Trixie would let go the brigand's watch from the night before. He needed at least ten dollars to properly work a table.

Trixie smiled when she saw them, stood beaming and

started bouncing in place as they got closer. She took to the mules right away, set to stroking them and scratching behind their ears. The animals grew more lively under her ministrations.

They were packing the saddlebags –Trixie wanted to get them out of town as quickly as possible– when the Native man rode up on a stout pony the color of dirty straw. He looked like a giant on the beast, but it made no sign that he burdened it.

He dismounted. His pony had colorful stones braided into a nearly white mane. Some of them had strange glyphs on them. The man whispered something to Trixie, and she appeared delighted by it.

"Red Club is coming with us. He says the signs favor our journeying together. This is good. Very good."

"Red Club?" The man looked at him like Cecil insulted him by speaking his name.

"Yes. Don't stare, Cecil. Red Club Raised High. You can call him Red if the name troubles your tongue. He knows more about living from the back of a horse than most folks. I'd say his joining us more than doubles our chances of staying alive out there."

Cecil swallowed hard. She said it so lightly. In spite of everything, he still hadn't given serious thought to dying on the trail, felt like staying ahead of the law until he had outrun its reach was the only thing he need worry about.

"I'm Cecil." He extended his hand.

Red Club didn't take it.

"I know. I can hear you two talking." He set to checking the bindings on his saddle.

"He speaks English just fine. He just doesn't like to. Don't worry, he was stiff toward me when first we met. He'll come round."

"I guess as long as he doesn't cut my throat between here and Gardner, that's good enough."

Red Club turned and stared at him a moment, spat on the ground.

When they were finally ready to go, Trixie had to help Cecil, to show him how to ease himself atop Tuco, so as not to upset the animal. It took some effort finding his seat, and from the corner of his eye he caught Red Club shaking his head.

Trixie took the lead on Judas, and it sounded like the animal purred as she leaned across its neck and whispered something to it. Then she sat up.

"Let's go."

The three of them began an easy trot to the west end of town, to the trail that would take them to Gardner. They rode well into the evening, having started late. The trail was much more sparsely ridden than the road from Franklin. A mixed blessing, really. There would be no more celebratory airs, yet there was a safety to the solitude. News would travel more slowly and the chance of being caught thinned substantially, but the dangers of trail life were even more numerous, and thoughts of bandits and wolves and Natives even less friendly than Red Club scraped their fangs across the nape of him.

Still, it was as a knot slipping loose and undone, when Cecil looked back and Independence was fading to little more than a speck. The sun was beginning its fading, and the heat was less of a weight on his back. Though mules didn't move quickly, their gait made for an easy ride, and he imagined Red Club's pony must be practically tiptoeing to keep to their speed. The man rode at the back as it was the only way to keep from running far ahead. Gardner was yet thirty miles on, and they would not make it at one stretch.

The path had a lonely sort of peace. The road to Independence carried most of those who would divert there for the Oregon trail, and while Gardner also nearly intersected, it was not near as popular a starting point. Generally, the Santa Fe was less crowded, which suited Cecil just fine, but he found himself missing the company a little, leastwise those he had traveled with. That and the whiskey. It gave him an anxious shiver thinking too long about it.

"What's going on with you, you gone mute or something," Trixie yanked him from his thoughts. She was trying to poke him with a stick she had picked up somewhere and just then jabbed him in the ribs.

"Ouch." He snatched at the stick, too slowly. She eased her mule back, then forward, and whacked him in the back of the neck.

"Remember this was all your idea. Least you could do is try to be proper company." Trixie puzzled over the boy. His desperation was easy to read, but there was little else. If he didn't ease up, he would wither and blow away before they got near to New Mexico.

"Just tired is all. I didn't know if we'd get out of there, still hard to trust it."

"Sitting on your ass worrying isn't going to get you nowhere," she laughed. "Don't waste your time thinking about what's behind you. It will either catch up to us or it won't. Staying alive out here is going to take all your attention." She whacked him across the back and then tossed the stick aside before he could grab it.

"Hey," Red Club grunted, and when they both looked back, he motioned with his eyes and with a nod. There was a man riding up on them at a steady clip.

"Hoy there, strangers." He rode an Appaloosa, light brown and white, and looked too clean for a cowboy. His chaps were a light calf skin and not a scratch was apparent. His white shirt was buttoned to the neck and a short scarf of blue silk dangled from his neck. He was clean shaven, and his teeth and the whites of his eyes gleamed under the shade of his broad brimmed hat. He didn't so much as acknowledge Red Club; his eyes lingered a moment on Trixie and then he turned his attention to Cecil.

"What are you youngun's doing on this dismal road? If you're looking for Oregon, you're way off course."

"We're headed to family in west Kansas, my sister and me are riding ahead of Ma. She had business to tend to."

"It's a dangerous road to go unaccompanied. Your Ma should've known better."

Cecil didn't know how to respond. It was forward of the man to say what he did, rude even. And there was something generally unsavory about him, the way he held that steady smile and his gaze didn't waver.

"We won't be out here long," Trixie interjected. "Gardner's naught but a short ride."

"A short ride, sure, missy, but not one you want to make at night. Don't wait too long to make camp. There's more paltry accommodations the further along you get."

"We'll be fine." Cecil was resenting the man the more he spoke.

"There's a set of hills about a mile yonder. If you go over the first of them, there's a clutch of trees that makes a nice windbreak. Probably about as good as it's going to get for you out here. A lot of folk don't like the reds much out this way, so you'd be better off camping where you have a bit of privacy. They ain't all as broad minded as myself." He smiled even bigger at that, showed too many teeth. "Well, good evening anyway," and he tipped his hat and was off.

Cecil and Trixie debated on the merits of what was said, on whether the man could be trusted. Red Club rode up between them, parting their mules.

"He had a stink. I don't like it."

The light was fading, and the hill he had described was just visible in the distance.

"Whether he was good or bad, I see no sign of him and not much of a choice. Sleeping off trail seems the best idea for more reasons than he could know, and we aren't going much farther."

The other two silently accepted the truth of his statement, if reluctantly, and Cecil felt a little rush at having fallen into the role of leader. Decisiveness was soothing.

The folly of the decision came clear late that night. The fire had died down as he was dozing, and Cecil woke to a blazing conflagration.

"Wha… what?" He rubbed sleep from his eyes.

Above the crackle of flame and the wind through the trees was the sound of metal on metal, ending in a loud click. Then the cold steel, a crescent of it stinging the skin behind his ear.

"Turn, real slow." He knew the voice.

He did as he was told, and turning to his right saw the same man from the road. He had another pistol trained on Trixie, who still slept.

Across the fire, Red Club was lying prone, his face turned toward Cecil in an agonized grimace. Another man had a boot to his back and pointed a shotgun at his head.

"What do you want?"

Just then, Trixie shifted, slowly opening one eye and turning toward the man. "Well, shit."

"That's right, darlin', now let's just all be nice, and we can part ways as friends. You just keep lyin' there, real still."

He tapped Cecil's cheek with the gun barrel a few times.

"We want everything. We're children of the Lord, like yourselves, so you can keep the clothes on your back and the animals. We got no use for lazy mounts and Injun ponies aren't good for nothin' but eatin', and we ain't that desperate."

Cecil thought of his pepper box pistol. It was deep in the pocket of his coat, which he was using as a blanket. Even if he could get to it, the man would cut him down before he could do anything with it.

The men cleaned them out. They took what little money Cecil and Trixie had left. They even got the money in his boots.

They took all the food, left only the canteens. Took the haversacks and the saddle bags from the mounts.

Cecil managed to roll aside his coat when they were having him empty his pockets and they must have mistaken it for a blanket because they left it alone. His pepperbox pistol remained in the pocket. At least he wouldn't be disarmed.

The one with the shotgun brought the stock of it down hard on Red Club's temple, then they retreated slowly and rode away. It was yet an hour or more to first light, and there was no way they were going to catch the bandits, and what would they do if they could?

They set out early that morning. Red Club was still dazed from the blow, and even Trixie didn't have much to say, other than to show Cecil the watch that she had somehow kept hid. It wasn't nothing, maybe enough to buy in to a game and earn some money. A slim chance but not nothing. About three miles on, they found their bags. Cookware and some extra clothes were strewn about. Cecil found a sock in a nearby bush but couldn't find its mate. They gathered what they could and moved on. By noon they could see Gardner in the distance, and they trotted their mounts past the sun-faded welcome sign in the mid-afternoon.

17

THE ASYMMETRY OF THE HUNTER'S WAY

Charlie stared at the message. The telegraph office in Independence was adjacent to his hotel but seemed a world away from his breezy room on the second floor. Fire raged in the potbelly stove in the corner. It was much too big for the space. The air was close and stifling and he felt a trickle run down the narrow between his shoulder blades. The old man looked perfectly comfortable in his shirt sleeves. Charlie felt like he would wither to a husk before he could wrap up his business.

Boy killed again. Dangerous. Contract goes up five hundred per body. Send two hundred more for expenses. Will take payment as agreement to terms.

It was too long. Would cost too much and give up too much.

He licked the tip of the pencil and began crossing out letters, any unnecessary vowels were the first to go. When he was done, the message he slid across to the bespectacled old man at his desk was much shorter.

Boy killd again. Contrac up fiv hundrd. Send two hundrd expens as agreemt

The man charged him a buck and a quarter; took his money and made change without so much as a glance at his face. Something about that bothered him, but he was too tired to care enough to do anything about it. He didn't know what day it was, had passed beyond the sleepy kind of tired and instead of returning to the comfort of his room, he wandered the street, letting his thoughts align themselves.

The rooming house was a shithole. Still, the old lady described the boy well enough. She told him he should talk to the sheriff, that there might be a bounty on him and the girl he had left with. He knew the boy was afoot when the poor couple parted ways with him, and when he took his own horse to the stable, he met a man -Greeley- who was a veritable fount of information. He already liked Independence much more than any part of this journey so far. People took one look at him and gave up all pretense of subterfuge. Their tongues loosened completely when he tossed them a few coins.

Greeley spoke of the girl like she was some mercenary seductress, said he had watched more than one lowly soul follow her to perdition, crossing himself as he said it. He liked the boy, he said, and felt sorry for him for having fell under her spell, as it were. Said he gave the boy a deal on a pair of mules and that he had departed west along the road leading to the train station and the Santa Fe. Greeley reckoned the Santa Fe was the destination, because there was no need of mules if he were to take the train, and Charlie saw the wisdom of this assumption.

It wasn't much more than he had already assumed, but it was good to have the evidence. He didn't think he could bear another long ride for nothing.

His wandering had taken him well away from the pretty part of town, farthest from where his hotel and the telegraph office sat, and he found himself on a rutted street full of shoddy, clapboard structures. Few of them had glass windows and instead had wooden awnings that were propped up during the day for light and air. Many lacked proper doors. They were the kind of places drifters and cowpunchers went to gamble and fight, and Charlie thought he might use some refreshment to turn his mind to a sleeping mood.

He knew the kid was a gambler, son of a gambler. That wasn't a great help, as there were just too many places to check. Furthermore, he figured there wasn't much to learn from them that he didn't already know. Besides, the steady stream of men in and out of such places meant he would have had to do something memorable to get noticed. His youth might make him stand out, but not enough.

Charlie stepped through the doorway of the first place that appeared adequately ventilated. It had two of the awnings on either side, and the light spilled around his back as he entered, so the edges of his vision were more clear than what was right before him.

He moved toward the lump shaped like a bartender, and the man only appeared more shapeless the closer he got. He was like chewed gristle, a thing that must have been half formed at birth and only got bigger. His round face was bounded by puffy sideburns and the hint of a beard. His skin pale and freckled, and he had only wisps of dark hair atop his head.

Tall beer in hand, Charlie retreated from the sunlight to a far table, painted in shadow and tickled by the slightest bit of sunlight. As soon as he sat, he thought he should have ordered two and saved himself a trip.

By the third beer he suspected it were too winding a path to a quiet mind, and an uncertain one at that.

"The beer ain't workin', seems my restlessness is more than a match for it."

The bartender was scraping the foamy head from atop beer number four. "Well, I've got whiskey if that would suit you better. Puts me right to sleep when the rheumatism gets into my hands."

"I don't take to liquor."

The man started to laugh, but it died in his throat when he looked at Charlie. "There's a sporting lady or two around if that would suit you."

"It might. Is she clean?"

The man shrugged, an ambiguous gesture Charlie hesitated to inquire further of.

It was a blonde gal who appeared at his table just a few minutes later. She wore a dress but no bustle, and her belly was visibly round.

"I'm Delilah. Walt said you could use some company."

"Are you with child?"

"Sometimes," she laughed. It was high and nasal, and he hoped he wouldn't elicit another. "You wanna poke or what?"

Charlie nodded, decided the less talking the better. Delilah led him by the hand out the rear of the building. There was a little storage shed about twenty feet off from the saloon, and when they rounded the far side of it, he saw she had set a blanket on some straw there. She had a bucket, half-filled with foamy water, and some rags.

"Let's see it," and she opened her eyes wide in expectation.

He relieved himself of his pants and was grateful for the thorough inspection she gave, leastwise he could assume every other man got the same treatment. Then, she took a rag and gave it a dip in the water and washed his privates. It was a little embarrassing, and Charlie was not often embarrassed. She got a grip on his wet member when she was done and gave it a few tugs. It was all the encouragement he needed and by the time she shrugged out of her dress, he had firmed up quite well.

She was a tiny thing, despite the round belly that he was now fairly sure was a child on the way. When he entered her, for a brief moment he pictured the thing in there. It put his mind to his mother. Images forced themselves on him, of all those dirty dicks batting his little body around when he was growing inside of her. He started to go soft.

"Oh no you don't."

Delilah threw her legs behind him, pulled him into her with a surprising amount of strength. It was enough to bring him back and he set to working up a sweat. Once they got into a rhythm with one another, thoughts of her unborn child and of anything else were like a puff of smoke on the wind.

By the time he finished, he was nearly out of breath, and when he rolled off of her onto his back, he exhaled from a deep place, like expectorating all the miles and frustration from the last few days.

"You got a lot on your mind, huh, honey," She propped up next to him on her elbow, smiled. "That'll be ten dollars."

"Ten dollars is New York prices, darlin," but he was already fishing for the bill from his balled-up trousers. "I guess Independence is what you'd call a seller's market."

She seemed surprised as she snatched the bill from his hand. "I should have asked for twenty. You're some kind a high roller."

"Nothing of the sort," but he smiled at the compliment, anyway. He put on his pants and started making his way around the shed and the saloon, heading back to the street, and to the waiting bed that he finally felt right in the mood for.

"Come back anytime, honey." She was still laying where he left her and laughed again with that nasally laugh. It didn't bother him so much this time.

18

THE DRAW

The ashes of the first fire humanity ever built. They yet glow an angry red, their embers yet radiating unyielding heat. They burn at the bottom of every one of them. Their haunting glow casting shadows that tell the oldest story, that in each thing man creates, there is in the secret heart of it, the seed of their annihilation. Knowing he cannot last forever, jealous of a future denied him, he desires its undoing. The endless burning, a fever dream, whose shadows find their way into every promise, every hope for conciliation, for peace, because each knows that same fire burns in every other, suspects it burns the worse in the weak and the suffering. For they must be the more hungry, for being so vulnerable. The strong trample the bodies of the weak to make firm their position, and from there, snipe at any who might rival them.

It is ash renewing ash, pain begetting pain. Blood, blood, and more blood. The rocky soil is veined with fleeting life. While it, lonely in its perfection, finds sustenance in the barbarism, and sweet satisfaction in the shame that drives them to conceal it.

19

DEATH FROM ABOVE

"I'll ask you again, what good are you to me if in your company I can ride my men into a god damned ambush?" Autie's muscles twitched with unrelieved frustration. Flowers for Hair sat across from him, her tent too close to contain the violence that begged for an outlet, for an excuse.

"The Lechuza is a wanderer. There are some whose place is known, whose ways are known. I have only heard whispers of this thing. None have heard more."

Fire burned behind her eyes. She wanted to say more, and Autie would have been grateful for the pretext. He'd never hit a woman before, not even a Native, but when he thought of the boys he lost. There were five. Well, four and a fifth unlikely to make it. He had been nearly burnt to a crisp, smelled like burning hair, and worse. Most of the skin had come off his feet when they pulled him out of his smoking boots. Summerfield, that was his name. He thought about the letters he would write, for him and for the others.

"Why don't you have some tea?"

"I don't want your damned tea. I need a clear head." He did want the tea, wanted the opiate balm of certainty that rode across

114

his mind and his skin like a warm bath. He wanted other things. Staring at her face, the flowers, the place where her crossed legs emerged from her skirt, liminal. He wanted things he didn't dare to name.

She loathed him. He knew it, knew deep down that she would undermine him if she could. If it were on the sly so none could be certain it was her, she would sabotage him, his campaign, without a second thought. But she must know too, her safety was a tenuous thing, and he the only one holding the men back from treating her the way they would any hostile.

She began grinding her herbs, lay a few more twigs on her tiny fire. The sound of stone on stone and the occasional crackle was hypnotic. The kettle popped and sizzled, already rested near the flame. Shiny copper, anachronistic to the rest of her spread.

"Fine, the day can't get any worse. Make me some of your brew."

He watched her delicate movements. As his mind relaxed, the events of the night rolled slowly in, a dismal tide.

When they had spotted the great owl, the men had at first mistaken its size, thinking it was much closer than it actually was. A few of them took shots at it with pistols, but they were far off the mark.

He had been lost in thought, having only just stopped to make camp, and in the dusk, at first he didn't see what the commotion was about. It was an army on the move, and gunfire was routine.

Summerfield had been the first to raise a rifle, and Autie finally saw the bird as it careened from the impact of the bullet in its wing. But instead of crashing to the ground, or trying to escape, it had recovered its trajectory and made for the private.

He must have been shocked by its aggression, so that he

never took a second shot, instead flinching and ducking away. As the bird came closer, its actual size was monstrous. Its body was larger than a grown man, its wings near the size of wagons. It dove toward the boy, and as it nearly touched him and then swept to the left, a great flash of blinding light obscured the two of them. For a moment, he thought he saw through the man's skin.

Autie felt the hairs stand up on his arms. A deafening buzz ripped through the air and his ears popped. When he got his sight back, black spots dotted his field of vision. The smoke rising off the boy was clear enough, as was the fit he was throwing on the ground. His legs bounced and kicked, and his head was jerking to and fro.

Most of the men nearby had been too shocked to react, and Autie immediately drew his pistol and ran it dry. He saw just one puff come out the thing's back, one hit out of six.

Sullivan had come up beside him by then and was doing more precise work with his lever action, but the monster soon disappeared into the darkening sky.

They looked at one another, and without a word both began reloading. Autie quickly running his empties out and pressing fresh rounds through the loading gate of his revolver, and Sullivan topping off the Winchester. There was a general uproar as a panic spread through the unit, and as them that were nearby tried to give aid to the fallen man, or crowded around him with arms at the ready.

Screams rang out from the other side of camp. Sullivan broke into a dead run and Autie followed him. They found a man with his throat ripped wide open, helplessly pawing then clutching, trying to contain the blood that was emptying out of him in great spurts. There was another with his guts spilled on the grass, already gone pale and still.

"Tighten the men up."

Sullivan nodded in understanding and began shouting orders.

Autie ran for one of the wagons. He had only used a

Hotchkiss once and was grateful to find the guns loaded and ready. He drew aside the tarp and waited.

In a moment, there were more screams. He leveled the gun in the direction of the sound and let loose before he even looked. *Thump thump thump thump*. The Hotchkiss was loud, the wagon's wood floor creaking in protest and his hands immediately numb. It beat all thought from his head, and it took great effort to direct his attention to the task. He had caught the creature in the wing, and this time when it momentarily slowed, he was able to adjust the aim of the big gun and dark, arcing jets come out the back of the great bird. Finally, it fell to the earth.

"It's very bad luck, this thing you did."

The smell of the tea and the sound of her voice brought him back, and he found the little cup already steaming in front of him. Flowers for Hair sat, not quite staring, not looking away either. She was looking beyond him, through him.

"You should be more concerned with what I might do next."

"The Lechuza." She ignored his threat or else didn't hear it. "The great owl is a mystery. It is said she can mark you. Those who have seen it and walked away, none of them stay on the middle road. It is a blessing or a curse. Killing one…" She nodded and spat. "It must be very bad for you."

He blew over the edge of the cup, took a drink. He didn't want to lose control, fought to ease himself back from the red place, the great flame of him.

Looking at her, slowly exhaling, softening the urge to hurt and to maim, he felt right at the edge of something else. Something that was more dangerous than the tea, maybe more dangerous than giant birds that threw lightning bolts.

Flowers for Hair got up. Unlike him, she was small enough to stand erect in the tent, and her skirt flapped gently as she moved, eye level to Autie and very close. Her smell was more intoxicating than the tea at this distance.

He grabbed her hips and pulled her closer. She didn't resist.

He couldn't see her face. In his mind, her expression shifted into a little smile. A gesture he had never seen from her. His forehead rested on the slight round of her belly.

He licked the place below her navel. Salty and sweet, untouched by the road dust. Here was the ineffable thing he forever sought, its beauty and its strength. Pulling open her skirt, he took her into his mouth. His heart beat heavy as a blacksmith's hammer on an anvil, and he felt a sort of panic. A feeling uncommon to him, a strange tension. He trembled, gripped her hip with his left hand, felt himself stiffen. He didn't know what to do, and the terror was another kind of intoxicating. As he felt her grow inside him, he was delivered to a place beyond thought, of musk and violent grace.

He began stroking her with his free hand, taking the length of her in and out of his mouth. She tensed, and he tightened his hold on her hip. With each stroke, he pulled her more tightly against. him. He wanted to drown in her, to suffocate. The air between them was a sin that dwarfed any he was committing.

Time slipped, immeasurable, shapeless and meaningless, whether from the magic of the tea or their union. The tea was for sure acting on him some. He could taste colors on her, the orange of the morning sun on the bluffs, the reds that limned the clouds in the evenings.

He let go with his right hand and began stroking himself through the heavy fabric of his trousers. It was only a matter of seconds when he spasmed and the warm jet spattered his leg.

She came soon after. It caught him by surprise, and he choked and coughed. He couldn't help but swallow most of what come out of her. He spit the rest on the ground, wiped his mouth on his sleeve.

She stood quietly for a moment. When he leaned his cheek against her thigh, felt the sweat of it sticky against his head, she withdrew and returned to her seat.

Her eyes were a silent judgment, a tangible shift in the power between them. She held in this intimacy a thing that could undo him. He waited for her to speak. A long and pregnant moment. She gave nothing but that vacant stare. Clarity was ice cold, as sticky as that mess in his pants. He felt his face go red and ducked out of the tent without another word.

Most of the men were distracted. Caring for the wounded boy, and the dead, and each other. Out of the corner of his eye he saw Sullivan, caught his expression shift when Autie didn't turn to acknowledge him.

He moved as quick as he could to his tent and pretended to fall quickly to sleep, lest someone come to call. But sleep was delayed and fitful that night. Mostly he stared at the dark canvas and the thin moonlight it permitted, until early the next morning, when he drifted in and out of dreams stiff and breathless.

20

THE FRIAR

He didn't look like much: more like a skeleton draped in rags than a trail boss. Like the weathered and stained beaver hat he wore might at any moment tip him over.

Cecil watched him move toward the bar like it were a planet drawing a meteor to its annihilation. He watched the barman over the man's drooping shoulder, like he could almost see through him, insubstantial as he was. He was tall, but with a slouch that went a long way toward hiding it. The barman leaned close and whispered to him, slid him a glass of brown liquor and pointed to Cecil with his eyes. The man nodded with his whole body, and shuffled across the creaking boards and spiraling dust.

Cecil had been working the tables at The Final Insult, as the saloon was named, for three days when he worked up the nerve to start making inquiries. He had turned the paltry sum Trixie got for the dead man's watch into a small fortune, and his confidence grew apace with his winnings. No one smirked anymore when they called him "Kid," and some would up and leave the table as soon as they saw him.

The barkeep, Jonas, had assured him that he shouldn't judge by looks alone, and it was illicit business they were after. As the man approached, even in the dim light and at the distance, his face was lightless, lifeless. His clothes dusty and threadbare, like he and they were of a piece. He didn't have a hurry in him, and meeting Cecil's look did not hasten his shuffle. The glass danced with a tremor, whose silent rhythm beat in his free hand as well. He didn't spill a drop, though. The closer he got, the stronger the argument against his being of any help.

What choice did he have? Cecil and the others needed a guide. The path seemed simple enough, but a map couldn't tell you where to divert from a trail to avoid an army fort or encampment, what areas you could pause a day or two for a rest and which ones you best push through, even if it meant trekking all night. And how to avoid the scoundrels, the highwaymen. From the looks of him, this man knew them all by name.

The card tables had been much more profitable here than in Independence, but he knew they could lose any fortune within a day or two if they ran into the wrong company, and the word was that this man -despite his flaws- was just what they needed. Looks aside, he was no more outlaw than they were, and possibly less.

Not just any guide would understand their requirements or be comfortable fulfilling them: discretion, speed, to go unnoticed. Jonas and a few of the card players had said he was without scruples, had worked with smugglers and outlaws before. He had the knowledge and the skills. Most of all, he had a proven track record of living on the trail for months at a time. And if what he was told was true, the man had a need almost as great as Cecil's, and perhaps no lower in stakes. If he could be relied on to survive the journey. But no one could count on tomorrow, the less so with each mile further in this unforgiving land.

As he closed on the table, his eyes locked with Cecil's, and it appeared the man yet contained some grit. Whether this was fostered by the contents of the glass in his hand or whatever fortunes the barman had intimated to get him here, or whether there was something more to the man, remained to be seen.

"Hey, Friar, why don't you bless my cards?" A red-faced man shouted from one of the nearby faro tables. He was sweating and wild eyed. The whole game erupted in laughter.

Not quite to the table, the would-be guide shuddered, pressed his glass between both hands like a supplicant in prayer. The liquor sloshed up the sides but not over. He closed his eyes and in a moment the shaking relented. He took a seat.

Softly, evenly, he spoke.

"I understand you're in need of a guide." It sounded like he was pushing each word separately into the world as a baby bird falling from a high nest.

"I might be." Cecil hadn't expected enthusiasm, but this was something else altogether. Reticence.

"I'm Thomas." He slowly brought the whiskey to his lips. Drank half and gently set the glass to table. "Thank you for the drink. I assume Jonas told you about me."

"Yes. Well, some. I need someone who can get me and mine to California, to the coast."

"That's simple enough, why not just join up with one of the convoys? Get you a military escort and the comfort and safety of numbers." He pulled at his hat, so there was only a narrow gap between eyebrows and brim. The tip of a bandanna slipped down like a shock of hair.

"I'm hoping to avoid all that, especially any who might be coming from back east. I don't know if there's trouble following but can't afford to find out."

Thomas raised his eyebrows.

"What kind of trouble?" He held up his glass and eyed Cecil through the amber, then drank down the remainder.

"Maybe not the worst kind. Pretty close. The only kind that really matters."

"The mortal kind," he smiled. "Well, that will command a price."

"How do I know you're worth it? That you've got it in you? And why'd that man call you Friar? Religion got no place where we're going."

"You needn't worry. God and I parted ways some time ago. I was a missionary of sorts. Dispatched to bring Him to that desolate hell. Part of the grand design to civilize the Native folk. I wound up at an outpost in the New Mexico territory. Really a glorified encampment. Didn't have a proper name. That should have been a clue. Men name the things they wish to remember. They promised me the world to get me out there. Do my time and then they'd give me a mission on the coast. Church bells and the cries of gulls playing gently on the cool and salty air. I could taste it. Vanity. We rise on our fantasies to come to ground harder."

He pulled at his hat again.

"The soldiers returned from a patrol one day in high spirits. Don't know which day. We measured time by the patrols then. I did a service about every three patrols. They had found a group of Natives and corralled them back to the camp. It was a motley crew, a mixed lot of survivors of several bands, I think. Mostly they were tired eyes and saggy skin. Half starved. Other than a few injured braves it was old men, women, and children. What was left, meat stripped down to bone. They would have traded their freedom for a warm meal if given the choice, but by then the time of choosing was already done."

He fiddled with his glass, then with his hat again. His eyes were roving and a little wild, searching the room for the scattered pieces of his story.

"What's this have to do with what we're discussing?"

"It's getting there, just settle down. Maybe I'm evaluating you. Maybe I've already decided you need me a lot more than I need your money.

The next day, the grumbling started. We didn't have the provisions to care for them all. Supply lines were drawn thin that far out and that early in the war. I did my best to minister to them. A few were already converts and my efforts brought them a little solace. Seemed so to me, anyway. On day three, some activity started up on the far side of the camp. I didn't pay much attention at first. They were always building or repairing something. Nobody cared to tell me what it was about. I thought maybe temporary barracks, but that didn't make much sense. Maybe a frame for a tent.

Day four, the officers started dispensing whiskey to the enlisted men just after dawn. That was unusual. Later in the day, a crowd started to form around the construction. Curiosity finally compelled me, and I made my way over. What I saw made my heart freeze in my chest and my stomach roil. It was a gallows, and such an engine of killing as I had never seen. A broad platform with ropes for fifteen. Stacks of sandbags and smaller coils of rope were piled just behind the apparatus. A few men leaned on shovels in the shade of the nearby wall. I could smell the freshly turned earth beyond them."

"Mister, I don't need to hear all this." Cecil tensed, leaned away from the table to the limit of his chair. Then he slid his own drink across. "Here, take it."

The Friar adjusted his hat again, winced. He took up the glass with a steadier hand than before. Drained it in one gulp.

"No. You listen. You listen and then tell me if I'm fit to guide you.

Like I said, the Indians were half-starved, weak. Still, they got a sense of what was happening. A few set themselves to what weak resistance they could muster."

"What did you do?" Cecil gripped the edge of the table. He was starting to feel sick.

"What could I do? What could they do? It was a well-equipped militia against a bunch of unarmed Natives already half dead of starvation. The ones that ran made it about halfway to the entrance of our little camp and a loathsome young corporal, this shitheel of Biblical proportions, shot them down with his revolver. He stripped them and scalped them himself and had their bodies strung above the main gate. A cloud of black flies buzzed around them so thick, it put my mind to Legion and to Har Megiddo. No one resisted after that.

The rank and file started splitting the rest and marching fifteen at a time across the camp to the gallows. It was all very orderly despite so many of the soldiers already staggering in their drunkenness. They strung them up one by one, and many were so worn away by age or hunger, or just small owing to their youth, that they affixed a sandbag to the feet to give sufficient weight so their necks would snap when the ropes went taut. So thoughtful of them." He spat out the words, and Cecil saw there was some fire in him after all.

"I followed the men on burial detail. As they tossed the bodies into a single pit, I offered up blessings for the dead such as I could remember. My mind was so wild with the pain of it, the wretched inhumanity. The crack of those little neck bones echoed in my skull. Prayer was all I could think to do. And all around me was this machine of death, passionless. Murder by rote.

The captain came along with the fourth group of bodies. Someone must have told him what I was up to. He ordered me to stop, told me it wasn't good for the men to see me treating these savages as though they had souls like unto white men. It might give them pause or make them suffer in their duties, and couldn't I see that their lives were hard enough without me undermining them or burdening them with doubts.

I listened to him, nodded, and returned to my work. He warned me again and then marched off. Naive as I was at the time, I thought that was the end of it. Thought there was some protection in my position. And what else was I to do?

The bodies kept coming until late in the night. Finally, my work done, I retired to my tent and fell into a deep sleep, wrung out as I was. I awoke in the predawn to a lot of shouting and shoving. They yanked me from my straw mat. I don't know, maybe five or six of them. The corporal was there. I remember his malignant smile and the stink of liquor all around -breath and body. His blonde hair was long and curly and kind of bounced on his shoulders as he man-handled me. I don't know why that part sticks out. It was strange, like some kid's rag doll possessed of an evil. The captain stood back, wasn't smiling, wasn't drunk. He told me matter of factly that I had chosen this outcome by subverting his authority. He said that my love of the Natives put the whole outpost at risk. Love. I guess when you live in a slaughterhouse, any small kindness looks like love. He tossed me a little wheat sack, let me pack what possessions and provisions I could shove in there. Then as soon as I was dressed, they marched me right out the gate.

Even then I saw some nobility in it, blind as I was. I thought, having done my duty, having served the Lord God as best I could, that He would see fit to protect me, and I set to walking east, toward the nearest town, knowing it was tens of miles away. My first night out, they found me. It was a small group, five in all. Maybe related in some way to those that hung, maybe just a coincidence. I tried to tell them. God, how I tried. That I, too, saw the wrong in what was done to them and theirs. They were angry. Either they couldn't understand me or wouldn't."

The Friar removed his hat then, set it on the table, pulled loose the bandanna and set it beside. The hair on the side and back of his head was a jagged horseshoe of greasy straw. Above it was a bald, red pate. Raised in places. Deeply scarred, most noticeably where his forehead gave way to it.

"They scalped me. Left me for dead. I crawled bleeding and parched out of that desert four days later. There are some that would call that miraculous. But there are no miracles. Just wounds that kill you from the outside in, or more slowly, from the inside out. The Book is full of men finding God in the wild places. Losing him is a lot easier. I haven't felt his presence, his voice, since I walked out of that hell. Maybe he was just hiding under my scalp all along. Time punishes each in turn and the faithful most of all."

He laughed. "Anyway, this lot took to calling me Friar, after Friar Tuck. They never tire of the joke, and who am I to look down on a simple pleasure when life offers so few. I'm so distant now from the man who bore the name Thomas, anything else is a better fit."

He caught the boy's eyes, held them.

"I know the territory. I know its dangers. I know that there is no room there for kindness and no God to save us but ourselves. You get me what I need, keep me flush, I'll get you where you need to go."

"Whiskey? I'll give you as much as you can take and remain upright in a saddle."

"Ha, my boy. My boy, so much to learn. Whiskey is the bread, and man does not live by bread alone, but by every word that proceedeth out of the mouth of God. The word is laudanum. The holiest of spirits."

21

THE SIDE GIG

Charlie felt born again when he rode out of Independence.

A few days in the hotel, spending the Branaghs' money. Of course, they paid. The more storied this pursuit became, the grander their sense of importance, of duty even. He had ruined a shirt in his little scuffle on the Oregon, and it was beyond the abilities of even the finest laundry. Most wouldn't accept the job and the one that did, wouldn't accept payment for what they deemed substandard work. It was with a look of apology that Miss Valentine at the hotel returned it to him when she relayed the message. No matter; two hundred dollars would buy a lot of shirts, and he had one fitted, along with a fresh pair of trousers, the day before he rode out. He still hated that the job was pushing him further west, but already looked forward to a return visit on his way back through. Maybe he could talk that sporting lady into trying a few new things, though he had to admit she was pretty good at the old one.

He was several hours riding, the sun on the soft side of its apex, and he figured he was at or near the halfway point to Gardner. If he hadn't been so contented, the man would have never rode up on him so easily, never have gotten so close before he wheeled around. As it was, Charlie gave him a start, turning to, as he did. The man had to draw tight his reins, so his own mount came up a little on its rear legs.

"Whoa, stranger. Didn't mean to give you a fright." The man was a clean-cut sort of dude. His clothes were cheap but nearly as fresh as Charlie's. His chaps and boots had gathered some burrs and grit, but his white shirt was unstained, his blue silk scarf unblemished. He had a scruff of beard Charlie found wispy and unsettling, and wore a bowler that didn't shade his eyes enough to hide an appraising sort of gaze.

"It's the horse. She's finicky about them that ride too close."

"Huh," the man chewed his thoughts for a moment, unsure if he was witness to a joke.

"You look like a fresh enough pilgrim, just come off the train?" The man was forward for Charlie's tastes, clumsy with whatever maneuver he was trying to set up.

"That's right," he sighed. "If only it ran all the way to Gardner. You seem fresh yourself."

"I like to stay neat. The frontier sucks at the bottom of civilization like a catfish does the river. Too easy for a man to let himself be pulled along. Anyway, my name's William." He extended his hand. Charlie looked at it a moment, and when he didn't reciprocate, the man retrieved it, looked straight ahead.

"What's her name?" He nodded at Charlie's horse.

"Who?"

"Your horse."

"Horses don't care nothing for names."

"Seems to me a man should name a horse. This here's Bucky."

"He throw a lot of riders?"

"No." Again the man paused, not knowing if he should be riled.

"People just like naming things. Out east some of them name

their houses. A feller who names a horse, next thing he's telling you about his rifle named Laura Lee. It's embarrassing."

William glanced at his holster for a second, and grunted. He was growing tense. In the heat, Charlie hoped he would either tire of the company or take a swing.

Instead, the man talked at him for a while, droning about the trail and all the pilgrims that got ate up by it. Made a display of piety and may God rest their souls. They rode side by side. The man shifted the conversation to Charlie, asking for a lot more information than he gave. Charlie played along, painting the picture of a hapless rube. By the time William, or Will as he insisted his new friend call him, made his play, Charlie knew well where it was headed.

Still, he turned from the trail where the man pointed, made his way to the little clutch of trees hemmed in by the hills, and laughed to himself. A man could creep on you from any of three sides without you knowing he was there 'til he was near breathing on your neck. Of course, Mr. William couldn't camp with him, much as he would have loved to. He had a band of orphans or a fluffy ewe that fell down a well to tend to. Charlie had stopped listening by the time he submitted his excuse.

The wood provided a bit of shade, for which Charlie was grateful. It was an hour or so yet until sunset, and he enjoyed a dinner of bacon sandwiches Miss Valentine had packed, gave his horse some corn and oats in a nose bag. He hobbled her a little way into the tiny wood, didn't want to risk any harm to her with what was to come. Then he swapped out his clean shirt for the already stained one, packed some branches under his blanket and rested his hat at the top. It was a fair approximation of a sleeping man when he was done, and he slowly crept off through the woods. He made his way around the nearby hill, found a tree with the right kind of lean for him to recline against, and waited.

He didn't have to wait for very long. They must have thought a lone tenderfoot were easy pickings, because it was only just full dark when he heard them.

Pulling himself on his elbows, he crawled, snakelike, to a cluster of rocks, just as a big fella stalked into the campsite. Will was a few paces behind. He might not be cautious, but wasn't foolhardy either. The big one pulled a shotgun from under his serape. It was a beast of a coach gun, short of barrel and from the size, Charlie estimated a 10 gauge, maybe even an 8. Overkill for most work.

When he had leveled the barrels on what should have been Charlie's face, buried under his blanket, Will came sauntering over like he had just won a pageant. He lifted the hat and whispered something. Then he pulled the hat all the way off. He must have been the smarter of the two, because he stood stock-still then. Struck by knowledge of what was come upon him, only too late to help.

Charlie rested his pistol on the boulder and put a shot dead center in the back of the big one's head. In the flicker of flame, he could see the gore paint a swatch of William's face. It were nearly black in the dim light. The whites of his eyes were like polished bone, small beacons of fear, of the ending of any good thing that might ever happen again.

Finally, he cried out, like he was waking from a bad dream, and dove behind a tree. It wasn't much for cover, and Charlie put three rounds into it, one of which glanced off, throwing bits of bark and eliciting a squeal from Will, as it tore through his shoulder.

He cried out again, and Charlie heard the whinnying of upset horses. A scarecrow of a figure came running into the clearing, with a trio of mounts trailing behind him on a long lead. When he came into the light, it was clear he was the oldest of the bunch by a wide margin. He had a white beard and shortly trimmed white hair. The bulbous, ruddy nose of a long-time drinker formed a bullseye in the center of his face, and his back was bent slightly.

"What's going on, Will?" The man near shouted. His hand shook where he held the lead.

"Get out of here, Pa," William yelled with a tremble to his voice. "Garrett is dead, and I'm shot."

The old man let go the lead and drew a pistol with a tremulous hand. It was a hulk of a thing, and even at range Charlie could see it was one of the old massive cap and ball guns the army had handed out to cavalrymen, back before the war. He fired a shot into the blanket, nearly hit Charlie's hat where Will had dropped it. The big dragoon smoked like a locomotive and made near as much noise. The horses reared behind him; they turned but they didn't run.

"Over here." Will yelled out again.

The old man dove to the ground and immediately cried out. "My knee."

"You hit, Pa?"

"No. I think I hit a rock."

Charlie watched the old man crawl with his hands and his one good leg, join his son in the brush on the other side of the tree.

"How bout we have ourselves a palaver," William's voice had evened out a bit. He had a better grip on himself with his father in relative safety, it seemed. "Now I think this is all a misunderstanding."

"The misunderstanding was yours, hillbilly. I've heard a hundred men lay a better set up than what you were selling."

"Be that as it may. No reason anyone else needs hurt here."

"And your proposal?" Charlie drew his back up gun and set it on the rock, set to clearing the chambers and replacing the rounds he had shot off in his primary. Let the man talk while he prepared.

"We can all just walk on out of here. You kilt my brother. Pa and I are willing to let that go. Even Steven. Right, Pa."

"Yeah, that's right," The older man spoke with a defeated tone, had a more honest reckoning of his position than William did.

"My brother is worth seventy-five dollars. Much as it pains me, I'll let you take him to Gardner for your trouble."

"Right generous of you." Charlie began to work his way along the ground, pistol in each hand, belly crawling toward the horses.

"Well, what will it be then?"

Charlie holstered the smaller gun, gathered the lead in his free hand. It had snapped back when the animals turned and was on the far side of them from Will and his father. He rose to a crouch and walked them back toward the rocks quick as he could manage without exposing himself.

"Hey, what are you doin'? Them animals ain't no part of no deal."

Charlie secured the lead to his boulder. "Well, let's make a new deal then."

Bang. A round pinged off the rocks. The three horses shrunk back but stayed fairly steady.

"I need these horses."

"What could you need three mounts for?"

"I'm not hauling three bodies to Gardner with my one horse. She'd never forgive me."

"You sum bitch." Will came up fanning the hammer of his revolver and spraying lead everywhere. Charlie ducked behind the boulder, an unnecessary precaution. The rounds went wide. Out of six shots, only one came near to Charlie, throwing up some dust in the earth a few feet in front of the rock. Another hit one of the mounts. Got him in the eye and he went down quick. The other two horses made a hell of a racket, but the old man done a good job of braiding their leads, and the dead one kept the others anchored.

Will's gun was run dry, so there was only the dragoon to deal with, and the old man was reluctant to make the kind of display his boy had.

Charlie took a shot at his little campfire. The wood scattered and the alcove darkened considerably. He was more annoyed than he was scared, and began a slow and deliberate belly crawl around the hill, to come out in the wood beside the two.

The younger man whispered something, but the only words that rang clear was his Pa saying "Shut up."

Will was nervously trying to reload when Charlie closed on them, and doing poorly at it.

Aiming careful through a gap in the trees, he put two shots in the old man. He pitched forward, and then Will stood bolt upright, and lost his gun. He panicked, tried to make a run for it. Charlie put a round neatly through the man's right calf, and it must have hit the bone because he went down hard and commenced to crying and pawing at his leg. He was lying on his back, tears gathering the pitiful starlight on his cheeks when Charlie approached.

"How many you run like this through your trap line?"

"What?"

"How many you reckon you robbed or killed with this little scheme of yours?"

"Which one? Robbed or killed?" He was breathing heavy, and the words came out staggered.

"You choose."

"Well, Pa was always better with numbers," and his breath sped up on mentioning his father, like the reality of it had just hit him again. "Let me think."

Charlie kneeled down, slid his Bowie into Will's throat. He sat back on his heels and watched the man's eyes as he sputtered and choked. He wished there were fire to see by, to watch the twinkle of life fade and go out. He'd seen it enough times he could imagine it now, but imagining was a sorry substitute. Charlie looked up at the cloudy sky, at the few stars that shone there. One day they too would all be gone. He smiled at the folly of men, their ineptitude, and the implacable darkness.

22

THE HOUNDS OF ROCK PORT

It was near a week of uneventful days when the troop edged its way toward Rock Port. Autie kept close counsel, and kept his visits with Flowers for Hair as businesslike as possible. Mostly, he talked to her while they rode. At first it was hard for him to look at her, and it was only when he felt sure that none had noticed his momentary lapse -as he had come to think of it- that he began to relax. Through what conversations they had, he was building a rudimentary map of the territories and of some of the abominations known to dwell within them.

After five days of dusty riding, he had finally succumbed to boredom and taken some of her tea. It made for an enlivening few hours in the saddle. The prairie grass come to look like melted ice cream and the scrub and trees stretched and blended with the blue sky. He was grateful for the sobriety of horses, as he clung hard to the reins. Finally, as the world slowly resolved back into itself, he felt his demeanor calm also, felt some of his usual self-assuredness come back on him.

Sullivan had been riding ahead and returned with word of some strange goings on. The citizens of Rock Port were near apoplectic. Tools had begun disappearing, and they suspected Native thievery. It were a strange thing: a man left a good axe buried in a stump and come back to find the handle resting on the ground but the head gone. The tin roof of a shack was wore halfway to nothing overnight, like a hundred years of weathering all at once. The final straw was the mayor had the fine wheels and brass fittings of his coach stripped in the night. And there was a strange howling that coincided with these disappearances.

Flowers for Hair had heard of a thing that been known to do such vandalism as this, said it was a trifle. If people could be convinced to lock away most of their metal goods, or sprinkle a little pepper or ground sage around them that were too big to be so sequestered, the things would move along, more than likely scatter in the nearby hills, or follow Rock Creek to the Missouri River.

Even when Autie made it plain that this were not a thing they would let go, she was reluctant. When he told her that the alternative was to round up whatever Natives were still loose in the hills and put them to the sword, she finally relented. To attract the animals required nothing more than a cache of metal, iron being preferred and steel being passable. Autie had made a habit in the wild country to always travel with a passel of axe heads, knives, and other tools for trading, and they took up that night five miles east of town, with all their trading goods in a great pile, twinkling like some mythical treasure in the setting sun.

Flowers for Hair still didn't understand or fully accept the specifics of the mission and her role in it, because having failed to convince Autie of the unnecessary nature of this particular approach, she dismissed him from her tent with a wave of the hand. He laughed as the flap fell to, behind him.

Even with all he had seen so far, he could scarcely believe there were an animal could eat metal like she had described. And so, he found his heart sped in anticipation while he lay in ambush on the far side of their wagons, waiting for whatever might appear that night.

He had men prone in the grass in a broad arc, their rifles trained on the bait pile, and others had piled brush and other debris soaked in fuel oil in a tight arc on the far side.

It was a long night. The first hints of dawn were just an hour or two away, and Autie was chilled to the bone with the sense of imminent failure. He considered telling the men to give up the vigil, and try to get what sleep they could, so they might try again tomorrow. Then he heard the howling. It was a low tone, like a slab of stone being drug over hard ground. Or like this great brass horn he once saw in an orchestra at the Point. He felt it inside his chest.

The first ones to appear, he thought they were just some wild dogs. A little smaller and leaner than the coyotes he was used to. More and more of them came into view and when the first of them arrived at the pile, one turned so it was more or less facing him, and nearly disappeared. From the side it had the rough shape of a dog, but from the front it was impossibly narrow, particularly in the head. Its eyes bugged out at the sides, so half the orbs were protruding from their sockets. Where the animals set to attacking the pile, it was a kind of mechanical grinding sound, and then the night was lit up by sparks. Little showers of them sprung up and glowed bright where teeth met metal.

Another chorus of discomfiting howls, and then the larger group fell on the cache and the grinding sound became a cacophony. The sparks criss-crossed the night sky like fireworks.

He was lost a moment in the beautiful absurdity of it, when Levi appeared at his side. "Sir?"

"Yes, yes. Commence the attack."

The fires went up, and the glow made long shadows that played on the beasts' impossible bodies, describing fiendish shapes that stretched and flickered. The men took up their rifles and commenced to shooting. Autie was concerned that bullets would do little to harm a thing that could dine on metal, but when the first of them went down, these worries vanished.

Facing fire on one side and the wagons on the other, the animals went into a panicked stampede toward Autie's position. He only had one man on a Hotchkiss. Had thought even that would be overkill for putting down some mangy curs, but he was glad to have it. The gun came to life, and barked its mechanical death into the night. He watched as dogs came apart not more than ten yards away. Those a bit farther out turned back toward the flames, but it was soon just a confused mass of furry flesh running in circles, howling and barking their distress, and the men picked them off one by one.

Satisfied that the skirmish was well in hand, Autie retreated to camp.

A low grinding sound drew him to Flowers for Hair's tent, and when he pulled back the flap, he saw that she was seated, cradling a pup, who lay on its back and chewed the edge of a small cast-iron skillet.

When she saw him, she sheltered the thing with her free hand and scooted away as far as the tent would allow, but there were nowhere to go.

"Let it be. Your men have killed the rest. Let this one live. It can scarcely do any harm."

"I know mongrels. You leave them be, and in a few months, a year, there are a thousand of them. How can we civilize this place with these little monsters eating our tools and terrorizing our people? What happens when they find their way to a railroad?"

She held the beast close, and as Autie approached, he noticed it had rows of tiny teeth, like a bit for drilling rock. He yanked the creature from her, and it let out a squeal. Holding it by the scruff, he ducked under the flap. Flowers for Hair cried out, and it pleased him he could affect her. She had seemed so impassive, so unflappable until that moment.

He held the thing to the ground. It was a male, and made water right there. A little trickled onto his boot and it stank like rust. He planted a heel against its narrow head and snapped its neck. Leaving the remains to set just a few feet from Flowers' tent, he wiped his boot heel on the grass and walked away.

23

SKUNK APES

The Friar said he had preparations to make, which Cecil suspected meant tying on one last ferocious drunk before the austerity of trail life forced him to keep his indulgences in check. He grew increasingly impatient as the sun crawled toward midday, until he reached a near certainty that the man wouldn't show at all, and felt embarrassed for not knowing better. He was cursing the Friar, when as though summoned by the denigration, the man finally appeared. Parsimony of movement spoke to a likely hangover, but he seemed alert enough when they headed out. Who wouldn't be at that hour? Still, he rested in his saddle with a substantial slouch. It reminded Cecil of a picture he had once seen of Don Quixote, and he wondered if this man's world might be similarly fantastical, skewed as it was by strong drink and the other. Maybe it was naught but windmills out there, with the monsters mainly in the heads of them that rode. But the quiet was predator enough for Cecil, a thing of endless fangs and appetite.

"It looks like we were fortunate to leave when we did." The Friar pointed to a great cloud of dust whose distance was hard to judge. He dropped back to ride between Cecil and Trixie.

"What do you mean?"

"Well, that there's a great pack of settlers, no doubt some rangers or other militia men mixed in. We will want to steer clear of it."

"Would it not have been better, then, to ride out this morning?" Cecil was already beginning to doubt the man's qualifications, if not his sense.

"They'd have caught up to us. You and the girl, your animals are going to keep us to a modest pace. There'd be no avoiding them, then. Now, we just cut through a little wild country. The Santa Fe turns south about twenty miles out. We'll ride southwest and find it there. Just add a few days."

"Won't we risk running into the same group again?"

"No," and the Friar looked at him a long moment. "There's something you should know about this place, something I reckoned you lot might already have figured out. Time and distance are fuzzy out here."

"I don't doubt they are when you're tipping the bottle every few minutes."

"Don't lean on me, boy." And there was a bit of fire in the man's tone, such that Cecil cast his eyes away.

"Haven't you noticed that the maps, the miles, and the time it takes to get from place to place don't always add up?"

Cecil thought about Independence to Gardner. The terror of the events that night had taken prominence in his mind but thinking of it now, it should have been a day's ride, maybe just a hair more. It had taken them nearly two full days.

"I see you chewing on it. On the trail proper, it's usually just little shifts, subtle, but the further off trail you go, the more it can stretch, or even compress at times."

"Why? How? It don't make no sense."

"Not to your eyes or mine, but there are other eyes that watch here. Unblinking and eternal, and with an appetite we can't comprehend. Sometimes you can feel it pulling you, and you must be vigilant when your body says that a way seems easier, like walking down a gentle slope when none is there."

"What does it want?" Trixie was spooked, her voice hitched a little as she spoke, and she her eyes roved all about the terrain.

"Best I can tell, it wants the worst of us. The frightened, the hungry, the tired, the vulnerable. Scruples drop to the wayside in the throes of deprivation. And these pilgrims that swarm the plains, they're deprived already.

The cutting edge of the empire has always been those with empty bellies and no property. Whatever watches, whatever moves in this place, it seems to delight in their abasement. Each atrocity binds our spirits tighter to the land. They'll even tell themselves it was worth it, as the cold thing from below coils through them, diminishes them."

Red Club had been quietly listening, and Trixie was beginning to tear up. Cecil was rendered mute by the Friar's words.

"We need to take great care riding off trail. Watch the landscape close, every rock and every tree. You don't want to get lost out here."

Red Club had come up alongside Trixie and took hold of her shoulder and squeezed. "Don't worry. We'll find our way through. We must take care not to give it a handhold."

She smiled slightly.

"My people speak of this place too. And every legend is a warning to stay away. But now, many cross, and I see many were here before the white man. Don't let the hunger into your heart. Don't take more than you need. I think it will look elsewhere if we don't bend to it."

"He's right. I've crossed the untended spaces many times. Small footprints. The gentle way is the best. There's a darkness here, but it isn't the only thing that moves, just the thing with fangs and claws. Ahh, and there it is. I know this tree." And the Friar gave his reins a little tug and departed the trail just to the right of a gnarled oak.

Cecil swore it resembled a man, and he saw an agonized face in its rutted bark. He imagined signs like this would multiply the further they went, for it were a certainty he would live in the bosom of hostility until the journey's end.

They were four days on when they ran into the party, already a day beyond the Friar's estimate and, as far as Cecil could tell, still nowhere near rejoining the Santa Fe. There was no means to hide or get away, so they waited and watched them approach.

The men were filthy. A half dozen of them and they looked like some mirage, an elemental spirit conjured from the dark soil. From their trousers, they looked to be wearing old uniforms, but in their filthy state it was impossible to discern union blue from confederate gray. What difference did it make? Their place in the war bore little relevance to what they had become since.

Their clothing was patchy, repaired everywhere with crudely sewn skin - deer maybe. And each wore a fur over his shoulders and down the front and back, like a serape. The man at the front cantered his horse closer, and what at first appeared to be more skins draped over its haunches, was in fact a string of scalps. Instead of hair, the scalps bore a close-cropped fur, dark gray, some with a black stripe.

"You all get lost? What are you doing wandering alone out here. This here's dangerous territory." He held a large bore pistol, and on getting closer -seeing the group was no threat- slid it into his saddle holster. He let his hand rest there.

"We got separated from our group, just hoping to reconnect with the Santa Fe up yonder." Cecil squinted up at him, wrinkled his nose. This close, the man had an unsavory smell.

"You what?" The man laughed. "The Santa Fe is near 50 miles hence. Other side of that mountain," and he pointed behind him and to the right, without looking. The territory itself was an extension of his skin.

"What are you up to out here, seems you've been on the range a piece?" Cecil squinted, looked beyond the man to the hilly terrain.

"We're hunting whatever comes. Skunk ape mostly, around here. Better hope you never run into one, poorly equipped as you are. I've lost four men already on this expedition, good ones. Lost some good mules too." He drummed his fingers on the butt of his pistol, stared off in the distance.

"I don't know what you mean, mister."

The man patted the rump of his horse.

"The scalps fetch twenty-five dollars apiece, that's five times what we get for an Indian, but these bastards are hard to find and fight every bit as hard as a brave, even lacking anything more sophisticated than a rock or a club."

"You seem to have dispatched a goodly number of them."

"Yes, but as I say, not without cost. Still, we have the awesome power of God behind us, so we cannot fail. And until every savage thing is laid low, we can't properly claim this wild country for Him." His eyes lingered on Red Club as he said the last part.

There was a terrible howl from the foothills a mile or so distant. It was a hatchet through the air, like it might split the barrier between this world and another. Cecil had never heard anything like it and prayed he never would again. It spoke of a mix of sorrow and anger, a pain that could know no resolution.

"Looks like we missed one or two," and smiling, the man turned his horse and whistled. He brought a hand up and circled it in the air and pointed in the direction of the howl, that was only now beginning to fade. "Let's go men. More work to be done."

Cecil, Trixie, the Friar, and Red Club could not decide among them what to do. The only way back to the trail was the same way the men had rode and they were in no hurry to follow, no hurry to see what might have made such a sound. They decided to camp, but all were uneasy, and the old man especially. He had seen enough to know to a fair certainty what lay in the hills. His uneasiness brought out greater unease in the rest, as the conjurings of their minds were already frightful, and now they knew what was out there was beyond even their darkest thoughts.

They dared not build a fire that night. Cecil and Trixie shook in their blankets in the desert cold, which took hold as soon as the sun had fallen beyond the horizon. Red Club was standing watch, pacing to keep warm. The Friar was still as a rock.

Cecil didn't sleep a wink and couldn't imagine how anyone would. The thoughts that played at him sent a chill deeper than even the cold wind, until he finally gripped the blanket together at his chin to stop his teeth chattering.

The wind carried sounds on it. Some he had heard before, and others more subtle. There was coyote, and then a deeper howl following it. They carried on, back and forth. Late in the night, he swore he heard men screaming and someone yelling "no," over and over. As it turned in his mind, he couldn't be sure what was real and what was just his fearful thoughts finding music in the wind. He hoped it was the latter.

He must have just fallen asleep when the Friar nudged him with his boot. He felt like he hadn't rested at all. His bones ached to the marrow as he turned to face the rising sun.

"We need to get going." The Friar's face was a rictus, and suggested to Cecil he hadn't imagined the screams. "Try to cross those hills while we have light, and we need all the hours we can muster to have a chance."

Cecil scanned the territory between them and the hills. Part of him hoped to see the men from the day before, or to smell them. Preferred their menace to the other, if only slightly. But there was nothing.

They ate dry biscuits as they broke camp, passing around a water skin that was concerning in its lightness. At least he still had his canteen. Maybe there was water in the hills. They looked green enough.

Each hour of silent riding heightened his dread. As far as he could discern, they were getting no closer to the hills. Finally, when the sun was directly overhead, the ground softened somewhat and began to steepen.

They made good progress and crested the hill in another hour or so, and Cecil could see the plain beyond. Where it flattened out on top, it was wooded, which slowed their progress some and forced an indirect path.

Red Club stopped suddenly, stiffened, and paused to take a long look from left to right. That was when the smell hit Cecil. It was like unto the foulness of those men the day before. A mix of urine and sweat, of men not bathed in time beyond reckoning. But there was something else. Like the taste of a penny on his tongue, and the sickly sweet of meat starting to turn. It grew in strength the farther they moved until it was near overpowering. Trixie dismounted and retched, leaning against a tree, but nothing but a ropy string of sputum came up, and when she tried to spit it out, it clung to her chin.

They rounded a slight curve, where the land dipped before them, and the scene made Cecil instantly dizzy. He had nearly tripped over the first body. And body was all it was. The head had been pounded flat, until it was a meaty puddle completely separate from whence it came. Brains glistened wet, and Cecil stood there frozen by the implications of it.

When he recovered, his eyes were like a gossamer net utterly distinct from his thoughts, so he captured everything, but it didn't fully reach him. Like he might be a carrion bird high up, surveying the carnage with no attachment to it.

The men -all six of them- were spread around the space about thirty feet in diameter. It seemed most of the horses had escaped as only one was wedged against the far hillside, legs stiff and straight. The bodies were dismembered, and their naked torsos and limbs snaked in a spiral that ended in the body Cecil had nearly tripped over -and that body was the most intact. Entrails connected the parts each to one another, so the spiral was unbroken, and every part must have been torn loose with brute force, as each ended in jagged flesh and exposed bone.

The Friar walked among the corpses, and at first Cecil thought he might be performing last rites, or some blessing for the dead, but then he made his way to the horse and dug at the soil where its body met the hill. He walked slowly back toward Cecil and Trixie, who stood agape at the horror, each unable to fully make sense of it.

"All the gear is gone, except this," and the Friar held out the saddle pistol that had so impressed Cecil the day before. It was intact, if caked with dirt. "No extra ammo though."

The Friar slid the pistol into the back of his pants. "Even the scalps are gone, but no surprise there, I think we all know who did this."

Red Club bowed his head. He whispered something unintelligible to himself -a prayer or a curse- then walked over to the horse. He rested a hand on its muzzle, then brushed its eye closed.

"You think maybe another band of rangers?" Cecil was hoping for some sanity to this, knew the answer before asking the question.

"They told us what they were hunting. I've heard of these creatures before. Brutes, but not without a culture, rituals. They bury their dead, cover them in wildflowers from what I hear. I guess they didn't take kindly to the scalpers and their predations. Good riddance," and he spit on the headless man.

"Now, we should move on, and quickly. I don't plan on betting my neck on the mercy of those that did this."

24

A THICK SKIN IS INSUFFICIENT FOR
THE TASK

Gardner was too small a town for the boy to go unnoticed, and it hadn't taken long to track him to the saloon. The barkeep had seen him, and a few unhappy gamblers were only too happy to offer up what they knew. They put him together with a local drunk who was said to know the territories, whose scars and vices would make him stand out even on the trail. The party must be four now, and what a motley bunch. He doubted there was loyalty enough to the little band that any of the others would put up much fuss when Charlie caught up with them, which he expected to be soon. If they did, he'd prize another hundred or two from the Branaghs. The outcome would be the same.

The bounty on the three he'd delivered to the law had brought him another $275, which made it well worth the inconvenience. Long hours in the saddle were taking a toll. Having grown weary of the journey, he was loathe to stretch out the pursuit much longer. West of Kansas, the towns were further apart and short on luxuries, and the terrain grew much less forgiving.

Garden City was not far off, and beyond that, the Santa Fe

149

branched. This presented two problems. The first was in not knowing which way the group might go. A wrong choice would mean a significant delay until he would recapture their trail. The other problem was that each branch presented a set of hazards that he would need to provision against. To the north, it rose through the mountains. It would be colder, especially at night and would take longer to traverse. To the south was the Cimarron route that led more directly into New Mexico. It was less populous. Larger groups avoided it for the lack of water. It would be cold at night and hot by day. It would be easier terrain to track them through and pick his moment. If he didn't catch up to them before that point, it would not be his choice to make, and who could know the mind of a drunkard trail guide? He could have any number of reasons to take them either way.

The uncertainty was a weight on his back, and he drove his horse hard, though she was clearly tiring. Any chance to close the distance was one he must commit to.

The trail was fairly close, with some shade and windbreak from Oak and Maple trees. Autumn had stripped many of these bare, and their naked branches hung long and brittle in places, so that bits would scratch at his arms and occasionally snap off and stick to his trail shirt, or to the horse's withers and mane, so he was frequently picking off pieces and tossing them. The messiness was a grave annoyance.

It was hours on the trail when he came to the hills. He found a place where the soil was churned, and all the track led off trail at that point, so he followed. The wood began to thin a bit. The hills were further out than they looked, and it took him more time than he liked to get there. It was close to sunset, when he began to climb. He hoped he might find the highest vantage before making camp, so that he could best see where the party might have gone.

Picking his way along, he felt a stir in his chest and a slow clenching of his gut. The feeling was familiar, it called him to pay closer attention. Something was out of sorts, and he needed to figure out what.

The first thing he settled on was the quiet. He hadn't heard a bird song since he started up the hill, not so he could recall it anyway. The track became strange as well. In places, it was downright chaotic, as though one or more horses had panicked and set out at a full run. Then the smell hit him. There are all kinds of animal rot, but any who have smelled a man, dead several days and left out in the open, can scarcely mistake that smell for any other.

He set heel to his mount, put her into a trot. He would rather get well out of range of whatever was throwing up that scent before making camp.

When he emerged on the clearing, and set eyes on that great spiral of meat, he nearly fell off his horse, so hard did he pull on her reins. Dismounting, he guided her slowly behind him as he walked the full length of the savage scene. Parts of men, disarticulated limbs, guts. The buzzing of flies alone was maddening. He could hear nothing else, even his own thoughts grew scattered. Against a little hillock lay a dead horse, still saddled and with part of the man who rode him beneath. Charlie vomited. It came as such a surprise that he was hardly able to steer it away from his shirt. Stringy phlegm and bile hung and dripped from his mouth and nose, and he wiped at it with his sleeve, much as it bothered him to do so.

He wondered if the boy were among the dead and decided he would have to take a thorough inventory of the various parts. The thought of the project near made him vomit again, but he found his hard center. It was always there. That place where he had learned to retreat, stepping further inside until it was like he was outside of himself, and no longer a part of this world. He had first found the place in boyhood, sitting all night in the cold outside Mabel's shack. The full measure of that hardness evident when he was ten, and made his first kill. A lowly son of a bitch he found beating her.

Retreating to the beginning of the spiral, he began his examination. All the big pieces, the ones he could identify, came from grown men, so unless the boy had sprung up in the last few days, he wasn't among the dead. So, what the hell had happened? Investigating was a slow process, and demanded he push aside loops of intestine and other gore to do the checking. He probed with his great Bowie knife, was only halfway through when he heard the first howl.

The sound cut through him like a winter's gust in the Sierras. It was low and loud, drowning out the buzzing insects. It must be close to be that strong, he thought, and whipped his head around, looking through the nearby woods for any sign of movement. Then came another howl, this one from the other side of him. He swiveled his head, turning to scan in all directions, frantically looking for the source, and still finding nothing. To be so loud and not nearby was all the more worrisome.

Then it was a chorus, and all around him the woods echoed with low howling, and it was like some great percussion instrument the way it moved through him. His chest hurt and his guts twisted, and he thought he would shit himself if he stood there much longer. Even the flies had begun to scatter.

He mounted quickly and threw heels, put his horse into a full run. The trail was close, and he thought of the track he had found, and how little good that panic had done them he had followed. He was sweating and his breathing shallow, like he couldn't draw enough air. His singular thought was *run*. Run as fast as she could take him. Run her to death if need be. Only to take leave of these hills and be free of the wretched howling, that sounded so close he expected to feel some fetid breath at his back any moment.

His horse was soon lathered in sweat, foam gathering at the bit. She must be scared as well, because he hardly had to push her to keep her galloping full speed. She stumbled twice on the decline to the plain. The second time he clenched his jaw and tensed, prepared for the fall that almost came but didn't. Then they were on level ground again. The howling grew more faint. She began to slow, and he dug heels into her sides. It sped her up a few minutes and then she began to slow again.

Charlie drew his pistol and fired three shots in the air. She put on speed. He ran her another hour, then slowly, his head began to clear. The planning and plotting Charlie -grown up Charlie- reasserted control. If he played this horse out, or even worse, killed her, he would be utterly stranded. He would never catch up to the boy before west Kansas. He wheeled her to a stop.

Dismounting, he drew his telescope from the saddlebag. It was dark now, and not enough starlight to see by, so he soon gave it up. Instead, he stood and stared at the landscape behind him. He watered the horse, filled her nose bag with oats and strapped it to her.

Finally, with one last glance at the way behind him, he began walking her along. He had completely lost the trail. They would walk until he no longer had the strength for it, then they would sleep.

25

A CLEANSING FIRE

Fire was the veil their work was hid behind -Autie and his men- and often its medium as well. The bustling masses that swelled the cities of Missouri and eastern Kansas were ever pushing outward, westward. The dreams of free land, of property, a powerful narcotic that relieved them of any sense of caution. Where most of them came from, or were at most a generation removed from, land was a thing reserved for the aristocratic -either by birth or fortune.

The land must be made ready. Prairie grass was no diet for cattle. It must be burned away. The trees and scrub needed cleared so the pilgrims could plant their crops in the ashes. It was a paradox, to covet a thing and want to destroy it in equal measure. Most of the homesteaders still associated land ownership with something like the divine right of kings. Maybe they hated themselves a little for the want of it. Maybe they looked at each misfortune as a punishment for subverting the will of God.

Autie eased his mount forward. His eyes burned and the smell of woodsmoke lay thick in the moist air of morning. The fire had been going all night, and neither he nor the men were well rested on account of the stifling heat of it, and the unforgiving light.

"We'll never see the like of it again." Sullivan rode up alongside him.

Autie let out a long sigh. "You beginning to regret coming along on this mission, Captain?"

"No sir. Better to be the last one to see a beautiful thing. It stirs something in me. Even God's angels were called to bear the banner of ruination in their time. Your word is the word of God as far as I'm concerned. It just makes me feel old somehow."

"You feel it move in you," and he could sense the tension in Sullivan. "Don't worry, son, it moves in me too. This thing that draws us, only them with the power to withstand it are so called. It's destiny that pulls us ever westward."

"It's worrying, sir, feels the strongest when I'm freshly stained with blood." He spoke in a near whisper, a confession.

"Didn't blood mark them that God passed over, when he killed the sons of Egypt? Why would it be any different now?"

"These things we're doing, the things we've seen, how can we return to the world of men after this?" There was a sadness, a resignation in the man's voice. It was sour to Autie's ear.

"Never shed a tear for being a stranger to the world of men. Ours is a greater destiny. Take heart, son, for there will always be another frontier, and each day you prepare for the next."

The public, as far as Autie was concerned, was a feeble-minded child. Let the politicians and newspapermen worry about the whims of wretched masses. Their adoration was a pleasant balm, but Autie scarcely relied on it. And a public that had accepted the eradication of the bison, and with such enthusiasm, what would they care about some scrub and the stray rodents and deer and whatever else burned with it? Herds a million or more strong shot down, so their rotting carcasses drew clouds of insects that blotted the sun. Their skulls piled like mountainous shrines to death. And people bought the hides for blankets and coats with nary a complaint. As long as the way remained open to the bounty of the west, no one dared complain about a thing he or his men did out here. And scraping the ground bare was a way to reveal those things otherwise hid away.

Some they never saw, never would see. In the billowing conflagration, they might hear a desperate cry, bestial, strange to their ears. Some unknown creature that prowled the wood. The fading echo of these cries in his ears the last trace before the thing vanished completely from this world. To be such a creature. To know the end is coming and that none can hear your pleading but the one who has put you to the sword. Each sound, each dying proclamation, a thing he owned. He, and just these few others. There was something worth coveting.

Flowers for Hair had become more reticent, withdrawn, as it became apparent to her the breadth of his intentions. She must have thought he would be more surgical in his operations, owing to the information she was able to provide. He had recently taken to visiting her nightly, and had begun to worry that she might poison him with her tea. Some nights, the visions were less comforting than others. She told him the tea was always the same, and if he felt unsettled, it was what he was doing that haunted him.

He also had begun to more regularly seek her out for that secret pleasure she had given him, that they had shared. For he knew in her trembling, in her spurting seed there was an enthusiasm, no less real for how well hid she kept it. Sometimes he would let the tea fully take hold and then, on his knees before her, he would take her in his mouth and then stroke himself while stroking her. He looked up at her one night, having settled into a rhythm, jerking at his member and working his tongue around the head of her cock. He saw that she was crying, and he drew back.

"If you're so heartbroken, why don't you ask me to stop?"

She looked at him, wiped her cheeks with the back of her hand.

"I am your prisoner. Anything I deny you, sooner or later, you're going to take it. Men like you. If they are made to wait, they always take more."

"I'm not a rapist." Even the word seemed to stick to his teeth. He hated it. She must want this as much as he. Hadn't she smiled the first time?

"It pleases me to show you who you are, what you are. I'll keep showing you until there is nothing left, until even you can no longer deny it."

"I am a soldier and a servant, and here I am the hammer of God. You have nothing to show me."

She let out a little giggle then.

"See, you have cheered me up now," and she pushed her cock against his teeth.

In a few moments, he came, tensing and closing his eyes tight. She withdrew and he felt her seed squirt onto his bare throat. He looked down and the front of his deerskin shirt was stained and sticky. He shoved her away, buttoned up his pants. He could hear her giggling again as he made his way under the tent flap.

He had almost arrived at his quarters when he saw Sullivan for the second time that day.

"Sir."

He had no choice but to stop.

"We should make it to the butte tomorrow, but I'm thinking about the river. When do you want to brief the men?"

The thing at the river was beyond the reach of prairie fires. It would likely be their greatest challenge so far.

"I'd say it's a week out or more until we make the river. Still. Set a watch and tell the men to be ready at sunrise. Gather the other officers and assemble by my tent at dawn. I'll go over plans and each of you can dole out assignments. Once we are mounted up, I'll talk to the men. Until then, I don't want to be disturbed."

"Yes, sir. Sir?"

"What is it?"

"There's something on your shirt."

Autie could feel himself flush. He chuckled, nervously. "Must be some soup from tonight. I wind up wearing some of my dinner more times than not."

But there had been no soup for dinner, and Sullivan stood a moment. His silence and blank expression were their own sort of indictment.

"Tomorrow then, sir." He spoke haltingly, then turned and walked slowly away.

26

THE DRAW

Under the excitement like decaying meat and bones beneath the soil, the rotten root of all the manic urgency. It is the thing, the same thing that has sniffed their footprints and examined closely the sign of their making. That gnawing desperation that closes on them when they finally stop. So they can't, won't stop, until the land gives out entire.

The limit of each, of their fate or destiny in this carnivorous world, is measured in how far they might go until their bones are ground to dust. Their hunger is a thing of the eyes, a disease that shrinks and winnows the world, that they might digest it but never be full.

They will slice and parcel what none can truly own, and that hunger will leave them seeing everywhere what should be theirs, until they see in every one a mirror, and in that mirror none but fear and that same implacable hunger.

27

HOOP SNAKES

The cook fire had long reduced to weakly glowing cinders that threw no heat. The ground had lost all trace of warmth, and the moon -though bright- lent no comfort. Cecil crowded the pit, let his boots rest in the dirt near the ashes. Tuco and Judas were sprawled, and one of them snored. He struggled to tell them apart. Trixie leaned on one and held her knees to her chest. It was just him and Red Club and the Friar with nothing to say to one another.

The sky stretched in furrows of gray and purple and maybe the two of them felt an awe that made speech superfluous. He only knew it struck him mute.

There is a quiet on the plain that Cecil didn't know possible. The susurration of gentle breeze, punctuated by the occasional cry of the coyote or a bit of birdsong. Little more than a whisper in the greater void. He wanted its message to be true, that there is peace to be found somewhere, here, that nothing can hurt him in such a gentle place. To come to a truce with the quiet, to be able to dwell there.

He heard a shushing then, like leaves on an autumn wind, but there were no leaves, only scrub and prairie grass, and the pearl of a moon dangling over the nearby butte, and a glittering, twinkling of the light playing on the rock.

At first, he thought it might be gold or silver, and the legends of prized nuggets just sitting on the ground to be picked like wildflowers danced briefly in his mind. Then there was movement, and in the movement a shifting of the color that flashed there, iridescent, like insect carapace.

A closer sound: small pebbles and grit working their way down the slope. The flashing sparkle moved closer too, began to fall down the nearly vertical wall of the butte like a gentle avalanche.

As it moved closer to them, descending, picking up speed, it began to take a clearer shape, disparate masses, like great hoops, and by the time they reached the flat they were moving with such speed that it tricked the eye, multiplying their apparent number. Phantom hoops spun and trailed from each. There were so many. He stood and stared, mouth open.

The desert floor around Cecil and his camp came alive. Rabbit and rodent, frantic in their movements, and tiny deer who sprang many times their length with each bounding kick.

The Friar grabbed Cecil, pulled him close. Red Club moved quickly to cover Trixie with his body.

"Stand perfectly still, boy," the Friar whispered his whiskey breath into Cecil's ear.

Cecil ducked, leaned into the man, but kept his vigil.

One of the hoops came apart then, and as it was fairly close, it was evident by now the thing was taller than any of them. It opened to a crooked line that flew impossibly fast. Passing just a few feet from he and the Friar, so he felt a slight breeze come off it. Then, it collided with one of the tiny deer. The creature was in mid-stride and the collision sent both tumbling to the desert floor in a fury of dust. When it came to a stop, it was a broad triangle of a viper's head that latched unmoving on the deer's neck, and then its long body coiled and coiled around the thing until its furry body was lost in a ball of scales that shone brighter than ever under that beautiful night sky.

Snakes. Snakes unlike any he had ever seen. All around them the creatures spun furious and graceful in their feeding. There was no accounting for it. What other wonders and terrors might lurk in this wild land?

The Friar squeezed his shoulder gently, and Cecil was grateful for the small comfort.

Suddenly, the night erupted in thunder and flame. Behind him, in the direction of the road, the sound of metal on metal like a steam engine, fast and explosive. Something buzzed past his ear, like an angry insect.

The Friar threw both of them to the ground, pressed Cecil's head to the earth, where it was stuck staring at the snakes feeding and those still tumbling down the incline.

"Don't move."

Then the hill exploded, chunks of earth and stone thrown up cracking and pinging. In the moonlight, a dancing tempest of dust, bullets -it seemed like thousands of them- homing in on the sleek bodies, cruel and inevitable.

He watched in mute horror as the serpents came apart in their descent. The storm starting high, at the rear of the pack and working its way down the butte and towards them, where the lead reduced the snakes already feeding, and them they fed on, to a pulpy mass of skin and blood and bone.

It went on for minutes -felt longer still- the thunder and the blood, and Cecil held his breath, tried to press his body closer to the ground, to make himself small, to make himself disappear.

There was a high-pitched whistle, that he knew in his bones to be some animal breathing its last terror, drowning in blood. He knew this the way all animals know the common tongue - of suffering and the bitter end of suffering.

When it stopped, the silence was a jolt, as startling as what came before. Sulphurous smoke tainted the wind like the gates of hell themselves had been thrown open, and maybe they had.

Cecil eased himself, first to his elbows, and then slowly rose on shaking legs. The Friar stood silently beside him, and Trixie was standing next to Red Club. The mules raised their heads and did not stand, but only leaned into one another as though the effort to be upright was too great for either to take on alone.

Smoke rose in the distance, and the smell of spent gunpowder and the metallic whiff of blood wafted on the desert breeze. In the haze, he could make out two wagons, and four narrow plumes of oily black drizzled up from them. Then a lone figure appeared, waving at them from between the wagons.

"Should we go, or should we run?" Cecil knew the answer before he asked.

"Boy, you don't say no to what we just saw. You don't imagine choices where they are not."

The three of them made their way to the wagons, while Trixie stayed and comforted the mules. The soil, freshly tilled by the storm of lead, made for slow going and Cecil did his best to avoid stepping in the worst of the gore.

As they got closer, he counted seven men in military uniforms, but none acknowledged their approach, and instead were in spirited conversation with one another, laughing and talking loudly.

Finally, the one who had waved -his head now half buried in the apron of the nearest wagon- raised up and turned toward them. He was a handsome man, with blonde curls and a feathered mustache, and with great shining epaulettes glittering on his shoulders.

"Hotchkiss rotating cannon, a miracle to see it in action, isn't it? A bit temperamental, but only the best for our friends there."

Cecil stood silent, and the Friar hung a few steps behind with his head down, hat pulled low, and averting from the full torchlight of the improvised encampment. Red Club stood by him but didn't duck or turn his head.

"Sorry, son, for catching you in our tussle here, but honestly, who camps way out here on their own?"

Torches glittered in the distance behind them on the ridge-line, and after a while, larger fires glowed. The Colonel insisted they all break camp and return with him to his larger party. He talked to Cecil mostly; spared glances at Red Club, and more often, at the Friar. He asked Cecil how they had come to travel together, and whether he or the girl had been bothered.

"What's that," he changed the subject, pointing to the distant blazes.

"Cleanup. The damned things nest up there. Might be young'uns or eggs. Need to burn them all out." He spoke matter of factly, like he were describing a dull chore.

Cecil sighed. The reality was suffocating.

"The man looks desperate, and I dare say loathsome. Is he a relation to the two of you?"

By now, the Friar and the others trailed far behind where he and the Colonel walked. The animals had been tied to the last wagon and Trixie rode, while Red Club and the Friar walked alongside. The Friar kept his head down to avoid the meager light of the torches that jutted and rocked as they crawled across the uneven terrain.

"It's ok. They can't hear us, boy. If you're in danger, or she, out with it."

Cecil looked at the man. It was important to meet the eyes of his sort, and grateful he was again for the gambler in him, a face that he hoped would reveal nothing he didn't want.

"Sir," he gulped hard. "It's nothing like that. Sissy and I were set adrift when our Pa took to drinkin', and that man and his Indian are helping us find our way to family New Mexico way. He was a friend to our Ma, may God rest her, and has been nothin' but good to us."

He looked at the boy, looked back at the others.

"Hmm. It's strange, the man looks familiar to me. I've been all over this damn country, so I suppose we could have met somewhere, but it's something else. I don't trust him. I think the lot of you will have to stick with us until we pass a proper town. I want the law to set eyeballs on him before I feel confident turning you loose."

As far as Cecil knew, the Friar was the only one among them who didn't have the law looking for him. It didn't matter. They were trapped now, and the four of them together, the odds were stacked against them not being recognized, at least one of them, and maybe more.

"So, what happened back there?"

"I'm going to need you to forget all about that, son." And the Colonel withdrew a book from his jacket, opened it to a dog-eared page, that he then carefully tore free, before replacing the book. He strode with heavy steps to the wagon that rolled slowly ahead of them and set the page alight by one of its torches. He beheld it pinched between his fingers until it burned nearly to them, as flakes of ash glowed orange and floated away, disappearing into the air. Finally, he released the last of it, and Cecil watched it wither and burn to the last.

"Sir, I don't understand."

The man nodded toward what lay behind them, the plain and the butte beyond, and he turned. In the near distance, he reckoned close to where they had camped, another orange glow now wavered, and in its light he could see silhouettes of men, busying themselves around it.

"There are things that should not be. That cannot be. Myself, these men, have a mandate to erasure and I will turn even the memory of every blight on this country into ash. I need for you to help me. To erase this night from your mind and to make sure your partners understand the need of it, as well." He was polite, but his words were stained glass bordered by lead.

Cecil was certain the Colonel and his group were connected to what they had witnessed in the hills the day previous and hoped he would be able to talk to the others before anyone whispered a word of it. They wouldn't be free of danger until they were free of this group, and they must all set themselves to finding the means to quit it at the earliest opportunity.

In the distance, he saw the trail, it must have turned this way after the hills, so they had mistakenly camped fairly close, even when they thought themselves well away. The land was tricky, ever retreating from understanding.

He walked with the Colonel in silence after that. The man wore a calm on his face that Cecil found discomfiting. After all he had witnessed that night, he saw little cause for soothing.

As they approached the trail, it was apparent the two wagons were but a small part of the total force, which was spread beside and along the road for a good hundred yards. Civilians clustered around, but not too close. All wanted the protection these men afforded but none wanted to be under their scrutiny. The military did as it pleased, and especially here where there were none to tell them otherwise or to bear witness to their excesses.

The Colonel insisted they make camp well within the perimeter of his troop. Whether he suspected Cecil was misleading him or not, it was clear that he had a mind to preventing their departing.

"It's late, and I've already done enough to interrupt your resting. We'll speak again tomorrow." And the Colonel left him, whispering something to a nearby soldier, who stood watching Cecil and the others after the man had left.

Their animals left with the wagon, the four of them huddled together. None were so close as to hear them so long as they spoke quietly. Red Club set to building their own fire and then laying out his bedroll. Trixie looked at Cecil, and her eyes were tired. She lay down as well.

"We need to get free of this lot as soon as possible." The

Friar's voice broke on the words. His eye was twitching, and he held tight to the lapels of his jacket to steady his hands.

"I know. He intends to hand us over to the law at the first opportunity."

"It's worse than that. I know the man, and sooner or later he will know me. I can't say what will happen then, but it will certainly undo any tale you've been spinning."

"No. It can't be. Of all the soldiers out here riding and killing. You're telling me…"

"He was younger then, but it's him. He was most enthusiastic in that massacre and in putting me out to die on the prairie after. Maybe he thought me dead. That might slow his recognizing. That, and how withered and broken I've since become. But we can't count on that luck holding out."

The Friar withdrew a bottle from his pocket. His hand shook so bad that Cecil wrapped his own fingers around the man's and steadied the bottle to his lips. Helped him take a great gulp and then stole a sip himself.

"You're right to be scared," the Friar whispered. "There's a darkness in him I fear has only grown more malignant with age and rank. What they're doing out here is beyond my ken."

28

AWANDER IN FRIGHT

He told himself he needed to get back to tracking. Again and again, he told himself, but the urgency of it were removed. Every few minutes that stern voice called from the immutable present. It said, *every moment lost, they move further from you, closer to the mountains or the desert.* There was his mother's voice in there too, cajoling him. Telling him to be a man. Had she ever said such to him? Or had he just filled the void in their home with an imagined adult when it was clear she was unfit for -had no interest in- the job?

It was for naught, because something deeper, that piece that been silenced since he was too young to properly remember, moved him now. Its power over him was nonverbal and nonnegotiable. It spoke in feelings he had thought long dead, those he denied so long, starved of attention until they withered, until he was unable to feel them at all. Howls and unanswered cries echoed in his mind, magnified, and he flashed on visions of tooth and claw and of the undoing of all those men who came at his mother, the ones she must have loved more than he. He saw himself turned inside out, and his insides folding over and over again, the black nothing of a bottomless well, for there was nothing in there that spoke of warmth or humanity. He was left with none but a chill that shook his entire body, until he thought he might be struck by a fever. Looking over his shoulder at the road behind him and truly haunted for the first time by the irrevocable darkness of what he was.

He wandered because it was all he could do. He didn't bother to ride; the urgency to be any particular place was a hollow echo. He walked side by side with his horse, held her reins with one hand and stroked her withers and scratched her side with the other. He started talking to her, and the hard part of him was at first sickened by what gave that older part comfort, but need had the upper hand.

"How you doing, Daisy," for he had decided if he was going to talk to her, he might as well name her. "You just let me know when you need to take a break."

It went on like that. Every time he crossed a little water, be it a small pool or a trickle of stream, he would stop, let Daisy drink her fill, and find a place to sit under a little shade, or lean against one of the larger rocks. He took notice of the warmth of the sun caressing his skin, the tickle of an occasional uptick of the breeze.

On the second day, he started to talk about his life, the things that had happened that he had never said out loud before. He talked about all the nights he spent hungry and cold because his mother was entertaining some vagabond and didn't want him to spoil the mood, didn't want to spend her whiskey money on vittles.

He told Daisy about how he still couldn't say no to her, still sent her most of the money he made, that he hated himself for the weakness of it, but couldn't make himself stop. Finally, he told her things he'd never fully understood, that the money was nothing if he could just make her love him. A hopeless dream, because it would mean going back. The past can no more be changed than reckoned with. We are all of us captive to it, damned to spend our lives trying to undo what can't be undone.

Daisy, for her part, warmed to him. She would lean into his touches, and at some point on the second day he looped the reins over the saddle horn, and she just kept on walking side by side with him. He had never felt such affection for an animal, two legged or four.

He woke on day three under a cypress bough. A small bird whistled and chirped in the branches above. Daisy was idling nearby, pawing dirt with one hoof and wild feeding near a little brook. He sat a moment watching her. Watching and listening and enjoying the warmth of what sunlight trickled through the branches. Searching himself, he could not find that desperate fear that held him so tight even the day before. It struck him that he yet had a responsibility, a job to finish and his reputation in the balance.

Setting a small fire, making coffee, he went through the rituals of waking with a feeling of peace. Ate some jerked beef. Then he kicked dirt on the flames until they were fully stifled, mounted up, and rode north. Sooner or later, he must hit the Santa Fe, and he would pick up the trail from there. The inevitability of all things was itself a sort of confidence.

It was at least five days from Gardner to Garden City, probably six or more for them riding mules. But he had already burned up near three days, and it would be hard riding if there were to be any hope of catching the boy and his friends.

Daisy was well-rested, and what's more, she was now of a mind to serve. His gentleness had made her an ally, and she took to the route with vigor. Charlie pushed her, but not so hard as he had that terrible night just a few days past.

The terrain was mostly flat, and for that he was grateful. Once he hit the Santa Fe, late that same day, it was easy going. But an easy ride and a long ride can be its own kind of terror. Quiet trail, unquiet mind.

Charlie kept coming back to that dread night, and the feeling that he had lost something he couldn't quite hold. A part of it was the apathy, that the only thing driving him now was his work ethic, that he was no longer thinking about how to turn the job to his greater profit. He wanted it to be over. That was the least of it. A general feeling of uncertainty filled him, and concerns about right and wrong burrowed like mealworm larvae into his heart. He'd never much cared about morality or virtue, leastwise he never thought he did. But as he inventoried his past, the work he had taken his time with, that had given him some measure of joy, it had always been when he felt he was performing some duty beyond a line item on a receipt. Them boys on the way to Gardner, for example. Killing them that prey on others. More than that: them that prey on others with no sense of craft.

Maybe he should change his line of work a little. Hunting bounties could enliven his spirit, give him a little more of that joy. It was a silly thought, childish, connected to that part of him that was slowly settling back into the recesses. There was the matter of risk and reward, and these jobs for wealthy folks always came up the best in that cold calculation. But he hated the folks he worked for. What's worse, he knew they hated him. He was another embarrassing secret of their lives, another body to bury where none would find it.

He rode with these thoughts, and for two days he wished he would catch up to the kid. Lacking that, to encounter any hardship that required his attention and efforts to navigate - a storm, some highwaymen - if only to have something more pressing to engage him.

As the sun was starting to dip on the second day, he came around a little bend in the trail. It was heavily wooded in this part, and he wound through some skeletal maples, branches up like fingers crawling from a grave. The leaves crunched under Daisy's hooves. The sound was satisfying. He wanted to crunch those leaves himself. In about a quarter of a mile, it opened up, and off the path there were half a dozen wagons and a string of ponies. He made a clicking noise with his tongue and shifted just a little in the saddle, and Daisy turned off the trail toward the camp.

"Howdy, stranger," an older man, heavy set, with sunburnt cheeks, leaned on a cane.

"Howdy."

"If you come in peace, you and your mare are welcome to camp with us." He smiled. He didn't look the rube most men on the trail did.

"What'll it cost me?"

"Ha," the man winked at him, "Maybe your soul. We're unruly heathens out here. On our way to Californee. But if you've got any whiskey, we'd be grateful for a nip."

"I'm afraid I've got not much of anything but saddle sores and trail dust."

"Well, you're white and you're free, so you'll find friends here."

He set up his roll away from the main camp and set Daisy to graze, made his way back.

The old man was the ringleader. He was a southerner but lacked the accent. Charlie didn't pursue the story, didn't really care. There were three younger men with him, he figured they probably were little more than boys when they fought in the war, and the grey trousers they wore had been let out and patched until they were hardly identifiable.

Then, there was the passel of women. He counted ten at least, a few of them little more than girls. A few old enough to be his mother. They chittered among themselves. Tending the fire and the cooking, occasionally checking on Cole, as the old man was named, and the others.

Cole sat on a wooden chair like it was his throne, and the group clearly deferred to him. He didn't need the backstory. These women were in Cole's employ. He'd been a gentleman farmer, and when one flesh trade was taken away, had stepped easily into another.

"Would you like me to extend you some credit, son?"

"What kind of credit?"

"Well, if you don't mind my pointing it out, I see you've got an eye for my ladies there. I reckon you could use some of this beer and maybe a bite as well. It turns out, I need a lad like yourself to help us along the road."

"You can't afford me." He smiled. The banter was a welcome relief from the thoughts that had been swirling in him. A comfort.

The man's eyes lit up. He leaned forward in his chair.

"What brings you on this path, son? Visions of gold? The promise of land? These are pitiful illusions that tempt man away from the present. Lies. The only truth is that thing, that moment. You find it sometimes at the bottom of the bottle, but always you find it in that delicate mound that each of those ladies carries like a silk purse."

"You might be right about that. But what I need is information. If you've got it, I'll pay for it."

"Yes, yes, everything must have a price," and the old man waved his hand like he were clearing smoke from the air as he spoke. "What do you seek?"

"I'm looking for a boy, young. Waif of a thing. Traveling with a Native, a drunk, and a young girl. At least two of them on mules. Though I begin to think they all might be figments or mirages, the way they're forever slipping."

The man mulled it over. He wasn't much of a card player. Charlie palmed a ten dollar gold coin, passed it to him. He bit it, then pocketed it.

"Bring the man a beer, and some chow," he barked.

"I know just the ones you speak of. They camped near us just one night ago. Or maybe it was two. Regardless, they are with the Colonel now, about half a day or so west of here. Should be round about Garden City by now."

A woman handed Charlie a wooden mug and a plate of steak and beans. Some tortillas were stuffed under the steak at the plate edge. She smiled at him as he took it. She had thick legs and small feet that he noticed were unshod.

"Enjoy your food and we can negotiate dessert." The man smiled broadly.

Charlie set to his plate, thought about how much more he might spend before the night was over, what it would cost to get his mind back to where he needed it. Separating the boy from a god damned military escort. That was going to take patience and persistence, and every bit of cunning he could muster.

29

VISIONS

Autie stood impatiently, tapping his foot and glancing about. Flowers for Hair was the only one other than he who had a full tent on this expedition. He could not -would not- invite her into his, but since the last run in with Sullivan, he had again grown reluctant to spend too much time in hers. There were whispers, the seeds of gossip that could hamstring his command. She was the only woman attached to the troop, and a Native. He kept the men away from her, and any time alone with her was therefore suspect. Sullivan was a problem. The young captain's eyes were ever watchful, ever judging him since that night.

"Please sit down, spare the roof of my tent." It was true. Standing, his head pushed against the canvas. It was unlikely to do harm, but only drew more attention to his presence.

He sat awkwardly, it seemed his pants never fit right when he was in front of her.

"You know why I'm here, so get on with it."

"Yes, it seems you have quite an affection for my… tea," and she looked up at him, eyes wide and with a hint of angle to her lips that made his face hot.

She pulled some bright blue and some yellow flowers from her braids, crushed them over that earthenware cup, so they stained her hands as she sprinkled them. Then she retrieved a beaded bag that hung from her neck and tapped the bottom with one finger, so a fine powder fell into the cup also. She motioned with her head and her eyes, and Autie leaned forward to pass the kettle from the fire. Taking it from him, she poured slowly into the cup. Wisps of steam rose and disappeared in the light.

The smell was sweet with an edge of camphor. The last two times he had noticed that as soon as it hit his nostrils, and it set him to salivating. She took a delicate ring finger in her mouth, closed her eyes as she cleaned it of residue, then looked at him as she slipped it into the cup and gave it a stir, handed the cup to Autie.

"Let it steep a moment."

He turned the cup again and again in his hand. It was hot to the touch.

"Why do you really come to me, what need do you have of this?"

"I see things. I don't know if they are my destiny or a glimpse of what might be. I'd be a fool to say no to what hints of fortune lie in that cup."

She giggled, like a tinkling of glasses, and raised a hand to her mouth.

The medicine does lend itself to visions, but it is not what's out there you see. It's what's in here." She pointed at his chest. "I have told you this and yet you do not hear."

"Nonsense. Maybe your people lacked the ambition… what I have seen is greatness, victory."

"You have seen a small man who wants to be a big man." She whispered. He wasn't certain he heard correctly.

"What?"

"Pay no mind." She shook her head. "Let me tell you a story while you sip your tea."

"Go ahead," His tension began to ease as he slurped a tiny sip. He could taste the clay of the cup and the bitter liquid. It spoke to something ancient, some vestige from a time outside of language, something before. Before before. Whatever it was that preceded the dominion of man.

"Among my people there was once a man named Silent River. He was quiet, showed no strong feelings, which often means one who is a storm on the inside."

"Maybe, or just one who has found the peace in himself, like me."

Again, she giggled.

"Yes. Well this man was not so great as yourself. He fell off a horse, fairly young, and damaged his leg so it stopped growing, became useless to him. The others came to him and said, 'oh, this is terrible, what will you do?'. He answered them, 'Who knows what is terrible and what is good?'

As he grew older, unable to join the hunting or raiding parties with the others, he would stay behind. In this way, he was able to find a bride and he became closer to the elders.

Everyone said to him, 'this is very good, you are becoming an important man here.' He replied 'Who knows what is terrible and what is good?' His way was cold, strange to many, but he was important, and they accepted him. For a time, it seemed his evenness was desirable, as his counsel was simple and clear. Later, he had a son. The boy was born with a crooked back and struggled from the beginning, could not do the things other boys could. People came to him to offer blessings for his misfortune, as it appeared the boy was ever in pain, would never be a great hunter or a warrior. Silent River's answer was the same as always. When your people came into my country, all the men gathered into a war party. All except this man and his son, who could not tolerate a long ride or fight from a horse. Those that rode off to war were slaughtered a few days later by your army."

She closed her eyes a moment, gestured a crooked line upward, tracing the invisible smoke.

"Those who were grieving their sons, fathers, and husbands said to him 'at least you still have your son. How fortunate for you.' And again he said 'Who knows what is terrible and what is good?'"

"This man sounds like a stoic. A good man, a wise man," Autie said.

"I don't know your word stoic. This man was lacking a spirit. To put oneself outside of feelings of loss and of wonder, is like to removing your skin. How can the world talk to one like this, who cannot feel the wind, the cool rain, or the warm sun? It is to be cut off, entirely. And so it was for Silent River, as even his own son and his wife could no longer bear his emptiness. The elders too, decided his lukewarm counsel was of little value, for he had shared in the decision to send the men to war but bore no pain in the outcome. In the end he was completely alone."

"A great stoic said, 'If you are distressed by anything external, the pain is not due to the thing itself, but to your estimate of it; and this you have the power to revoke at any moment.' Seems to me the wise men could have learned from this Silent River."

"I don't doubt this impresses you, for your people are like him in a way, but with much greater illness."

He drank from his tea which yet simmered, as did he.

"There is the light and the dark, and each of us has both. Medicine can help you see this, help you find the balance to live with the two. But if you will not see, then the dark comes to look like the light, and then the light is meaningless, and then you are a very dangerous person because there is nothing inside you to say 'don't do that,' no corruption you cannot accept, so long as it serves your belief. And then you see yourself as at the center and the rest of us," and she swirled her finger in the air and looked around, "we are no longer real to you."

Autie grunted, set down the cup and staggered from the tent.

He could feel her words clinging to him and wanted the bright sun and what might be revealed in the sky to burn them away.

His limbs tingled, and the whole of him softened, as though the gravity of the earth itself might no longer hold sway over him, and that he would float a few feet off the ground, or higher. The sky went crystalline, agitated by shapes that moved across it. Great flying things, born of those he had seen and destroyed. And ye,t here they swam in winged grace, and he had to will himself to look to the ground, as he nearly tripped.

Pulling. Again, he felt the current pulling him west, and where his feet touched soil they sank into grass soaked a deep red. And the gore, too, was as a stream that gently bubbled west, an effluvium of all the dead things that brought him to that moment.

Looking -to be sure none had taken note of his staggering- he put all his attention into each footfall, placing it as carefully as he could afford without acquiring an unnatural slow gait. He crossed himself as he fell into his tent.

He lay down and closed his eyes and the visions played out in bright flashes, lightning in the dark leaving sinister shadow impressions. He saw the end of the Santa Fe, his band reduced to few and haggard, but he still leading proudly at the front, with his lance caked with the dried blood of formidable beasts he had vanquished. He felt a star, hot and bright inside of him, and knew -was certain- that nothing would stop him.

30

CECIL'S DISCOVERY

ecil was performing his best impression of a curious child exploring the camp when he saw the Colonel. He watched as the man disappeared into a tent, like unto a teepee, but more squat and with steeper angles, small and nearly closed at the top. He hid behind a wagon wheel nearby. Sat in the shade of the wagon and waited.

Emerging several minutes later, the man was unsteady, with an unsure look. He stared at the sky a long moment, then began walking clumsily. Nearly tripping after just a few paces, he caught himself and then walked more slowly and carefully. Cecil had seen men do similar while very drunk, but no man could get drunk so quickly.

He followed so none could see, walked at angles to the Colonel's path, so it might be coincidental that each moved ulti- mately to a similar trajectory. He watched the man return to his own tent and lie down. It was early yet, and strange to be returning to bed just as most of the camp was waking. He edged closer, at an angle, so he could peer through the flap as it waved gently in the early breeze. The man was indeed lying down, but he was talking to himself. Cecil couldn't make out the words, but they spilled from him at a constant and heady pace.

"It sounded like he was praying. Fevered, not like any prayer I've born witness to." Cecil hoped the Friar would have some insight into this latest development.

"I don't recall Moorland being particularly devout. That would require a humility utterly alien to one such as he." The Friar had a puzzled look, he squirreled up his face like he was physically wrestling with a problem. "Quite the opposite. To my mind, he could scarcely conjure a higher authority in the universe than himself. Of course, men like him talk about God, but only to paint a veneer on their ambition."

"What, then?"

"Well, as you describe it, an alteration of some significance occurred at this other tent. Perhaps the route to an answer lies along that path. It certainly wouldn't hurt to have some measure of the man's madness. I think it best if you and the girl take up your investigation. Whatever orders bind us here, it is Red Club and myself that are the subjects of its greatest scrutiny."

The Friar discreetly took a pull from his bottle and Cecil noticed it was nearly to the dregs.

"You take care with that, I'm not sure when I'm going to be able to get more."

"That's a trifle, son. What about the other?"

Cecil slipped him a tiny flask. It was the only way he had found to dispense the laudanum with any discipline. The Friar would consume whatever quantity he possessed until it was quickly gone, so Cecil had to mete it out in portions that would keep the man steady without pushing him clear to the other side.

The Friar took a sip. "Body of Christ, body of Christ. Bless you, my boy. Yea though I walk through the valley of the shadow of the bootheel of the U.S. government, I will fear not, for thou art with me," and he kissed the flask and slid it gently into his jacket pocket.

"You take care with that. I won't be refilling it today."

"Of course, my boy. Of course," and he patted the outside of his pocket.

Once Trixie was up and had a bit of coffee, she became enthusiastic about their mission. Still dressed boyishly, she shook her hair loose of her hat and untangled it as best she could with her hands, fingers spread wide in a makeshift comb. Producing a bright red ribbon as if by magic, she tied it in a bow.

"This should dazzle them that bother to look."

She took the lead to the tent, skipping across the dusty tarmac. Cecil had only to follow her and play the hapless older sibling trying to rein in his charge.

Those soldiers that paid notice at all, spared them little more attention than a glance and a chuckle, and the ones who looked to Cecil seemed satisfied when he returned their looks with a shrug and a frown.

Trixie was clever, didn't make her way directly. Instead, she zigged and zagged past and then doubled back, taking her time to exhaust the attentions of the troopers. She paused at each obstacle, feigning interest in what lay behind it. When she finally ducked into the tent, it was so quick that to Cecil, it was like she had simply disappeared. He walked slowly and deliberately in the general direction of the strange tent, took several minutes making his way past it, then backtracking.

She was already sitting cross-legged, next to a Native woman, when he climbed in. A swatch of light from the narrow aperture above illuminated the two of them, and little else. Trixie was giggling and chewing on a piece of jerked meat. Cecil felt his stomach grumble, took a seat across from them.

"This is Flowers for Hair. Isn't she beautiful?" Trixie beamed.

Cecil nodded. Her face did appear lovely. The cone of light from above lent a pleasing angle to her nose and cheeks. But feminine features didn't move anything in Cecil, much as he wished that they would.

"Trixie told me that you had questions. About the Colonel? And what is your need?"

"I'm sorry, what?"

"What do you hope to accomplish? You must have a sense of who the man is by now and what he is out here to do, but where do you place yourself and your companions?"

"As far from here as possible, ma'am. I want to understand the man so it might ease our escape from him."

"To get away from him where? For his domain is the whole of this land, what he intends will scorch the earth unto its ending in the great water."

Cecil fingered the document, the contract, in his pocket. The dream of San Diego and what might wait for him there. "Well, that's where I'm…, where we're, headed. To the ocean, to be as far from the reach of men like him as possible."

"Impossible," Flowers for Hair sighed. "My people tried running as well. Still, we must each learn our limits and how tight the ropes that lash us to our fate. But I also see in you something of him, of one who would hollow himself that his body might float."

Cecil felt heat rising in his cheeks, hoped it wasn't obvious.

"I'm nothing like that man, if that's what you're saying." he took his hand from his pocket, crossed his arms. "How dare you? You have no idea what kind of man he is, the things he's done going way back."

"I know exactly what he is," and she stared unblinking at Cecil, her eyes glittering green in the light, until he couldn't hold her gaze and looked down.

"Then help us. Help us get away."

"We really need any help we can get," Trixie turned to the woman and smiled. "Cecil and me, we've got more immediate problems than whatever the army is up to out here. If the Colonel hands us over to the law, we're done for."

Then she went right back to chewing the piece of dried meat with great enthusiasm. Trixie was unflappable, Cecil thought. She would be grinning even if they did put a rope on her, as long as she got a chance to kick the hangman in the shin first.

"I am as much a prisoner as you. More, as the Colonel finds me useful to his endeavors, and a pleasant diversion from them." She looked down, paused. "But he has grown addicted to his own grand imaginings, and I hope that soon he will grow reckless enough to stumble into his ending. I will do what I can to help with this. As he grows more bold, the net that holds you might loosen. Pay close attention, and plan for this."

"What about you?" Trixie asked. "Do you want to come with us?"

Flowers for Hair smiled, reached over and stroked Trixie's neck. "You are kind. But I see that my fate is intertwined with this man, and I will carry the burden of death with me even if I outlast him. My path must be a lonely one, for any near me might catch the ending that is meant for me. Death has poor eyesight, but is a relentless hunter. He frequently alights on the one next to his intended. Now, you two go, and don't come back here. The Colonel is a jealous man, and jealous men are always in search of a reason for violence."

31

THE WAITING IS THE HARDEST PART

He followed at a fair distance, cautious beyond any apparent need. Charlie had never seen a military troop move so haphazardly. Cavalry was scattered with no real formation. Scouting was little more than an afterthought, as there was rarely more than one man riding ahead, and he must have been covering quite a range because he would return hours later, slouching in his saddle, his horse moving at a slow gait, man and animal exhausted.

Every now and then, he would stop when the terrain provided decent cover, either by a thicker band of trees, or a bluff. Even better were those places of unaccountable feature, where the terrain appeared perfectly flat, but held nooks invisible from a distance. The west was a bandit's paradise. In these places, he would let Daisy graze a while and study the group with his telescope.

He knew the boy immediately; he and the girl rode the mules, who were attached by a long lead to the second wagon. The kid would glance about regularly, while the girl often dozed. She would periodically jerk awake in her saddle, mindlessly scratch at the mule's head and withers, then pitching forward and holding the animal's neck, would start to doze off again.

The other two must have rode in one of the wagons, because aside from the younguns, and a Native woman who rode far in the back, everyone looked military – if a somewhat shabby example of it. The commanding officer spent a good deal of time talking with the woman, but her role was unclear. If she were a scout, she should be riding ahead, or at least riding point.

Aside from the formation, there were other signs the group lacked discipline. Through the telescope, the uniforms were ragged and stained. Positively savaged by road dust and grime. And their colors were nowhere to be seen. No flag bearer, no bugle boy. Really the only thing that looked proper was the artillery. They hauled a couple of big guns, whose great wheels rutted the earth, and he imagined their creaking protests so vividly he could almost hear them, even at that distance. The covered wagons were a mystery. Some must be supplies and the prisoners. The canvas on two of them was slitted to open on the sides and he knew their purpose must be war.

The commander was oddest of all. The others were dressed in union blue, however wretched and worn, but the man in charge wore a deerskin shirt. It was fringed, and the little strings of leather bounced while he rode. He wore a hat that looked confederate. Mostly gray, it was worn and stained black in places. One side of the brim lay flat and the other was rolled up: it was a shooter's hat, to be sure. The man who wore it had known plenty of combat, learned the lessons that come to those who take up arms.

Late in the day, during one of his stops, he finally spied another Native through his glass. No doubt the one that had rode with the kid. He was leaning out of the rear-most wagon. He closed his eyes for a moment, closed his mouth and threw his head back like he was sniffing the air. Then, bracing against the gate, he leaned far out and opened his eyes.

Charlie dropped into the grass. The man had looked right at him. It was impossible at the distance, but when he brought the glass to his eye again, the man still stared precisely in his direction. Charlie shuddered. It couldn't be, shouldn't be. Ashamed of his lapse, of the chill he felt, he stood back up and looked again.

The man traced a convoluted shape in the air with his right hand, and then he spat, and receded behind the shade of the awning.

Charlie mounted up and fell back behind the train, even farther back than before. It was easy enough to follow the tracks. He needn't be able to see them, nor they him, leastwise not until he had a plan.

32

THE MONSTER OF THE RIVER

The column slowed as it rounded the bend. They had been running parallel the train track, and after a gradual ascent came to the remains of a bridge spanning some 100 feet over a slow-moving river. Here, the Colonel raised his hand and the whole mass came to a shuddering stop, first the horses behind him, whose riders broke like water on a rock and poured to either side until they were a line facing the ruined bridge. Then the wagons broke off one by one turning left and right until they ran perpendicular to the horsemen.

They formed a crooked line. Imprecise. Nonetheless, an imposing wall next to the river that surged below. Canvas was pulled back, and the Hotchkiss guns' barrels protruded and hung down with the quiet menace of sleeping giants. Men unhitched and maneuvered the field pieces, oriented them toward the river's edge.

Trixie and Cecil spilled from the mules. Cecil nearly went straight to ground, his legs were so stiff from the day's riding. Trixie untied Judas and Tucos' reins from the rear and Cecil walked to the next wagon to get a closer look at the guns. They were impressive up close, with wheels of thick gray wood that came up to his chest. He picked at one with his nail and found it was impregnated with some kind of lacquer. The gun itself was a dull bronze, the patina nearly black with road dust and the staining of long use. The bore was near the size of his head. Having witnessed the carnage from the smaller Hotchkiss guns, he tensed and drew a deep breath, resting his hand on the sun-warmed metal.

A youngish soldier, with a fuzz of beard, gave him a long look, as he dropped a metal ball on the earth beside the cannon. It fell with a hollow thud and sunk an inch or two deep. Cecil decided he should collect Trixie and the others. Whatever was happening here, he wanted to be ready to leave if cause and opportunity presented itself.

The Colonel was handing off the reins of his horse to the man on his left, and stepping down from his saddle, caught Cecil's eye. Trixie and the others would have to wait.

"Ho, there, where's the girl?" His eyes darted left and right.

"She's taking care of the mules. Are you trying to find a way around?"

"No, no. We are right where we mean to be. You see the bridge," and he cocked his head toward it.

Looking closely at it for the first time, what Cecil had previously thought might be sabotage of some kind was clearly something else. The metal was twisted in all directions. The wooden supports appeared pushed over from one side. But what could achieve such a result?

"We've built it twice now and twice it's been destroyed. The last time, there was a supply train on the track. An engine and three cars. We found them tossed like leaves on the wind. If you walk over that rise there, you can still see the pieces. But the last time there was a survivor."

"What happened?"

"We think there are caves, something vast and ancient, under that river. The one who survived was no greenhorn. He had hunted buffalo and men for the railroad. He was half mad when they found him, talking about a monster that came out of the water. We mean to get to the truth of that."

And just like that, a great racket erupted from beyond the line of horses, clang, clang, clang, clang. The sound of steel on steel. It rung in Cecil's ears and he felt it in his chest.

"I thought maybe the vibration would draw it. We're going to hammer those rails and see what turns up." The Colonel had a savage look in his eyes, something beyond contempt: the narcotic of annihilation.

"I'm, um, I'm going to find the others. Let them know what's happening."

"Yes, the lot of you should stay well behind the line, at least until we know what we're dealing with. Behind the wagons you will doubtless be safe."

When Cecil found Trixie, she was stroking Judas' muzzle with one hand, rubbing Tucos' ears with the other, and at turns leaning in to whisper to one or the other of them. She had a way with the animals, and they were soothed despite the racket that was beginning to drive Cecil mad.

The Friar arrived, with Red Club in tow, both looking solemn, and the Friar with a restless energy that set Cecil further on edge. The man needed a drink at the very least, and if he didn't get one soon, was likely to attract the wrong kind of attention. The Colonel always had one eye to spare for the Friar, as though maybe he knew more of him than he let on.

"We need to be ready." His eyes darted left and right. "Regardless of how things go here, if we have the chance, we should get away."

"Won't they just hunt us down?" Cecil didn't like the idea of running afoul of men disposed to violence, not more so than was necessary anyway. He wanted escape, but calculated, not panicked.

"They've got orders. Might go bad if they happen upon us,

but I don't think they'll break from their campaign to look. I believe they're following the railroad. If we make our way back to the Santa Fe, we can likely as not disappear, follow it at a distance and parallel until we reach its ending. Better for us than staying with this lot anyway."

"You have me there," Cecil had nightmare visions of his face on wanted posters, thought one might find its way to this troop sooner or later. "We stay long enough, and we might find a town where the Colonel can make good on his promise to ship Trixie and me home. That can only go badly."

Cecil glanced to make sure no one was looking, slipped a small bottle of whiskey from his waist band and handed it to the Friar.

"Here, I'm thinking you might need this to steady you. If your shaking is unnerving me, it can't do us any favors with the soldiers."

"Thank ye, my boy," and transferring the bottle discreetly to his pocket, whispered, "Sweet ambrosia." He continued mumbling as he drifted further out from the wagons.

"I'll keep an eye on him," Red Club was tight-lipped, impassive. Trixie gave him a smile, and he nodded almost imperceptibly and was off. His feet hardly disturbed the dust. He moved like a ghost, and Cecil knew he was preparing himself for escape and whatever came with it.

He and the Friar had only just disappeared over the nearby hill when the commotion started.

First, Cecil heard a distant splash, and then shouting.

"Stay back and look after the mules. Get their bags and whatever else you can."

Trixie nodded, scratching at Tucos' fluffy mane.

Cecil was rounding the outside of the wagons that held the Hotchkiss guns, when they erupted. Mechanical, rhythmic, so loud he could feel it in his jaw. The earth churned and pitted at the water's edge. The men who had been pounding the tracks dropped their hammers and were running for the line.

Boom.

An explosion sucked the air from his lungs and Cecil went flat to the ground. There was a great splash where the ball struck the water.

Rising on hands and knees, he finally saw what had set off the barrage. It looked like two snakes. Massive, reptilian heads raised a good eight feet above the water line. But no, not snakes. Long necks attached to smooth, ovoid bodies. Deep green, nearly black. Slick and smooth, like a salamander. They pulled themselves awkwardly along on great flippers.

The guns went quiet, and the air grew still. The Colonel stood in his saddle at the front of the cavalry, hand raised. The creatures reared their heads upward and howled into the hazy red sunset. It was higher pitched than Cecil expected, more like a cry than a roar, and then broke into short chirps and longer cries.

At first, he thought they were angry, and might rush the cavalry and the wagons, but one came over the top of the other's back. And it, turning toward the other, set both of them rolling over, so they crashed upon the sandy shore, necks entwined, squealing. It was a playful sound, benign.

They slapped at each other with their great flippers and tumbled apart toward the water.

Separated for a moment, they stared at one another and then at the line of horses and men, but seemed to pay scant attention to the gathering, and returned to their playful combat with one another.

Cecil froze, still halfway up and halfway down, he fell back into a seat. Apprehension clawed at his insides, and he wanted to run, because he could see what was going to happen next and the vision clamored for purchase among the mosaic of traumas that covered the cold and inhospitable center of him. He wanted to turn away, to spare himself one more unnecessary horror, but he didn't. He couldn't, no less a prisoner to this moment than those giants who played below.

The Colonel lowered his hand.

Having found their range, the Hotchkiss gunners loosed a fresh burst, which drew a dotted line across the soft belly of the creature to the right. A second gun drew a line above that one, and blood, thick and black, ran down the thing's side.

It let out a high-pitched wail that near ripped the heart from his chest, and then another boom left Cecil's ear's ringing and a cannon ball exploded just in front of the creature. The blast nearly severed the long neck of the beast, and its head fell heavily to the sand.

The other one set to wailing as well, loud and elongated cries that cut right through the noise of the guns and the ringing in Cecil's ears. Dipping its head, it pushed softly against the bulk of its twin, and when the nudging brought no response, it cried out again and began shifting on its great flippers, turning toward the water.

It had nearly put its back to the line, when another explosion shook the ground, and a cannonball exploded to its left and rear. When the smoke cleared, one flipper was gone and a great mass of tissue hung loose from the creature's haunch, swinging like a torn battle flag. The beast raised its head and cried out again, as the Hotchkiss guns raked what remained of its backside. Its tail, which broadened to a fin at the end, flopped on the ground, blood streaming off it.

Cecil clawed at the earth behind him, slowly pulled himself farther away, but still he looked.

The Colonel raised his lance and pointed it forward and the cavalry charged the wounded animal. Two of the soldiers rounded their horses to the front of the beast to prevent its return to the water. A half dozen others rode in a line, discharging their pistols into the wounded creature. They were whooping and cheering one another and soon the scene was obscured by the smoke of their gunfire.

When the thing had nearly ceased its movement and could hardly hold its head up, the Colonel dismounted and set at its neck with his lance. Stabbing at first and then gripping the stave just below the broad blade, he began hacking. The others set to chopping at its hindquarters with their own knives.

The cries grew quieter, the creature's head dipped lower, and finally it settled to the earth. The body continued to shudder, and Cecil hoped this was some reflex and not a sign that its suffering was yet prolonged, but the thought of the thing being at peace was a mercy that the world gave no evidence of possessing.

He realized then that he was crying, and went to cover his eyes, but there was no one to see him so exposed, and no consequence graver than the punishment of having witnessed this scene.

Cecil got up, turned away, thought the Friar might yet have a sip of whiskey, anything to numb the feeling that threatened to fill him to bursting, when there was another cry.

This was louder, lower pitched. Angry. A palpable wave that set him back on his ass.

The sun was beginning to set, and it was a silhouette he saw emerging from the center of the river. At first it looked like the other two, but the head continued to rise higher and higher.

One of the men called out, and the others turned their attention finally from their joyful barbarism, but it was too late. The thing wasn't out of the water yet, and its head was at least twenty feet aloft. When it brought it down on them below, it was with the speed of rattlesnake strike.

Its size became fully apparent when it ripped a man from the ground, and half his body disappeared behind a glistening line of dagger teeth, still slick and dripping from the water. The man hadn't a chance to make a sound as, with a jerk of its neck, the creature flung his broken body deep into the river.

The Colonel waved his lance to signal a retreat, and was climbing over his own men to make his way back to the line.

The thing pulled itself onto shore and crushed a man and the horse he was attempting to mount, under a flipper that was near the size of a wagon. Then it brought those massive jaws down on another, and took his head off along with most of his right shoulder. The body fell like it was bereft of bones. Horses ran in all directions. One went straight into the water in its panic, and set to swimming across the river.

The Colonel, having made his way to the line, ran past Cecil to one of the Hotchkiss wagons.

"Fire, fire," he screamed, "Why aren't you firing?"

The man nearest him pointed and shouted, gestured to the river's edge, where troopers yet scrambled, obstructing any clear shot. Then the Colonel drew his pistol and fired, and the man's brains were a dark smear on the canvas beside him.

There were no more protests. The Colonel turned his pistol back toward the enemy and the dusk was lit up, as the machine guns belched fire and smoke.

But these guns were poor match for the larger beast. Bullets ripped through two soldiers and wounds dotted the flank of the creature. It didn't register pain, or slow its attack.

It swiped at another man with a massive flipper and sent him soaring toward the wagons. He landed with a sickly thud and settled unmoving to the earth.

Another man fell to the Hotchkiss guns, but they didn't let up.

Boom.

This explosion was louder than the previous, even though it came from farther away, from the larger of the two cannons. A volley of grapeshot slammed the creature's chest, tearing it like wet paper. This finally slowed it, but it was not stopped. A cannonball took off half of its left front flipper, and still it continued its awkward climb toward the bulk of the troop.

The Colonel, mounted now, moved behind the line.

The beast made it to the nearest of the Hotchkiss wagons and, with its intact right flipper, smashed the center of it, so it collapsed to the ground, splintered and broken.

The men in the adjacent wagon abandoned their posts just before the creature's massive tail sent the wagon rolling end over end. It caught one of them in mid stride, and he disappeared in the tumbling mass that only narrowly missed the other.

Survivors from the shore were making their way back from the river now, and setting a steady barrage of small arms fire at the creature's rear.

Another blast of grape shot tore into the animal's side, exposing viscera that hung loose and trailed alongside as the thing slowed, but continued its crawling. One final cannonball exploded just below that massive wound and the creature collapsed into a mounded puddle. There was one last, great cry and then silence, shocking in the aftermath of such clamor.

Cecil was finally able to dislodge his attention from the scene and recall the plan. He pulled himself to his feet and ran to the nearby hill.

The Friar was already mounted. The bottle that dangled from his limp hand was stayed through some strange magic, the invisible bond of all things whose fate is tied together. His other hand held the reins of his tan pony. Red Club was mounted as well, and Trixie trailed just behind with the mules.

Cecil did his best to traverse Judas' saddle and found his way clumsily aboard. They set off at a trot, the Friar leading the way, slumped so severely he might have been asleep. He was like a serpent or some liquid poured upon the world, as though gravity were a disease and he more afflicted by it than the average man. Yet, he did steer his animal. Cecil looked to Red Club quizzically and the man offered the slightest nod to affirm they were following the correct trajectory.

The sounds that trailed behind them now could not be distinguished. Celebration or grief or the atavistic junction of the two, abandonment of reason when its fruits have spoiled. Any sounds of men meant they were not distant enough for Cecil to feel safe, and before they had reached the next hill, perhaps an hour later, a great glow to rival the recent sunset menaced behind them, and the smell of the smoke carried with it notes of burned flesh and of the sea. Cecil felt it squeeze his gut and his throat, and urged Judas onward. In the dark, he hoped no one noticed the tears that stung a cleansing path down each of his dusty cheeks.

Cecil had seen a book once about mammoth creatures of the distant past. It had seemed preposterous, but it said they had found bones that proved such things once lived.

What he had seen emerge from that river didn't seem monstrous at all. It was like a storybook, a miracle even, come to life. The army -the men- were the real monsters. Them who took such joy in wanton destruction. Is this what moved in him? Was he like unto them? These feelings of disgust he had. In time they might fade, and he would be left as hollow as them, and in the gnawing absence of him, what horrors might grow?

Escape from himself, escape from the Colonel and his wretches, both must be equally improbable. They had a little distance, but these men would not overlook their absence forever. The Colonel, especially. They might find their way back to the trail, but they could not long remain lost among a group of pioneers. Alone or in a mass, the dangers presented were different, but the odds were long on either. And they stood out, there was no avoiding that. Cecil especially. He would forever be separate, alone.

PART II

FREEDOM IS A KIND OF FALLING

33

RED CLUB'S LAMENT

In the chaos, Levi almost didn't see them leave.

The men were shaken, and it was only through a steady stream of barks and epithets that he kept the cannons to a regular blaze. When the thing crushed one of the war wagons -as he had come to calling the Hotchkiss platforms- he thought he might lose them altogether. Instead, it had the opposite effect. The men began working the big guns frantically, and he had to sooth them to keep them from making some grievous error in their mad rushing. A double load of powder could split a barrel -or even shatter it- and likely as not kill them all.

It was the mules gave it away, beasts that never found a labor they wouldn't protest. One of them brayed so loud Levi heard it between shots, and looking that way, he saw both the animals being led off by the big Native who traveled with the kids.

As soon as the monster from the river was fully down, unmoving in a great trail of its own gore, Levi ran for his horse and headed where he knew they would go. Off trail and to the south, for the hills to the north were daunting even to look at.

His instincts guided him true, and he was riding hard just a handful of minutes when he first caught sight of the party. They were moving as quick as the mules would let them, which is to say not very quickly. It was near full dark, and time was not on his side.

Levi had closed much of the gap between them when those sharp eyes appeared over the big man's shoulder and he turned the others with a high whistle. They all quickened their pace then, but not by much, and he could see them steering a course toward a bottleneck, where emaciated trees grew thick on either side of a narrowing path. Beyond the thin aperture, all that could be seen was the shadow of dense brush and scrub oak.

Stopping his horse, he drew his heavy-barreled Henry from its saddle scabbard. He didn't want to kill a one of them if he could help it, not without the Colonel's blessing. He drew a bead on the mule nearest the rear of the group and put a round in its haunch. The animal kicked and bucked fierce, and then the leg came down askew. It threw the girl in its violent thrashing, and then fell onto its rump. She was immediately up, if slightly dazed and wobbling from the impact, and she staggered to the mule's side. The thing let out a keening cry then, which rattled him. He wished he had put the animal down completely on the first shot. The other mule turned and come back to the downed one, refusing to keep its way to the trail despite the boy yanking at its reins with all he had.

Levi paused for a moment, waited to see if the scene would turn further in his favor. He was out of pistol range of the group, and confident they lacked anything bigger than sidearms, if even those.

The girl was steadfast, crouched by the wounded animal, stroking its crest and withers. It had settled into a low arrhythmic whine, and the other mule pushed its head against the fallen one. Now, it too began to whine. The boy finally loosed the reins and began pulling at the girl's arm, dragging her away. The uninjured mule wouldn't budge. Levi smiled. They could scarcely escape with the two of them afoot

The Native stood his ground astride his pony, while the others continued on their way. Levi and the man they called Red Club watched each other a long moment, and he had the feeling of something shifting in the air. A cold prickling rode his spine, and his heart beat in his ears, as if he had caught a rattlesnake out of the corner of his eye. He mounted up, his grip tightening on the reins in an effort to sooth his nerves.

Red Club knew the captain was behind them. Levi, they called him. The bigger of the two, with scarred hands and a permanent scowl. The one with the restless eyes, who had watched closely whenever he could spare it. He had known he would have to outsmart or outfight the man sooner or later.

He had felt Levi before he ever saw him. Felt it through the ground. Felt and then heard, and knew the man was working his poor animal to death, the beating of hooves so close together, so heavy. It made no sense. He could have crept on them. Red Club would still have known but perhaps not so early. But he, like the Colonel, was impatient. There was another who had been following the whole caravan for some days now, and that man was the more concerning, for he was more patient than any white man Red Club had encountered, which made him an unknown, and dangerous.

Red Club suspected the situation was hopeless, and then he saw the cleft in the scrub ahead, and thought if they could get there they might have a chance. The man Levi would have the wisdom not to blindly pursue them through a close and winding tunnel that could go on for miles. It wasn't a certainty, as he had learned that the impetuous are ever blind to peril.

When Tuco went down, and Judas wouldn't take another step, he knew there was but one chance left to them, thin as a blade of prairie grass, and he the only one equipped to take it.

He pulled his war club, with its great knotted head, deeply stained with layers of blood and scored on all sides with the markings of his victories. Its heft was a familiar comfort, and he gripped it in his right hand against the saddle. With his left, he drew the reins and set his pony to a hard charge toward Levi, as the others made their way as quick as they could manage toward the gap.

It was a hundred yards that lay between them, if even that, and the man froze for a moment when Red Club's pony threw a cloud of dirt as she turned and galloped. Only just a moment, then the man was mounted himself, pistol drawn to high ready, and moving to bypass Red Club entirely to flank the larger group.

Red Club flattened himself on his pony's back. She was an experienced animal, had already moved to correct course. There was the crack of the pistol, like a tree snapping amid the hoof beats. The buzz in the air told him it went wide, but not by much. He sat up in the saddle and turned his pony slightly as the next shot thundered through the air. This one was even closer, but his maneuvering saved him.

Levi brought his horse to a sliding halt, and leveled his pistol for a carefully aimed shot. There were only ten yards between them now. Time stood still, breath of man and animal commingling in the air in a rank miasma. Red Club set his pony to a hard turn, and with a few yards separating them, threw himself off his animal, lunging toward the soldier.

He felt the next shot in the same moment he heard it. Like a punch to his left hip and an all-consuming heat. It was not enough to slow his flight through the air, and he caught the man with the stem of his club across the chest and neck, took him to the ground, landing atop him.

Red Club's hip screamed on impact, bursts of bright light exploding in his periphery and then his vision darkening in a narrowing circle. He nearly lost consciousness.

Levi lay underneath him, quiet and still for a moment, then began sputtering and hacking. His pistol gone, he clawed at his throat with both hands. The club had broken some inner part of him. When Red Club's vision cleared, he saw a place in the man's neck had collapsed inward.

The soldier's eyes snapped open and he stared at Red Club, began clawing in the dirt for his weapon.

Red Club smashed the side of his skull once, twice, three times, until his face was like the quarter moon, and a halo of red stained the flattened grass. The wet warmth of it pooled under him, he had not the strength nor the purpose to withdraw from it, and he slipped away.

He awoke propped against a rock. His pony was nowhere in sight. A man stared at him, eyes shaded and hidden under the awning of his hat. But he knew those eyes even in their conceal-ment. Here was the patient man. Beyond him, there were the pointed toes of the Levi's boots. Red Club let out a slow breath. At least that one was dead. The patient man, the one who had been following, he was the final test. If he hadn't known better, he would have thought it was a vision, the man was so out of place. His black boots caught the light like still water, so bright it was hard to look at them. His suit, black like a preacher or undertaker might wear, was unmarked. Looked brand new. The shirt he wore under it was white as gauze. It was like he had materialized on the prairie, or was simply not part of this world, but of some other place divorced of nature.

"I carved your notch for ya," He was holding the war club, scratching at it with the edge of a Bowie knife that he was grip-ping by the spine. "I made it a nice big one since he's an officer and all."

It was the first and last time a white man would touch his club and remain standing long enough to revel in the folly, but the tool were a part of him, and he withdrawing further from all his parts.

"A captain, and not the first."

"No shit?" The man pushed back his hat and raised his eyebrows. He had a thin, red mustache and sharp features. So pale, like even the sun turned from him.

"Well, probably your last though, so I s'pose it's still an event. Looking at that hip of yours..." He clicked his tongue. "I think your days of countin' coup are over."

"I am Rewahle. My people don't count coup, we count bodies."

"Really, I thought you was all pretty much the same in that regard? Well, guess we got lots to learn about one another, and I've got all the time in the world. Seeing as you don't, though, I guess we should move along."

"What do you want?" He was growing tired of the man already, resented having to speak so much, and especially English, when he should be making himself ready for the crossing. He made an effort to move his leg, to test it, and even a little shift sent a wave of agony through his body, brought back the little pinprick bursts of light, peripheral darkness. He looked down, probed with his hand, and the grass around him was soaked and sticky with his blood.

"Well, sir. I'd really like to know where your friends are headed, especially the boy. There's a desert to the south there and I don't intend to cross it unless I have to. I'd be much obliged to know where they all want to wind up. Figure I can start there and work my way back if need be."

He smiled and it was like the snapping turtle, tight and lipless.

Red Club laughed.

"You have nothing to give me and nothing to take away. Move on, little man. Leave me in peace to my end."

"Everyone has something to be took away. Maybe I'll start with your eyelids." He dropped the club and rubbed his thumb along the edge of the Bowie. "We're all alone out here, and you've got a fair amount of blood left in you."

"I can tell you the truth or I can lie to you, and you won't know the difference until I'm long dead. Torture me and you'll be no wiser, but you might stain your pretty clothes."

The man flicked his wrist and the knife stuck into the ground with a thud. He slowly removed his jacket, lay it carefully over his saddle, and then began rolling up his sleeves.

"Don't you worry none about that. I'm pretty good at this, and well compensated. Buy me some new clothes if you bleed on these." He retrieved his knife.

"You're after the boy. And you're not the law. Someone is paying you. What did the boy do to be worthy of this attention?"

The man dropped to a squat, eye level with Red Club.

"I guess it don't matter none to share with you, since you ain't going to be talking much longer. He killed another boy. A boy of means. The family wants the eye and tooth the good book says is owed them."

"This is your work, fetching people for rich folks?"

"Something like that."

"And you think you're like them, these people who pay you. You dress like them, try to keep the land from touching you?"

"Not like them. Not like them and not like you."

"You're just like me. To them you're half Indian and half slave."

"Now just one minute," and the man's voice cracked a little. He seemed stuck on what to say.

"You dress like them. I bet they laugh about that. You're just a wild dog that they can throw scraps at to do whatever they like. And when they're done with you, to forget you ever existed."

The man lunged and stuck his knife in Red Club's left shoulder. He twisted the tip. Red Club tensed and clawed at the bloody grass. He did his best to stifle a groan.

"You'd be wise to shut the fuck up about that which you

don't know. I'm a respected man. People know I'm a professional. That's why they hire me and not just any filthy rabble."

"Yes. They know you know your place, in service to them. A mongrel who fetches and rolls over when told."

Charlie withdrew the blade, stuck it in Red Club's other shoulder. He was ready this time and didn't so much as wince.

"You should stop wasting time with me and go to the desert. You'll never catch those three, not unless the land wills it, but you should go anyway. Your polished bones will be almost as neat as that suit. Stupid white man. You think you control anything here? You are a bit of gristle stuck in the teeth of a beast. Go to the desert and find your insignificance. Your masters will forget your name and send another just like you."

"Shut up. Shut your stupid fucking mouth." Charlie raged, stuck his great Bowie into the center of Red Club, and the blade sunk deep, just below the breastbone.

Red Club could feel something important give way, saw a spurt of red when the man withdrew. He shifted, pushed out his chest and the geyser caught the man's white shirt dead center.

"Ha ha. I thought you were the patient one, but no. You're just scared." Blood bubbled from his mouth now, ran over his lower lip and spread down his chin and chest, but the sense of it, of its warmth or wetness, was already growing remote.

"Little man," he mumbled through the red foam on his lips, and smiled.

He began a low hum then, the soft beginning to his story, his last song. To call them to him, to let his wife and his baby and all the others know he was coming, with love in his heart and without regret.

Charlie raged, threw his knife with all the strength he had, and then instantly regretted it. It was a good knife, and he'd never find it in the grass and brush. He tore at his bloody shirt, buttons popping down the front, and threw the remnants of it over the dying man's head. The Native continued his humming and chanting. It rose and fell like the patterns of nature, birdsong and the susurration of wind in the trees. Charlie drew his smaller dagger, thought to stab him again just to silence the singing, but his anger was already running its course.

The man had gotten the better of him, earned the mercy of a death that was more or less on his terms. Charlie was angry mostly at himself. It had been many years since he had lost his cool in matters of business. And now he had a difficult choice with little knowledge on which to base it.

To the south was none but desert. He was ill-provisioned to ride through it for more than a day or so, and if he fell back to gather supplies, he would surely lose the track. And oh, how he hated the sand, how it got in everything and itched and scratched. He could almost feel it already, sliding around in his boot, so he would have to stop frequently to shake it loose or else be driven mad by it. The wilds were all of them places of madness, but the desert most of all.

To the west was Santa Fe, and the trail's ending. He had never been, but heard tell it was at least a fair attempt at a proper city. No Chicago or New York, but there were no doubt a soft bed and a warm bath and a shave to be had. He could post an update to the family and have them release more funds, get a new shirt, fresh provisions.

Whether the party stopped in Santa Fe or not, it would be a place to pick up their scent, and if they never showed, he could backtrack to the desert. If need be, he thought he would manu-facture sufficient evidence of the boy's demise. There were plenty of boys, with plenty of bones and scalps and fingers.

Yes, it was the best course for him now. Let the three of them crawl through the sand and fiddle with scorpions or rattlesnakes or whatever unnamable thing lay out that way. He would make his way to comfort and rest, and an ending to this insufferable mission one way or the other.

34

THE JACKALOPES

Autie squinted against the smoke. It was a great expanse of sage and mesquite and the ubiquitous prairie grass that he had ordered set alight. The dusky silhouettes of his men moved with purpose on the far side of the plain, now and then vanishing entirely in the haze. The wind had favored them at the start, then had shifted. Now it choked him, thick and acrid. He held a handkerchief to his mouth and backed his horse several paces, but it provided little relief.

He considered they might have chosen wrongly, the woman were ever more reticent with her assistance, and he thought it only a matter of time until she began to actively undermine him, if she weren't already. The flames were high and spreading fast, and there was yet no movement in the scrub, no sound except the crackle and the ever-present wind. When the smoke billowed higher and the heat began to beat at him in waves, he heard over the crackle and pop of the burning fuel a scratching and a rapping as of wood on wood. It conjured in his mind images of claws and of teeth.

The first to appear from the brush seemed to manifest from thin air, as if by magic, so perfect was their coloration suited to the environment. They were larger than he expected. He had seen the lean and elongated desert hares before; these were about twice the size, and with the racks of antlers, they were considerably taller.

Autie was mounted, had ordered the rest of them to fight from their feet, as he thought being horse bound would only encumber them for the task of killing such small game. The men had been prepared with sabers, knives and clubs, thinking these would be adequate to the task, but there was a general commotion at the sight of these creatures -and in such great quantity- as there were dozens now pouring forth from the smoking brush.

"Hold your ground!" Autie wheeled his horse and raised his lance high, then replaced it in its scabbard and drew his Winchester and set to. His horse was restless with the movement and the smoke, so that he had to lean over her neck. His bodyweight steadied her.

There was a general clatter, as most of the men hastily stowed their melee weapons and jerked pistols. This was shortly followed by the pleasant and familiar smell and sound of combusting powder. It charged him, reflexively. At first, Autie joined in the general barrage. Then, as some of the animals slipped past his men, he fell back and set to trampling these with his horse. She was hesitant at first, became more willing after he dug spurs into her flesh.

He had not prepared a solid battle line, had thought this would be an easy task, something to bolster the men after the terrible losses at the river. His folly soon became apparent. One man, having run his pistol dry, paused to reload. A particularly large specimen dug its feet deep and sprung with great force, its rack rebounding off the man's belly. It was immediately cut down by the trooper next on the line, and it appeared at first the injury must be slight. Then, the man dropped his pistol and took hold of his gut. He fell to his knees and on reaching out to slow his descent, released his grip. This barrier disrupted, his entrails spooled wet on the ground, and he fell to his side. He lay there in a slight spasm that Autie knew meant death, and not far off.

The ground was slick with blood and the metallic smell mingled heady with the increasing smoke. The sun was nearly obstructed by this point. Through the haze, the ground was a great pelt of the dead and dying hares.

As the larger ones began to thin, there came smaller specimens with less pronounced racks, and behind and beside them were the young. These lacked antlers, so looked more like jackrabbits with nubs before their ears. There were many, and they let out a collective squealing that sent a shudder through the line. It did nothing to slow the work, though, and Autie again was proud of his troopers' grit.

The men regained their hand weapons and set to cutting and bashing them that were left, as they had no need of bullets for these. Autie dismounted and joined them, slashing and thrusting with his lance. It excited him to see it drip with gore and the blood arced beautifully in the half light.

Soon the flames began to ease, as little of the fuel remained. Mesquite trees drizzled smoky plumes, but even the sky was beginning to clear, the sun a more distinct red smudge on the horizon.

The men began collecting trophies, hacking at antlers and the poofs of tails. Some carved the long ears and were busy stringing them on leather cords. They would burn the rest, but he felt he could indulge them this. As long as they only took parts, it would represent no evidence of the existence of the beasts, and that was the point.

He had lost two in the fracas. The one eviscerated and another who had taken a bullet. The trooper next to that casualty had been speared by an antler to the leg and discharged his pistol as he fell. He now bent over his fallen comrade, on his knees as if praying for forgiveness. He wept. There were no more the man could do, and Autie knew the others would judge him harshly. A half dozen more men had injuries: cuts and gouges from antlers, and a few bites. All in all, it was a great success, and he hoped it might put the campaign back on track.

Autie was standing near the glow of the dying flames. Some men were tossing remains into what little scrub was left, while others busied themselves gathering more fuel to burn all the bodies, for there were many. He heard a screech, and the creature flew from the smoke in a flash. The thing was all matted fur and charred flesh. When the blackened antler hit his inner thigh, he only felt a pinch. He reached down quickly and caught it on the rebound, swung the animal hard in a high arc, smashed it against a rock. As he pivoted on the wounded leg, there was an audible rip, and he thought his pants must be ruined.

He beheld the beast. Its face was grotesque, burnt nearly to the skull. It twitched and he smashed it again and this time its antler came loose, and he saw it was slick with blood. His right pants leg was soaked and when he took a dizzy step, there was a squish in his boot. He pitched forward, and then the whole world spun and winked out.

35

THE OLD MAN IN THE DESERT

They were nearly a week into the dry and desolate wasteland. The Friar's horse had give out after three days, and Cecil's feet had gone from a constant burning to completely numb. It were an infinite hell, and he wondered if he would even know when he finally expired or if his corpse would just keep marching, not knowing the difference. Trixie had gone distant and dumb shortly after they left the wooded path, and he was left to the company of his dark imaginings.

By the second day with no sign of him, Trixie knew that Red Club was gone. Her grief for him was doubled, knowing there was no other to grieve him, to remember the man he really was. It was the second time he had saved her, and since the first, their bond had been a thing of spirit, unbreakable by distance or time. A bond unbreakable even in death. She cried for the man he was, for the world that would be much reduced without him in it.

None of the others knew what he had lost. Theirs was a common grief -Trixie and Red Club- both orphaned in their way.

Her from parents and sibling and he from his entire people, his land, and last of all his wife and child. He had taken his vengeance out on those men he could reach, who had took from him, and then from many others who took. All notches on his club.

Their bond, unbroken, was now transformed, and would forever be a corrosive thing that stung her when she touched on it. To be added to those that came before: mother, father, brother. All her pleasant memories had a dull edge that excoriated, that trained her to not touch them too often or too close.

Cecil was wondering which of them would fall first, and how soon, when the man appeared as if from nothing. Some contour of the shifting sands so subtle that it went without notice, lost as they were in their agonal trudging. One moment, it was nothing but sand and weeds, those standing bristles that clustered in bunches of green and brown. Those, and the occasional cactus, erect and defiant, arms raised in hopeless pleading under that scorching light.

Then, in the blink of an eye, there was the squat cigar box of a cabin and then the man, frail and thin as the tendrils of smoke from greenwood. His skin was a tan and sagging sheet over a skeleton. His bones a blasphemy.

He didn't see them at first, and for a few moments Cecil thought there was hope. That they were no longer lost, and this just an old timer living on the edge of some greater community.

He held a makeshift broom. Cactus wood with a bundle of green weeds clutched to the end by a bit of fraying twine. He swept with a mania that made Cecil tense, an energy that seemed an ill fit to his withered body. His hair was long and white, and draped over his white beard like a veil. It was probably why he didn't see them until they were just a few yards away. Then he jerked upright, eyes blazing blue and nearly fell backward, caught himself in the low frame of his doorway.

"Heyo, strangers." He put a hand to his chest. "Did you ever give me a start." His beard shifted and he brushed his hair back to reveal a toothless smile that put no one at ease.

Trixie brushed past Cecil, "You got any water? We've been walking for days it seems," and she smiled a baleful smile, undermined by her chapped and cracked lips. It was the most animated he'd seen her since they entered the desert, and he was grateful for it.

Cecil put a hand to her shoulder, lest she march right into the cabin. Thirsty or not, he needed to know it was safe and she was clearly beyond such concerns.

"There's a dribble of a spring around back. Damnedest thing. Can't get more than a sip or two at a time but you're welcome."

Cecil tried to get a hand around her wrist. He didn't like the idea of her being out of sight just yet. She wrenched away with energy he could scarcely have expected, and had bounded out of sight in the span of a breath. There was no choice but to follow. He tried to keep an eye on the old man, but he stood still, as if challenging Cecil to go first. The Friar, who was many days now past the end of their laudanum supply and a good forty-eight hours without so much as a sip of whiskey, stood twisted and silent, head tilted down, eyes hidden by the brim of his hat. It was a sort of torpor came over him when the medicine's song went quiet in his blood. He would be of little use.

Cecil rounded the back of the structure and found Trixie on hands and knees in a spot of shade under the slant of the thatch roof.

"Want some?" She looked up at Cecil, smiling broadly. Bits of wet sand clung to her cheeks, and she held a kerchief gently in cupped hands.

"Like this." She held the cloth above her upturned face then and squeezed it until brown water ran and dripped into her mouth.

She returned it to the damp spot on the ground and pushed it down, handed it to Cecil a moment later and he did the same. It was gritty, tasted of soil and salt.

Only after they had each of them taken a few turns, did Cecil realize the old man hadn't followed them. Returning to the front, he found both men as they had left them, the hermit staring silently at the Friar. Trixie dabbed at his lips with the damp cloth until he finally took it from her and squeezed it himself.

"Well, you might as well come on in," the hermit spoke, and curled his fingers in a welcoming gesture, each knuckle grotesquely pronounced by the act.

Cecil followed, while Trixie tried to guide the Friar, who would not enter the building, and so the two leaned in the slight shade just outside it.

The hermit set his little broom carefully against the wall just inside the doorway.

"God damn this sand. More of it ever day. You could lose a whole lifetime just keeping it out."

Cecil glanced around the space, where shafts of light revealed the many gaps between bits of lumber in the walls. The floor was hard packed dirt. It was a peculiar madness trying to keep sand away.

"It's different dirt, inside and outside," the man had read his mind. "It'll bury this place if I let it."

"We're trying to find our way back to a trail of some sort, or a town. Some way to finish our journey west. I was hoping you might give a little guidance."

"Ha." The old many barked a laugh, dry and joyless as the endless desert outside. "If you figure that out, you come tell me. There's nowhere else, no way to anywhere from here, boy. Believe that I've tried. Used to be all I did was try. Plan. Try.

Plan. Try. Plan. You know, boy. God doesn't exist, but still he laughs at us."

"We've been trying to plot our way by the sun, been moving west for a few days now, going a little north each day too, but you're the first person we've seen in near a week."

"Might be the last person you see, too."

A threat? The man said it softly, like he spoke with regret. Cecil wondered how he was surviving in this great nothing, thought the occasional lost traveler might find its way into his stewpot.

"What do you mean?" And Cecil brushed his fingers against the pepper box pistol stuffed into his right pocket. There was only the slightest reassurance there.

"What year is it?"

"I'd say we're closing out 1883. Hard to tell the season this far out on the trail, though. Might be Christmas for all I know."

The old man slumped and sighed deeply.

"Can't be right," he whispered, Cecil could hardly make out what he was saying. He was mumbling. Numbers. Ticking off fingers as he went. "Can't have been thirty years. Not thirty years. He trembled, looked up at Cecil, eyes pleading. A desperate sadness wanting for tears, but there wasn't moisture enough to make them.

"You mean to tell me you've been out here since before the war?"

"What? What war?"

Trixie and the Friar walked in, she ushering him to a corner, guiding him gently to a seat. He was trembling now. It wasn't much cooler inside than out, but his chill was of a different kind. Trixie tucked a serape around him, and he clutched it tight.

"He's not well. He really needs some medicine." She looked at Cecil and then at the old man, eyes pleading.

"You know we're out. Not even a drop of whiskey left since day before yesterday."

"I don't have whiskey, but there's a cactus flower whose tea is balm for my headaches. Might give him some of that."

Trixie and Cecil stood looking at one another while the old man quietly started a small fire, poured about a thimbleful of water in a rusty kettle, and set to brewing. Both could sense the other's thoughts well enough. Neither wanted to trust this man but there was little else for them. When he was done, he poured the concoction into a clay cup. It was thick and fragrant, and Trixie sat with the Friar while he sipped. The shaking eased but didn't pass.

"Let me cook you some supper. No point wasting a fire."

He had a skinny rabbit and some herbs, and began preparing both for the pot with an expertise that made Cecil's heart hurt. How many times had he repeated exactly these steps in thirty years. His unease with the hermit didn't reduce his pity for the man.

"I swear I've killed this same rabbit 'erry day for half my life. He stopped trying to run from me years ago. Now we just look at one another. We're both of us victims of this hell. He knows. Knows I try to give him the mercy that none can give me."

Cecil felt witness to a ritual; preparing and eating the animal was like an evening prayer for the man. Who could blame him for his fantasies? For wanting to connect to something?

Trixie joined them for supper. There was just a bit of flour remaining, and Cecil managed a few biscuits. The old man ate his in quiet reverence. No one spoke until he had finished.

"How did you come to live here?" Trixie finally broke the silence.

"Huh. I wanted to be a mountain man, if you believe that. At least that's how I remember it now. The past gets to be like a loose tooth after a while. Like somethin' part of you but not quite. Telling myself the same stories over and over until they sound like they belong to someone else. Anyway, the house was already here. When I found it, I was so tired, so weary, I thought it a blessing. I was young and stupid, didn't know there was places like this. The land can be a hunter, no different from a wolf once it sets it's jaws on you."

"Couldn't you just go back the way you came? Save up some water from out yonder and then go?" Trixie's voice was up an octave, apprehensive.

"That was the first thing I tried. So many times. So many. I've near died out there more times than I can count, and the only place I end up is right. back. here.

It's the goddamn sand. You do 'errything you can to keep it out. I can feel it under my skin. The desert takes up residence in you like it does every damn thing. Until it owns you." The old man looked very tired.

The Friar took up a low moan then, like the wind howling through loose boards.

"We've got to get our friend out of here. Anything you can tell us to help. If there's a way in there must be a way out." Trixie looked desperate, begging for a sliver of hope the old man wouldn't or couldn't give.

"You don't understand. Things I've seen. I once crossed a goat skull out there in the sands, not much more than a mirage. I touched it. Don't know why I did but like I had to. Such a blank and lifeless place the thing needed to be real so's I knew I was still living. So, I touched it, and it came apart in my hand. Dried out like burnt paper, just fell apart and in a few seconds the whisper of a breeze had spread its dusty remnants to nothing, just the horns left stuck there like they was growing out of the ground.

I feel like that on the inside. The grit. It's in my blood, in my marrow so I can hear it, feel it when I move. Just whispering its slow erosion. If you cracked me open and touched my heart, it would collapse in a puff just like that skull did. I know it like I know I'll never be free of this place."

Trixie shook, retreated to give some measure of comfort to the Friar. Cecil had come to see that was where she often found comfort herself, taking on the needs of the frail and pitiable things. With Tuco and Judas gone, the Friar was the next logical choice. She removed his hat and dabbed sweat from his face with his bandanna.

"Do you know what it is to not trust your eyes? Your mind even? What is hell if not that. I cut myself with a rock once and it was a sandy sludge come dribbling from the wound. I touched it and it felt like silt between my fingertips? How can I know anything after that? We should rest. Sun'll be up fore you know it, and you won't be able to sleep then."

Just like that, the old man drew back to the opposite corner from Trixie and the Friar and left Cecil to wrestle with his confusing words.

The next morning, he was up before they were, had gathered some water in that cup of his and offered it up. They took it and passed it among themselves, taking sips. The Friar was more alert than the night before. He trembled now with an agitated energy, his face a knot of worry and irritation. There was an edge to him. A loose board slapped against its neighbor, and he tensed and yelled "fuck."

"So, what do we do?" Trixie's worry hadn't eased in the night. She looked to hardly have slept.

"What can we do? Just keep walking west northwest. We have to hit something sometime."

"Didn't you listen to a thing he said?"

"What do you want Trix? What else is there? We just take up in this here house? He's a madman, probably walked in circles for few months and then settled. How can we believe anything he says?" But it ate at Cecil. The things he'd already witnessed.

He saw his future in those hollow cheeks, those surrendering eyes. Could see a time, maybe not so far off, when he could no longer tell waking life from dream or nightmare. Maybe he was already there. He pushed the thought away.

"Let's get as much water as he'll let us gather and then go. The longer we stay the harder it's going to be."

They spent the next hour mopping up water from the spring and squeezing it into their canteens and skins. It was a grueling process and the old man stood staring while they worked, finally retreated indoors as their efforts grew less and less fruitful.

He remained silent when Cecil and Trixie stepped into the cabin to thank him and say their farewells. Wouldn't look at them or speak a word.

The sun grew hotter each step they took westward. Though it was early, by the time they covered a hundred yards the heat was already punishing. Trixie and Cecil walked side by side, the Friar a few steps behind, so Cecil was turning his head every few steps to make sure the man was with them.

A scream, otherworldly and desperate, split the air like lightning. Cecil spun in place and saw the old man, what was left of him.

Naked to the waist, his tanned body was monstrously emaciated. He had shorn his beard and hair as closely as he could, probably with the skinning knife he now held aloft. The blade's edge glowed in the bright sun like a dying star, and there were runnels of blood down his face and chest where he had gouged himself. He was closing the distance at speed.

The Friar went pale at the sound of the hermit's screaming. He stiffened, then wheeled and gripped the saddle pistol that hung on a cord around his neck like a great yoke. Trixie screamed and the gun went off like a cannon. A sluice of gore shot out the old man's back and in a moment that stretched impossibly, Cecil could see it glittering like sand before man and his contents came to a rest on the desert floor.

The Friar let the pistol fall, and where it brought the cord taut, it almost pulled him to the ground. Trixie ran to him and buried her face against his body, settled into a low whimper.

Cecil turned and looked at them. No one spoke for there was nothing to say. They turned, and continued their quiet trek. He told himself the man had got in his head, and that he didn't see what he was sure he did. It would be easy enough to know to a certainty, but there was not enough gold in California to get him to take a closer look at that body.

They had only quit the grisly scene less than an hour when Cecil spotted the jackrabbit. He had seen so much, and his body was becoming a collection of tics and tremor -aftershocks of the dreadful and fantastical- that the events of the morning were lost in the cloud of static that permeated him always, kept everything and everyone a little more distant each day. The scene replayed in his mind. The screaming, the strange jet of effluvia. All of it was soon no more real than the mirages he saw on the shifting landscape. Far off promises that dissolved to nothing the closer one got.

The jackrabbit was different. He first spotted it in the shadow of a many limbed saguaro. They were watching each other, Cecil and the others walking closer and closer, and it made no effort to move to greater concealment. Finally, he stopped about ten yards from the creature. Trixie and the Friar came to a halt beside and just behind him, only noticing the beast when Cecil slowly raised a hand to point at it. No expert on the various members of the Lepus genus, he yet suspected this was a rather large specimen, as they went. It was starved down to skin and bone but stood nearly three feet.

As they waited there, each sizing the other up, the jackrabbit stutter stepped into the light, revealing features previously hid.

Its flesh and fur was burned in places, and most significantly its face and ears, which were nearly black. Two jagged stumps protruded from its skull, yellow and brown and smooth like bone, with the rusty patina of dried blood at the tips. The Friar raised his gun for the second time that day.

"Put that thing away and let's go," Cecil said. "I don't want anything to do with the rabbits around here."

"You're going to wish we had some meat later and feel awfully dumb." The Friar had lowered the big pistol slightly but not released it to the cord it hung from.

"It looks sickly, and that's the last thing we need."

"Leave it be," Trixie spoke up. "I've seen enough things die for a lifetime and we don't have time to stop and cook it anyway." She stepped in front of them, and finally the Friar eased the pistol back to hanging on its leather cord.

It was three days walking when Cecil saw the creature again, and all of it the same desolate terrain, without a landmark coming into view even in the remote distance. They used up the water on day two and had taken to spending the day in whatever shade they could find, usually the meager protection of some thick manzanita or an ancient cactus. They were traveling at night. Cecil feared getting snakebit, but the unrelenting heat of mid-day made a stronger argument.

Dawn was just making its presence known, casting a half light on the sand, and they were scanning the rolling desert for a place to hide out for the day when he saw it. There was a thin bunch of dried chaparrals that caught his attention as possible shelter. Altering his course to get a closer look, the thin light caught an outline that was immediately familiar. He blinked hard and when he opened his eyes, it had stepped clear of the woody clutch. His mind reeled. He wanted to deny the reality of it, but there was no question it was the same beast. It watched him, possessed of a greater malice than when last they had met, and he thought of the old man and what he had said, that the rabbit he caught daily desired the release he brought it, and hadn't the old man done the same when he saw that Cecil and the others were intent on leaving him?

This time, he didn't alert the other two, and both were too tired and beaten to notice. Instead, he encouraged them to walk just a little longer, knowing what they would find and hoping he was wrong. Within the hour, they clawed up a dune that seemed intent on swallowing them by inches, and as they came over the top, Trixie let out a cry. Cecil ran to her side as quick as he could with his feet sinking every step, put an arm around her and they stood together staring at the cabin. She shivered in his grasp, and he knew they both would be crying if they had the water to make tears.

They spent the next two days at the cabin. Resting, drinking, storing what water they could as it bubbled up from the pathetic spring. Cecil half expected to see the old man again, that he might be resurrected like he believed the rabbit was, but the realization slowly dawning on him was something else. The man was an outsider here, as were they. It was everything else that never changed. And he began to think of what might be required for them to escape this endless waste.

On the second day, the Friar went out. He had settled into anxious sobriety and had a vigilant restlessness that rattled Cecil's and Trixie's nerves. He was glad to see the man take his bouncing limbs and roving eyes elsewhere. Glad until he heard the gunshot several minutes later. It was like a great tree limb cracking where there were no trees, and it gave the two of them a start.

The rabbit was dressed already when the Friar returned, and lacking its head and feet and guts and skin, it looked so like what they had eaten that first day with the old man, Cecil's suspicions were all but confirmed. Trixie wanted nothing to do with it, and for that he was grateful. He wouldn't have let her eat it if she had begged. It was an anchor the way he saw it. The Friar simply shrugged and sat down in the corner on the old man's pallet and ate the thin stew in its entirety.

———

The next day they set out to the north in the early morning. Cecil didn't want to happen upon the old timer's decaying body, or worse, the absence of it on the sands to the west. They hoped a new direction might reveal features pointing to a truer path, but it was all the same as before. Cecil felt a presence and kept glancing backward. It was only an hour or so when he first saw the jackrabbit. It was following them, not making any effort to stay hidden. It would move into easy pistol range and stand tall, staring with those black doll eyes, its charred face and the bony nubs on its skull like it just stepped from a tunnel straight to hell. It kept following them for three days, until they alighted on the cabin again.

This time, Trixie had to be persuaded even to drink the water, and Cecil didn't blame her. The place was cursed. She wouldn't touch the spring but finally let Cecil bring water to her. The Friar killed the rabbit again, and again made a stew. This time hunger outcompeted caution or superstition, and Cecil ate a little. Trixie sipped some broth. Shortly after, the Friar lay down and in minutes his light snoring was all that could be heard in the deep quiet of the desert evening.

"Trixie, I don't know how else to say this. We've got to leave him."

"That's senseless. What good would that do." They were both of them whispering but it sounded loud in Cecil's ears in the closed space of the cabin.

"I can't explain it. I just know. This place has got a grip on him. He took away its prisoner or its pet or whatever you want to name it, and now it wants one of us. It's the only way we're ever going to find our way back."

"You can't know that, not for sure. He's our friend. And the way he is, since the medicine run out, I don't think he can make it on his own." Despite her protests, Cecil could hear doubt working its way into her voice. Like water between rocks, set to freeze and crack her wide open in the cold quiet of the desert night.

"You know I'm right. It's why you don't want to touch the food here or drink from the spring. He's got no reluctance because this place already has hold of him. Look at how it's brought him to life. He doesn't so much as move like he used to. We have to go, and go now, while he's sleeping."

Trixie looked away and Cecil took her wrists in his hands and pulled her closer. Finally, she looked into his eyes, and he felt her shudder at what she saw there.

"If he was in his right mind, he would tell us to do this. I know it."

Trixie looked scared. She softened, let herself be led. They were nearly out of supplies and took only their canteens and serapes, which they had cut holes in so they could wear them and keep out some of the cold when walking the desert at night.

They were just over the first great rise of sand when they heard him. The Friar's voice carried over the quiet dunes like a harpoon cast against wild seas. Cecil could feel its steel tip searching for them.

"Trixie! Cecil! Trixie! Cecil! The raw desperation of it chilled him from head to toe, and he knew if it found purchase in his heart, or in the girl's, that would be the end.

Trixie moved, started to turn back, and Cecil took hold of her and brought them both to the ground, so not even a silhouette would be seen in the pale light of the moon. She shook and she cried, but she didn't make a sound. It was an hour or more, in which the pleas grew ever more desperate. Trixie covered her ears with her hands. Cecil listened as the man's voice shifted, grew more quiet, then finally stopped altogether.

They lay there another hour in the quiet before resuming their walk. It was near dawn when Cecil saw the thin outline of a distant mountain, like it was drawn in soft pencil lead on the landscape. He let out a long breath he must have been holding for a week, and Trixie looked up then and saw it too. Both of them began to cry, but Cecil knew her tears were from a gentler place than his. Regret was one more monster he had finally begun to outrun. He looked at Trixie and wondered for a moment if something happened to her, how it would be. Could he reconcile even that so long as he yet lived and was free? A part of him wanted to believe he couldn't, and he felt like his humanity hung by this flimsiest of threads. That other part of him suspected that being free might mean not caring about a damned thing, and that he was not only a passive recipient of the hollowing that began in Ohio those many months ago. Perhaps it was who he had always been. Keeping a fire alive is an act of vigilance. The darkness merely waits.

36

THE SLOW DESCENT TO THE
BOTTOM

"The field surgeon says you need to lose the leg. We should've taken it when you were out. Be a lot less pleasant with you fully conscious."

Sullivan looked pleased with himself, and Autie hated the man just then, wished he had never taken him under his wing, never made him a captain for damn sure.

"I'll be damned if you put a saw to me here. Santa Fe is not far off. There are better surgeons there, better medicine." He was sweating and feeling delirious, his thoughts like brittle leaves on the wind.

"You'll never make it over the mountains, let alone the rest of the way, sir. You'll die of that infection. Don't you smell that? You can't tell me you don't know what that smell means."

"You'll do as I say, damn you, as long as I'm in charge of this outfit. Have the girl prepare one of her potions. It will see me through the mountains and beyond."

"Her potions have corrupted you sir, we see it, all of us see it, and I fear the poultice she put to your leg to stave the bleed only brought further corruption to your flesh. She's an abomination, a part of the abomination we've been burning from the soil here.

231

And you've let her… change you. You aren't the man I followed into Virginia, not even the man I followed onto this god forsaken campaign," Sullivan spat, shook his head.

"You're insubordinate, trooper. Her ways have guided us, let us conquer this land and its monsters."

Sullivan laughed. "She's been leading you with her dark ways. Whatever it is you do in that tent at night. And through her meddling, you've marched boys to their deaths. We're down by more than half. Can't you see what's happening here? You cost me my friend, a man who served you faithfully since the war. Levi was the best of us."

Sullivan paused a moment, narrowed his eyes and looked straight into Autie's. "Didn't seem to affect you none. Just keep on the march. No plan, just charge blindly, slaughter and burn. But you can't make your failure disappear in the ash and smoke, not no more."

"You have no right to question me. This is mutinous. I could have you hanged."

"I used to think you were God's right hand, his judgment made flesh. But you were always a figment. I just saw what I wanted to so's I didn't have to make any choices for myself. I'm choosing now, sir. I'm relieving you of your command until you're well enough to lead again. And that leg is coming off."

Autie reached for his pistol, found the holster empty. He saw his lance and made to lunge for it, but rolled over on his right leg and the white-hot pain closed in around him so he was blinded by it, almost lost himself in it. He shivered, and fresh sweat broke out on his forehead, and he felt blood begin to ooze from the wound.

Sullivan leaned over slowly and retrieved the lance. He looked at it a moment, ran his finger along the edge.

"It's sharp, ain't it?" He stepped just outside the tent, so Autie could still see him. Stuck the point deep into the ground, held the far end and kicked it in the middle. It snapped with a loud crack, and he tossed the broken shaft into the brush.

"I'll fetch your girl. You can have whatever she's fit to make you. Better ask her to make it strong. The leg's coming off tonight. You can rest tomorrow, and we'll set off for Santa Fe the next morning. We've already lost three days to your fever and can't spare no more."

"You son of a bitch. You'll hang for this." Autie was still trembling. Trying to control it, to hold his leg still so it would stop oozing.

"Maybe so, sir, maybe so. But I'll be damned if I watch another man die that needn't."

Sullivan left, and Autie's mind swam, desperate, clawing for a way to reassert control. Time got away from him in his fevered thoughts, and it seemed much later that Flowers for Hair appeared. He didn't see her come in, she was just there. The light was dimming, and the air had a chill.

"I prepared you a special tea. You must drink it now. They come for your leg very soon." She had an impassive look, unreadable. He wanted to believe she was there to help him. Hadn't her tea been helping him all along? Sullivan didn't think so, but what did that man know. He didn't know Aurelius from Aristophanes. Autie giggled at his own joke and noticed Flowers for Hair's expression shift.

"I've seen men, whiskey drunk, scream for their mothers, crying like children when the field surgeon come. And I've seen men take laudanum until their lips were blue and they lay peacefully for the saw, but never opened their eyes again. I'll take your potion, take my chances, but if you kill me, know that I will haunt you to your last; and if you hurt me, it will be much, much worse."

She nodded, offered the cup.

"You'd better hold it, my hands might shake bad enough I lose it."

She did as he asked, set the cup to his lips and he guided the tilt of it with his trembling hand.

It was aromatic, had a sweet smell, tasted vaguely of wild blackberry, and was very tart. The sludge at the bottom had an earthy taste and he tried to get it all, didn't want to feel any more than he had to.

Flowers for Hair rose, turned to leave him.

"No. I wish for you to stay. Maybe you can help in some way if things take a turn."

The barest hint of a smile passed across her lips. It was gone before Autie had chance to consider its meaning.

His mind began to slip further, and he was grateful for the promise of that. The light of the fading sun, that penetrated into the space of the tent, separated into bands, colors that broke and jutted throughout the space at strange angles. So many colors, some he had no words for.

Flowers for Hair broke apart and joined the light, her multi-colored braids mixing and exploding in shifting patterns. A warmth spread from his center to his fingertips. The light and color shifted. Oscillated. Like a wave that broke over him with the regularity of his heartbeat. He felt a distance between himself and the world, his body. He was anchored, but at a long tether, like a kite drifting on the wind. The pain that gripped every inch of him in tension finally eased, a tide slipping away.

The clattering of instruments brought him back, and there was Sullivan and the surgeon. Rathskeller, that was the man's name. He was short, with thick arms and neck, and his hands were impossibly large and corded with veins like grotesque vines wrapping a tree. His fingernails were waning moons. Autie could see every bit of dirt that clung under them. There was a fire in his eyes that cast menace like a poisonous cloud. Like a wave, the tension and pain were returned to him, and the shift from low tide to high took all sense of calm with it.

Flowers for Hair stood in the corner. She was silent while the other two spoke. He couldn't make sense of the words, something about "should be easy... pulse strong... fully unconscious."

He wanted to correct them, to get some explanation of what was to transpire, and he found he could not move his lips, and his tongue was a swollen rag.

They cut away his pants, then pulled his leg straight. He tried to grab the man. The pain was excruciating. They needed to wait until the medicine took hold. He could not move his arm or his hand, could not so much as bend a finger.

He tried to blink and could not even do that. His eyes were fixed windowpanes, his world the things that moved in and out of that frame. A lantern burned somewhere, washed everything in thin light. Flowers for Hair stood vigil at the limit of his vision.

The surgeon splashed something on his naked leg. It was cold, and where it got in the wound, it burned like fire. Fire. There was a fire just outside his tent. Its flickers played in the soft light of the lantern, made shadows and half shadows everywhere. How could they not see he was awake. His eyes were wide open.

The first cut was the book of Revelation, was every Greek tragedy playing out in his flesh. The second was no better. He was more present in his body than he had ever been. Could pinpoint exactly where the surgeon's knife was, knew its depth to the fraction of an inch. By the third cut, he would have gladly forgone life to be free of the pain. But it went on. He didn't lose count of the number of times his flesh was parted so much as lose all sense of numbers in an animal panic that ran everything but pain -stark and immediate- from his mind.

When the cutting finally stopped, it was deliverance. He imagined -hoped- the ordeal might be over. Swirling, fevered desperation was still a closed fist on his mind, and when the cold truth settled on him of what else was to take place, he began a manic praying to any god who might listen: that it be over, that he be spared this one thing, that he lose consciousness. When the serrated edge bit into his femur, he prayed that he would die. He felt every pass of the saw, imagined it must be the dullest of instruments the way it sung across his bone. Each stroke only pulled him closer, more fully awake. A high-pitched squeal of a tone, that finally went dull, the blade bound up. Then rocking back and forth to free it, each punishment worse than what came before. Another eternity, the movement back and forth, a dread pendulum.

His mind flitted, black spots crept from the periphery of his vision until all was nearly dark. Still, it would not let go. His vision fading only made one less distraction from the pain, magnified it. He felt the limb come loose from him, saw Sullivan carry it outside, could feel the warmth radiating from what he brought back with him.

It was a large flat pan they used as a cautery, glowing red in the center. The brightness of it reawakened his eyesight, only to let his eyes burn from the heat. He made to blink and found he could not. Then, it disappeared from view and the searing pain, the smell of his flesh cooking, the sizzling sound - it was a thousand times worse than what come before. There was Flowers for Hair. She bore a thin smile; it was the most genuine lightness he had yet seen in her. Her joy was the final cut, the most painful, for it brought the knowledge that he had been made the most pitiable of fools.

Finally, all went black.

37

THE THORN

Flowers for Hair crushed the berry between thumb and forefinger. The juice -bright red and tacky- ran thick and dribbled to the ground. She painted a line with it under each eye, and two aslant on her forehead. The stain would last days, maybe weeks. The juice had worked perfectly, and she thanked the spirit of the bush, sang softly to it, the rhythm of the earth a sweet hum in her throat and across her tongue and lips.

She had watched, drank deeply of every moment, amazed that no one else in the tent could see the silent horror in the Colonel's eyes. She stood vigil, every second another evil reckoned for. Not enough. It would not, could not ever be enough, but it was something. She watched until the light went from his eyes, and then quietly slipped away from the camp.

Her people shared blood with the Black Hills, and she climbed like a spider, handhold to foothold, quick and quiet, scaling the nearby rock face, back to where she had gathered the medicine only a day before. Crouched on a slight overhang, she waited and she watched. They would not come for her. The man Sullivan was devout and would, if anything, be pleased at her absence, his only regret being that he was denied the satisfaction of killing her -or worse.

She had told the Colonel her intentions from the start. Knowing him, knowing he would be too arrogant to take her at her word. He didn't remember her. Why should he? Her little band had been one of a hundred, maybe a thousand, that he and his troop had laid low.

She remembered the morning like it was yesterday, and it was forever her yesterday. She had been gathering plants, and as she made her way back to camp, she heard the gunshots and the screaming. Slowing her pace, she listened closely, circled wide to the other side of the camp. Most of the men were gone, either having joined a war party or already dead from fighting in a previous one. From her vantage on the wooded hill, she watched as men in blue uniforms roughly herded the elders, the wounded, the women and the children to the creek that ran through the east end of camp. They huddled together in groups, holding one another. Children cried, and she wanted comfort for them, for all of them. Then the shooting began in earnest.

It was a volume of fire that could not be separated into individual shots, but rather bent into one continuous cracking, like rock splitting apart. Like the mountains -the backbone of her people- was being broken. And it was. The undoing of her friends and family was complete. In a matter of minutes, the creek ran red, and the screaming quieted to just a few weak voices, desperate and dying. The men closed on them and finished their work with rifle butts and knives.

She felt as dead as those below, like her body still moved but the life had gone from it, floated down that bloody creek.

Watching, waiting, reclining in her perch until the soldiers had finished their looting and desecration. Then she did what she could for the dead. Praying, gathering, burning. Inside, she would always carry the fire from that day, her lungs forever filled with their ashes. Her every breath a cry for vengeance. She made her way to the prisoner camp, because there was yet life there, even if it was a half-life.

Often, she had dreamt of the man who led that massacre. She had seen their paths intersect so many times that it was like another dream when he had finally arrived. It had all come back, everything she saw. It had never really left. And the oath she swore to the dead was like her own name, was a fire that burned through her, all that remained of her spirit. Yes, she had told him her intentions, because she knew it would not dissuade him, and that it would make him suffer more in the end.

It was easy bending him to her will. The tea brought his weakness to the surface, put it on display. Her seed was powerful medicine, too. So she let him suckle her, bit her lip and pushed down her disgust. It only blinded him further. It pleased her to see him nearly beg for it, too, to see in his eyes that hunger for her that made him hate himself.

She thought over all these things, lay back against the rock. The song of the plant gave way to the song of her people, of revenge, and she let it spill from her, down the mountainside, and into the sky, while she rested and waited.

The Colonel lay on a blanket. Grey wool, stained deeply, crusty and dried, the blood unnaturally dark. His clothing was sweated through. His stump was wrapped tightly in bandages but had bled through those. He was pale as packed snow. She had been sitting on the ground watching him for over an hour when he finally began to stir.

His eyes rolled around a while, his breath irregular. When he finally looked at her and tried to speak, he let out a raspy cough. She offered him water from a canteen. He took a little swish of it and tried to spit it at her. She sat back and watched it dribble down his chin.

"Sullivan." He tried to yell but his voice cracked and all he could get out was a whisper.

"You." He glared at her. "I'll see you cut piece by piece until there's nothing left of you bigger than a teacup." He coughed again. The effort to speak was taking a toll.

"Sullivan!" She yelled as loud as she could, smiled. "Your people are gone, Colonel. They've left you."

"That's not possible."

"It is. You've been sleeping a long time. The medicine I gave you. The part you remember is just the beginning. After that, it slowed you down, took you to the foothills of death, made your blood go quiet. They might have buried you. You could count yourself lucky then. Now all you have is me."

"My men would never." He looked down, his terror at the absence of his leg registering anew.

"I've been out there," and she pointed upward with her eyes, "the better part of three days now. Your men went east yesterday, what was left of them. They even took your tent. I guess they didn't want a grave someone might come looking for. Better to leave you to the scavengers. That's what they thought of you, Colonel."

"So what, now you kill me? It won't be easy. I've killed hundreds like you." He sat up, gritted his teeth. The strain was obvious, and he was very weak.

Flowers for Hair leaned forward, slapped his bandaged stump.

"Aaghh." He tensed and tried to lunge for her, but she easily sat back, out of his reach. "You red bitch." He leaned back on his elbows. "Just do it then."

"I told you. You would have been lucky for your men to bury you. Killing you is an easy thing. I could have done it that first night, or any of the others you came to see me. Could have done it any time you drank my tea. No. You are breaking, and I will watch as you keep breaking; every piece of you that falls away is remembrance of something you took. There's not enough of you, not nearly enough to pay the balance, but I will keep you alive until the last threads of you are carried away by the wind."

She wasn't happy, because there is no happiness in the company of ghosts, but still she smiled. The dead must know she was satisfied on their behalf.

"I brought you something. I'm going to leave it here because I have preparations to make for our journey." She set the earthen cup just out of his reach, where he would have to move to get at it.

"Get your potions away from me, witch." He spat at her, but it was too thick to travel past his own chin, and it dribbled on his chest.

"It's just tea. To soothe your throat and your mind. I said I wanted you alive."

With that she got up and walked away, to gather the things to make a litter. Until she acquired a mount, she would be pulling him through the mountains. The terrain was uneven, it would be a greater discomfort to him than to her. He would drink the tea. Sooner or later, he would. There were still so many sights to show him.

38

THE ENDLESS LONELY SAND

The desert was unfathomable. They walked in the daylight, until the heat stalled them. Then they would rest under what meager shade the landscape would afford, and when they were rested, again they moved.

The silhouetted mountains in the distance had, in less than a day, become a mocking thing. With each day following, Cecil thought those peaks were more like the fangs of man's oldest god, vengeful and cold, as the endless trudging brought them no closer. What if they'd stepped from one trap to another? What would the desert demand that he finally be free of it? What would he be willing to do?

Trixie had become little more than dead weight. In shock, or just pulled into herself to deny the reality of their circumstance. Regardless, she hadn't spoken a word since they lay behind the dune, ignoring the desperate pleas of their friend. He looked at her and to himself, searching for pity that now resembled naught but a pale mirage.

He wished she would speak to him, even if just to scream recriminations in his face and spit her hatred in sticky spider web strands. Just to know she was still in there somewhere, that he wasn't totally alone. That there was something worth winning back. Once, when she had drifted back a ways, he had gripped her wrist and gently pulled her along. She wrenched free, looking at him with eyes that were wholly empty, stood with arms crossed until he began walking again, then fell in a few paces behind him.

Instead of conversation, there was only the company of his own thoughts, and these raced in stark contrast to the deliberate, crawling pace at which they moved. Constantly, he scanned near and far, looking for any hint to their progress. His heart froze with every rise and fall of the land, holding his breath in anticipation that the old rotten cabin might again come into view. That all hope would be lost. That he had abandoned the Friar for nothing.

The anonymous scrub, the saguaro and cholla, the sand: it worked at him until he could not say with confidence that they were not, at the very least, walking in some great circle. Part of some greater circle, and so on. That even getting clear of this obstacle was only entering a deeper part of the dread maze.

Even with careful rationing, the water ran out by the third day. They had no food, and of the other supplies they had taken with them, only the blankets, the empty canteens, a few useless dollars, and the pepper box pistol remained. His solitary reassurance was that they had not happened upon any of the things they left behind. Finding his spare shirt wheeling across the sand in the hot breeze would certainly have broken him, what was left of him to break.

Day five, he thought it was -or maybe six- he began to notice a subtle shift in the terrain. The sand began to give way to a dusty hardpack. Then, as the hours ticked by, the vegetation began to change as well. Mesquite trees -squat and grotesque- slowly replaced much of the cacti, then the spectral mountains on the horizon began to resolve into more distinct colors -cadaverous granite, sun faded brown soil, yellowing grass and scrub.

Finally, pine and juniper appeared in sparse patches, and he smelled water. Was it an illusion? A hope made manifest? It must not be. To die of thirst now, it was too absurd to consider. That water bore so distinct a smell was something he wouldn't have believed a few weeks before.

He watched the trees for a patch of brighter green that would indicate they were well fed, listened for a gurgle or a swish, and drank deep with his nostrils. He grasped at any sense that might guide them. And he hoped that it was not too late, that liquid sustenance might restore his companion, might restore her confidence in him.

The terrain gradually became rougher, rockier. He had to choose a path that wound between great jutting fingers and fists of rock, and he tried always to choose the path that was most wild with vegetation. He wanted to rest, but dared not. To stop now would be a quiet surrender. Trixie walked with her head down, her feet scuffing on loose rock the only assurance he had that still she was with him. His own gait became a stagger, each footstep an act of will against flesh that had long grown rubbery and numb.

It was near dark when he heard it, and so desperate by then that he felt sure it must be his imagination. Turning to Trixie, he saw a flash of recognition in her eyes and knew she heard it too. Summoning a last desperate bit of strength from a well run nearly dry, they both took to the thickening wood at a dead run.

Pine boughs bit at his arms and whipped his face, and he emerged on a decline of loose shale. He tripped, and nearly went sprawling, then caught himself and surged forward in a wheeling run. Reaching the river's edge, he careened, splashing into the chill water. A second splash to his right announced Trixie's arrival, and he set palm heels to the silt and rose up slightly to drink like a beast from a trough. Sucking great gulps until he coughed and sputtered, and as soon as he recovered, he drank again.

The water swashed and rippled around them, and they both sat soaking as the sun began to dip behind the cliff face that rose, smooth and formidable, just beyond the other bank. They sat until the water drew goose pimples, until their teeth chattered, as if even their skin demanded to drink of the moisture long denied it.

39

SANTA FE

Charlie set the bottle on the stained and unfinished table. Flickering lamplight from the nearby sconce enhanced every greasy fingerprint, every scratch. The whiskey had no label, and stood testament to the erosion of the place, the way edges were smoothed, and new edges made. The wood creaked and protested under his boot as he slid into the chair and deposited two dirty glasses next to the bottle.

The man could have grown out of the saloon. His skin was worn leather, and his face was cracked and lined like a dry riverbed. His eyes were like bits of coal sunk in deep holes. They gave away nothing. His mouth was a whisper of a thing behind a bushy white beard. There was a hint of a smile there, but it didn't extend beyond the lips.

"Pike?"

"Dr. Pike, if you please. Best to maintain the honorifics out here among the brigands." He coughed a little laugh.

"Good to meet you, doctor."

The man quickly poured the two glasses, amber sloshing up the sides.

Charlie, who rarely drank liquor -and never to excess-

decided now might be the time to start. He had never been so far out west, and the broad expanses, instead of filling him with a sense of freedom, felt like walls closing in. He had never felt so captive, so restrained, in the crowded cities of the east.

The old man took a drink, then slid something small and heavy, wrapped in a red handkerchief, across the table.

Charlie put the glass to his lips, drained half of it in one gulp. He wanted the fire of it, felt it surge into his gut and then start to come back up. His mouth was dry as he swallowed again, hard.

The old man's smile grew slightly.

Charlie didn't feel the equal of it. Setting down his glass, he probed the fabric delicately, unwrapping the package like some poisonous snake might be coiled within.

It was a pepper box pistol, sawed down, just like the one the boy's father described, the one the kid had took. He drained the rest of his glass.

"You can have the gun for fifteen dollars, and the cost of the whiskey, of course. If you want the story behind it, let's make it an even hundred."

Charlie was seven days into Santa Fe when he left the hotel to meet with the old prospector. There had been a letter from the Branaghs waiting for him when he checked in that eternity ago. The patriarch was losing his patience, how hard could it be to catch a boy with no experience running, and with no survival skills. He wanted evidence that he wasn't throwing good money after bad. Charlie had read the letter a hundred times and each time it dripped fresh misery, with his income and his reputation slipping from him.

He had worked his way through every clean whore in the city, and was making steady progress through the rest. Waiting, hoping the boy and his friends would show up. Each day a more desperate running and clawing away from the truth, that he would have to go back, walk into that forbidden hellscape of a desert, and find some sign, something that would convince his employer that the job was done. The last few days, he couldn't eat. Every time he closed his eyes, he saw his own bones bleached and shining like mother of pearl in that endless sand, the words of the Native man haunting him.

When he heard about the old doctor, it brought the thinnest thread of hope. He was said to know the desert like no other and if one were fool enough to venture there, he might provision them with enough knowledge to increase the odds of walking back out. Still less than 50/50 but better, nonetheless.

He picked up the pistol, examined it closely. The old man sloshed more whiskey into his own glass and a splash of it into Charlie's. He leaned back in his chair, sipped and stared. Charlie could feel the man appraising him, knew he was outmatched. If anything, the longer he sat and examined his prize, eyes wide and resolve softening as the booze radiated heat in his belly, the more the cost was likely to rise. This was a man who knew information held more value than artifacts.

Charlie pulled the little purse from inside his shirt, dropped it on the middle of the table, where the coins jostled and giggled at him. "Man makes plans, and the gods laugh. Something like that."

Pike covered the bag with his hand and frowned at Charlie, at the display, the lack of discretion. Then scooped the purse back to him smoothly, off the table, where his hand disappeared into his lap. He took a long sweeping look around the saloon and then topped off his glass.

"Where should I start?"

"Tell me the tale and I'll stop you if I need more details."

He was on a prospecting trip when he had seen them: the boy and the girl. Charlie nearly interrupted, then decided to wait. The other would make an appearance or he would not.

Dr. Pike was on a bluff near the headwaters of the Gila River, to the south and the west of Santa Fe. It made no sense that they had bypassed the town entirely, but there it was.

Pike made a steady trade on turquoise and whatever else he could find. "There are a lot of bits and pieces of long dead cultures in those mountains," he said, "and few who are willing to brave the risks to go looking for them."

Curiosity and the need to refill his waterskins won out, and he had made his way down to the river. It was midday when he caught up with them, walking along the riverside. The girl, ankle deep in the shallows, seemingly lost in her own world. The boy's eyes never rested, always glancing this way and that, to the woods and to the water. He spotted Pike and quickened his pace, yelled at the girl to keep up.

"Whoa, there," Dr. Pike yelled across the babbling water, for it was rocky near the headwaters. "Hold up, I don't mean ya' any harm."

The boy turned, regarded him straight on. The girl finally woke from her daydream and looked to the boy and then to the old man. Cecil slouched, resigned that he could scarcely escape the encounter if he wanted to, and how much longer could they last out here. They had no food, no means to acquire it, and no way to make fire. That first night, dripping wet from the river, they had nearly froze. Woke to ice crystals bending the boughs and their breath steaming white in the still air.

Pike splashed across the river in bounding steps. The water moved quickly, but was fairly shallow here. As he closed on them, the girl retreated behind the boy. He came to a stop in the sucking mud of the water's edge, not wanting to scare them off.

"What are a couple of young'uns like you doing alone out here? Where's your parents?"

"We got lost, my sister and me. Been wandering for days."

The girl looked at the back of the boy's head with an icy glare. He was lying.

"Well, let's get you something to eat and see if we can't figure out a way back to where you ought to be."

Cecil followed the old man, Trixie close behind. He fingered the pistol that hung heavy in his pants pocket -the pants that had fit him when he started this journey. Now, even with his belt as tight as it would go, the weight of the gun pulled them halfway down his hip, so he had to frequently pull them up. And the thoughts that thrashed in his mind. Those too were changed. They would have been just as ill-fitting to the boy who left Ohio those many weeks ago. But now? Now, they matched his grotesque features perfectly. His jutting bones and sunken cheeks, reminders that death is a persistence hunter. He wondered about Trixie, how she might react if he shot this man in the back like the one on that night when their paths converged. Cecil wondered if it even mattered. The old man would either help them or they would have to help themselves.

Dr. Pike didn't trust the boy. He kept one eye on him while attending to the camp. He gave him as much work as he could, simple chores to keep him occupied: gathering wood, getting the fire going, keeping it going. Pike didn't trust anyone with his kit, and did all the cooking himself. He watched the boy and the girl eat, for people tend to let their guard down when they eat, and especially ones as hungry as these.

The girl -Trixie, she called herself- ate with great enthusiasm. She had two biscuits and a plate of beans and bacon cleared before the boy finished nibbling on his first biscuit. Pike scraped half his own plate onto hers, and she spoke around mouthfuls of food while the boy sat silent and staring, chewing slowly. Like he was talking himself into something, or more likely already had, and was waiting on the moment.

"So, what kind of doctor are you?" Her cheeks puffed like a squirrel's.

"I was a surgeon in the war. Them who call me doctor now, do so out of a different kind of respect. I guess you could say I'm a doctor of the mountains, and the river, and the desert." And he waved his hand around to illustrate.

Her laugh was a bright sort of thing, high and tinkling. "I ain't never heard of a mountain or a river that needs doctoring."

"Some doctors just know a lot of things. I'm that kind of doctor. Now tell me what brought you out here. Really."

The boy swallowed hard and looked at her. She rolled her eyes at him.

"We've got some folks after us. Some crazy colonel got it in his head we needed rescued, and we had to run away before he handed us over to the law, maybe worse. We might could be doctors of the desert ourselves, having just escaped the worst place I've ever seen."

"Trixie!" The boy started to put his plate down.

"Now you just sit there and keep at your deliberate chewing, son. Whatever you have planned can wait until we hash this out."

The girl told him of the things she'd seen, and her eyes glistened wet when she told of them she'd lost. When she was done, she took a deep breath.

"I guess you probably think I'm telling stories."

"I spend a lot of time in these hills, little lady. I ain't seen all of what you tell, but I seen enough not to scoff at it, neither."

She smiled, fairly beaming.

The rarest thing in the wild places is one who can keep to themselves those things that seem a liability there, who know the value of them, their irreplaceability.

"I'm headed back to Santa Fe in a couple of days. I'd be happy to take you with me, get you back on a proper trail."

Her smile fizzled. The boy shook his head.

"No, they'll be looking for us there. That colonel knew we were headed that away."

"Well, this here is the Gila and if you follow it, it will take you to Yuma. Just this side of California. Mexico just to the south. You'll have some options there. I've got a spare knife, couple of blankets, a few sundries that should get you there if you take care. I reckon you ain't got much to trade. Why don't you show me what's been jangling in your pocket, boy."

The kid went ghostly pale then, knew a bad hand when he saw it. He slowly withdrew the pistol. Held its grip between thumb and forefinger and passed it to the man.

"That'll do." He took it. "You're lucky of the company you keep." He nodded to Trixie. "She might have saved your life more ways than one."

"So that's that. I provisioned 'em best I could and sent them west along the river. Get you a fleet horse and you can beat them to Yuma. Just tell me one thing."

Above the din of the bar, Charlie heard the click under the table, a sound as familiar to him as his own name. The whiskey had done what it did best, what he hated it for. Harden you and soften you in all the wrong places. "What?" He looked down at the table.

"Look at me. You're after the boy. You'll let the girl alone?"

He nodded. "Yes. The boy is my sole interest."

"Good. I only took this meeting because that's the way I understood it. That kid, she's got a peculiar kind of grit. The way of some things to hold onto the light when all they've ever seen tells 'em there ain't any light to be had. But what if she gets in the way?"

"You want some kind of guarantee. You're awful bold for a dried-up prospector." He poured each of them a glass and drank deep from his. He was starting to see the appeal, even if it did give the old coot the drop on him.

"I'll guarantee you something. I may not be a swish gunfighter or nothing, but I got ways you can scarcely understand. You regard the girl as the thing that bends the sails of your future. Her safety, one less reason to be forever troubled in your sleep."

Charlie downed his whiskey. "You got a way with words, old man, I'll give you that." But the cold depths of the man's eyes put him back in those hills, when the howling monstrosities drew the old fear out of him like a pitcher pump. Even now, he could feel it wanting to gush out of him, and he was chilled to the bone. It took all his effort to push back from the table smoothly and tread out of the dank saloon with a look of relative calm.

The Wandering Dharma

40

THE PILGRIMAGE

"Please, go easy. I'm bleeding again." Autie's wound was seeping through the makeshift bandage and the stump burned like fire. It was as if she found every little bump on the mountain trail and magnified it. She wasn't so much pulling him, as jerking him a few feet at a time.

Unbidden, thoughts of her soft thighs and strong calves flickered in his mind. How could such desire sit at the table of unspeakable contempt?

Silence. She had stopped answering to his complaints and his pleas. They paused when she tired of pulling him, and rested only long enough to restore her strength. She let him sip from his canteen, which now stunk of the herbs and flowers she milked hell and damnation from.

He had spat it out at first, but he was ever thirsty, and it was all that she offered, so he drank and was kept in perpetual fog. It was some in between place from which the world as he remembered it was now a distant vision, and a world of fevered scuttling, of chaos and devourment, played at the periphery. It was forever closing on him, threatening to force its way in at any moment.

Moving backward, ever retreating but not escaping, watching the world unfold behind, being pulled slowly across it. Few things were recognizable, it was rock and pine, and a trail that was hardly that. Neglected. She was dragging him along an ancient path long forgotten by all but the wild things of the world.

Every bump sent a flurry of stars, fireworks dancing in his eyes. And all the colors and the shapes of things shifted constantly and subtly, so that only his pain anchored him. Only his misery reminded him that it was not a dream that he could someday wake from.

The first night he asked where they were and where they were going.

"This ain't the Santa Fe. Not anymore. I reckon you're afraid of them we might cross paths with on the main trail."

"Do you not feel it?"

"Feel what? All I can feel is the throbbing in my bleeding stump. Thanks to you." And he realized just then that he had not felt the shifting beneath him since that day the wretched hare had cut him, could not feel it now. Whatever had drawn him before was no longer speaking to him.

"All of you are so full of the stories you tell yourselves: who you are, what you are. It finds the truth in you. Your secret shame. Makes a home of it until its movements in you feel like they come from you. Its wants become your wants." And she held out each hand and then put them together, moved them upward like a fish wiggling through water, followed it with her eyes.

"Enough of your goddamn riddles. You mean to leave me where none can find me. Why not just kill me. Leave me here."

"It's the energy. Lines of it. They all go west, but here it is very strong. It wants you. Makes the work of pulling you easier. Now, have some tea."

"Sooner or later, we're going to find some pilgrims and you'll wish you'd killed me when you had the chance."

She held the canteen to his lips. He drank because he could do nothing else. His head swam.

He didn't know when sleep came, whether it had crept over him, or he was still awake and only bedeviled by her potion. He felt motion, like he was coasting over the ground, only now he was facing forward, and the way was smooth and far too rapid. His stomach rose up in his chest, tickled him. The pain in his leg was distant.

Water. Water as far as the eye could see and he was coming at it so rapidly. Nothing had ever been so beautiful, so desirable. He must be flying in a direct path toward it. The Pacific. He had never seen it, but knew it, nonetheless. Salty foam lapping nearly white sand. He flew over a bluff and descended toward it.

The foam went dark as tobacco juice, and the water behind it was red. Endless red, beating against the sand and the rocks, and where it retreated, leaving stains and thick streamers of coagulate.

Then, the bloody water retreated entirely, and in the black depths it left behind, something opened. Like a great serpent's mouth, jagged stalactite fangs stark white against that endless black. Opening further, it was row after row of those poisonous teeth, and he opened his mouth to scream but could not. His terror and the sheer force of wind stifled him, and then he descended into that malign cavern. Then all went black.

He woke shaking, wracked by a full body shiver he could not suppress. Flowers for Hair was packing a blanket around him, tucking it carefully around his neck, arms, leg. She had a little fire going, and when she was done with him she fed loose mesquite and pine into it.

"What's happening? What did you give me?" His teeth chattered so he could hardly form the words.

"The tea is only a small thing. To open you. But this thing

out here," and she circled a finger in a wide arc, "it wants you. It grows impatient with me. I have never felt the draw so strong."

Her eyes were wide, and Autie could see it was awe, not fear, that danced in them. His shivering intensified, and he felt a warm liquid pour around his stump. For a moment, he feared the wound had opened wide, then realized he had only pissed himself.

She giggled.

There's a faint tickle, something she hasn't felt in so long that she can't immediately recognize it. An electric shudder that covers her, head to toe, like the breeze on the hilltop. The place and the time long ago, where she watched her people corralled and slaughtered. She never wanted to think of the place again and that this feeling recalls it, leaves her tense. But as the disgust fades, it leaves in its wake a lovely void, playful and wanting. Only as the tears stain dusty streaks on her cheeks does it finally hit her. Curiosity. It used to define her, the thrill of discovery. Collecting and comparing the oldest stories, trying to parse common threads. It was all aimed to a purpose once: to know. To refine her wisdom to a glimmering edge that cut through confusion and doubt, to know the world as an infant knows its mother's breast.

To fully and truly know was the dream of a younger woman. Because there is never a certainty. To be certain is the end of the search, it is to die a little death. Instead, it was her curiosity died on that windswept hill, replaced by the certainty that there could be no deeper meaning that would explain what she had witnessed, that could reconcile the horror to a world worth living in. A wanderer with half a spirit, less even than that. For so long she lived with nothing but a bottomless hatred that held no hope for being quenched. She thought she might already be dead when the Colonel came, would not believe in the gift being presented to her. From then, it had been the rage that moved through her. Hungry ghosts that seeped from her every pore, and she little more than a passenger, following their design.

This was different. She had never been so close to the center of it. This thing that her people had always recognized and never looked upon too closely. It was whispers and warnings. The fetid breath of corruption; let it in and it was an incurable disease of the mind and spirit. But here, now, her vocation and its will were conjoined. She knew only that the path lay before her and that she must follow it to its end. She would die having seen such things as she wished she hadn't, but the mystery was sweet intoxication, and she would indulge herself to drink deep of it.

41

MONSTER OF THE GILA

Trixie watched the boy, marveled at the difference in how the journey had shaped them. He had been the more naive of the two when they met. Maybe that was the key. Naïveté was a luxury, not afforded to her, and certainly not to Red Club or to the mad priest. Having come up from his den of warm ignorance, he had not liked what he saw, and retreated with what tools were left him, to the grim pragmatism of white men.

For her, tracing the path of the Gila was a soothing convalescence. They walked mostly on the gravel bar, or the soft soil nearby. She preferred the gravel -the shifting crunch of it under her feet- or sometimes the shallow river's edge, where she carried her boots, and the chill of water and the silt squeezing between her toes was enlivening. She could only play at this occasionally and briefly, for after a few minutes her feet would grow numb.

She followed him, usually ten or twenty yards behind. His edge never softened entirely, his gaze never resting in one place. Any crunch or crack in the woods would give him a start. She laughed the first time he ducked and tensed at the sound. The look he gave her after… she kept the laughter to herself from then on.

The close woods were dense sycamore and alders, grown tall and thick with the ample water supply. On the other side was mostly rock; sometimes the sheer wall of it rose beyond the limit of her vision, and disappeared into the white fluffs that crowded the sky above. There was plenty of shade, and in all but the warmth of midday sun, she walked with her blanket around her shoulders, neck and ears to ward off the chill.

She wondered if he felt anything about the two they had left behind, for he showed no sign of it. In the quiet of evening, when they had to huddle close to the fire and share what sustenance they had gathered that day, she thought to ask him. Something held her back. She had long realized that you must be willing to accept the consequence of such questions, be ready to live with the knowledge that the answer would burden you with, and so she didn't ask.

They ate blackberries that grew in wild brambles, and what fish they could catch with their hands in the natural traps the geology of the river sometimes provided. She didn't like the fish, the catching of them, or that they ate every part including the heads.

It was a few day -perhaps as many as five- into their journey when the river broadened into a fat belly, where it turned from southwest to west. Here there was a marshland that forced them into the trees. For hours, they walked alongside it. Trixie marveled at all the strange creatures that lived there. Blue herons stood vigil and alighted with great, powerful wings when she wandered too close. Turkeys clucked and strutted in the woods. Splashes in the water promised some other wild thing that seemed always too quick for her to catch more than a flash of pale skin and a disturbed, foamy ripple.

Cecil had stripped the leaves from an alder branch and sharpened the point. He tried several times to get one of the birds, but they were too fast and too graceful for him to get close, and instead he settled into spearing some mud-dwelling fish. He was using his shirt as a makeshift basket for them, and her nose shriveled at the thought of what that might smell like by the fire, later.

The marsh was thinning and the river beginning to narrow by the time they made camp. Cecil cooked the fish and hung his shirt from the spear he had now stuck in the ground, as close to the fire as he could get it. Trixie hoped the smoke might scare off some of the stink. She picked at one fish, while Cecil ate five others. Before long, he had dozed off, surrounded by the little bones like some fairy tale troll.

Trixie stared at the fire, her mind as agitated as the water she could hear lapping at the rocks. Where would it all end? She had never imagined they would make it this far. She would have been content to land in any one of the number of little towns along the Santa Fe. Now she might see the ocean, but what would it mean? Selling herself to merchant sailors and the like? No. Never again. Maybe she could find work on one of the boats. She could pass as a boy, which, while no great protection, might afford her a little breathing room. A job. She liked the idea of floating, of freedom in the vastness of the ocean, of being far away from this carnivorous land.

When she heard croaking, at first she thought it was the trees, bending and twisting in the wind. Once she turned her attention to it, though, it was clear it came not from the woods but from the water, and after the first, there was a second and a third croak, each slightly different in character. Then came a whole chorus of them. She looked at Cecil, still sleeping soundly, a slight whistling snore emerging from him at regular intervals.

Easing off the ground, she slipped closer to the water. The croaking continued at intervals. There would be a few, then many, then a period of silence before it all started again. By the fourth or fifth such cycle, the sounds became more fluid, rising and falling into and out of one another, so there was a musical quality to it. As she reached the marsh, she heard other sounds. Birdsong in the night and crickets chirping. A symphony. The croaking shifted in response to the other creatures' songs. The wild places were confusing, from terror to beauty in a moment, and sometimes both at the same time. Trixie was softening to it. A great wall around her heart had been soaked through and was giving way to the water. All the pain, all the loss, came rushing out, and hot tears soaked her cheeks.

Stripping her pants and shirt to keep them dry, she continued into the marsh. First tromping through sucking mud, and then into the river proper, where she waded out until the water was up to her chest. It was cold, and she trembled, teeth lightly chattering.

She found her way to the middle of the music. The sounds came from every side, and even from behind her now. She closed her eyes and listened. Moments stretched infinite. She was utterly lost, let the song carry her away, and for once she allowed herself to believe that it might work out, that she might find peace somewhere, cut free from all the horrors she had lived through, borne witness to. But gripping a moment is like to holding water in a closed fist, and the tighter she tried to hold, the more fleeting it became.

When she opened her eyes, dozens of black pearls gathered and reflected moonlight on the water's shifting surface. A pair of them near her rose up from the water and croaked loudly. It startled her and she almost fell backward. She swished her hands in broad arcs to get her balance back and waded toward the thing. It retreated as she approached, then another croak sounded near and to her right. Then another to the left. She lowered herself, chin beneath the surface.

Three pairs of pearls approached her, and as they got near, they became pools set in great, round faces. Like toads. Their skin was gray in the moonlight, covered in bumps around the head and neck. They bounced in the water, black eyes shiny and huge. The one on her right came the closest, brushed against her arm. Its skin was cold and slick, but the fingers that squeezed her for a moment felt not much different from her own.

The next time it bounced up in the water, it came halfway out, and its shape was like no toad she had ever seen. It had a long torso like a person, and the arms and hands -webbed though they were- had a human likeness to them.

The three of them advanced and retreated in the water, croaking to one another. Then there were five of them, then more. They began to swim away, stopping every few feet to look at her. She followed.

They emerged on a shallow, a pool where the water was just a few feet deep, with a gravel bed at the bottom. It hurt her feet to stand too long on it, so she made her way to the edge. Two of the toad things crawled out and squatted on a nearby log. Another made its way next to her. She pushed herself out of the water and sat on a smooth rock, feet dangling and kicking little ripples.

One of them nudged her from behind, sent her splashing back into the pool.

"Hey, watch out." She laughed, submerged, came up spitting a thin stream of water that caught her attacker in the chest.

It fell backward, rolled side to side in the mud, emitting a high-pitched croak. Those nearby began croaking similarly.

She laughed, splashed at the one nearest her in the water. They played like this until the moonlight started to thin as it passed over the cliffs. The river people watched her as she retreated. She tried to sign that she needed to go, hoped they understood. They seemed to. She made her way along the water's edge until she found her clothes, and got dressed.

As she turned from the river, she could see the campfire bright and bold in the woods beyond. It should have been reduced to embers. She pulled on her boots and moved as quickly as she could through the trees and brambles.

Cecil was standing, fully dressed, eyes wild, manic in the glow of the flame.

"Where have you been, Trixie? Goddammit, I nearly yelled myself hoarse. We need to go!"

"What's going on?" His look worried her. "It ain't nearly daylight yet…"

There was something dark on Cecil's hands and arms. It dripped from his right elbow to a slick puddle.

"Something's out here. It's not safe. We need to go right now." His eyes danced back and forth. His lip trembled.

"It's fine, I've been in the water, there's noth…" She let the words die in her throat when she saw what lay beyond Cecil. The flicker of the fire caught a pale, webbed foot. She charged, pushed him aside.

Those great black eyes, the life gone out of them. The fingers on its left hand still flickered. Blood ran, glistening, from more holes than she could count. That wretched spear of his. She nearly collapsed, fell against a tree.

"I woke up to it going through what was left of our dinner. The way it looked at me. I had to. Had to defend us." Was it a crack of uncertainty in his voice? There and gone. He stood tall, white knuckles clutching his stained spear, the toad's life drip dripping into that slick puddle.

Something irrevocable broke in her. All her hopes were but the crackling sparks that floated from the fire and quickly died. Truth was that poor thing on the ground. They were accursed: he, and she for standing with him.

42

THE RENEGADES

Flowers for Hair was weary of pulling the man, and of his constant complaints. She made stronger tea, and sometimes that quieted him. Sometimes it did the opposite, and he would mutter -incoherently and agitated- for hours at a time. Then it became harder to pull the litter, because it jostled constantly with his violent movements. The will of the land continued its pulling, incessant, under her feet, but its encouragement was just another annoyance, like a child who constantly pesters with questions of how much longer a journey might be.

She had bypassed Santa Fe entirely, and was making her way through the Black Range, when she encountered the first people she had seen since beginning this trek. The Ndee, one of the few bands that continued fighting. At first their leader, Baishan, didn't want to let her pass. He was afraid she was in service to the Colonel, that the two of them might betray his location to the Army that was hunting him.

"Do you not see the great dark weight I carry on my neck?" she said. "Do you not smell his wound? I carry him to oblivion and if I do not follow him all the way over the edge of that abyss, only then will I finally be free."

"We know this man. He is the white man's angry dog, the one who bites without thinking." The one who stood before her was scarred from battle. He had a round face, dark hair. Wore a ceaseless frown as well. Light colored shirt and skirt and leg wrappings kept most of the rest of him hid. He didn't blink, his eyes were claws that peeled away the veneer of words like bark from a tree.

"Yes. He killed my people. Broke us apart. And for that and all his cruelty I make him suffer."

"It would be better if you let us kill him. We can cut off his eyelids and leave him in the sun to go blind and crazy. Or peel off his skin and then burn him alive. Where you take him, there is no certainty. He might yet outlive you."

"It is my burden," and she met his gaze, matched it. "It is where my story must go."

"Dusty Bird has stolen some of the Army's horses just a few days ago. What do you have to trade, that your journey might at least be less difficult?"

She offered most of Autie's possessions, his larger pistol and belt, his hat, his spurs. The man's smaller gun she kept for herself.

Baishan placed the hat on his own head, slid the pistol into his belt. He tossed the other items to Dusty Bird, who looked them over as he walked away.

"He will find you a strong horse. It would be easier for you to ride away and let us kill this man, but he is yours and we will not stop you."

"Kill you all," Autie mumbled.

Flowers for Hair smiled, draped a blanket over Autie's head. He clawed at it, pulled it off.

"You must understand how vulnerable you are here. Quiet yourself."

"Just kill me already. Let them kill me, whatever."

Baishan raised his eyebrows, a hint at restrained cheer.

"No. Not yet," she said, and the man's solemnity was restored.

Dusty Bird returned, leading a stout, grey pony by a rope, let it drop and drag along the ground as he drew close. Flowers for Hair stroked its muzzle, and it leaned its head heavy against her. It was a squat, muscular thing, well suited to the mountain trails.

Baishan insisted she stay and eat with them, and while she did, he told her of his war with the whites. She told him of her own war, of its impetus, and also of the strange things she had seen since being taken by the Colonel. He nodded slowly as she spoke, and she knew he understood.

"These men don't know themselves, don't know the pull of the dark below, and so it finds a home in them, makes of them more of itself."

"Maybe they are descended from it, and for them it is as coming home. Does it not seem to have grown stronger since they came?" Flowers for Hair had been thinking of little else but the mind of that dread thing below. It was an unknowable mind, and her thoughts criss-crossed like spider webs.

Baishan nodded.

"This may be true. They are takers, occupiers, just as it is. When the first of us came out of the earth, we left the old places unguarded. I think it moved in, just as they move into every unguarded place now. There are not many of us, not enough to keep watch at all the places. So many of them, they keep taking. Now all that is left of us is to take from them what we can. It cannot last."

"Where will they go when they have taken it all? There are so many of them?"

"I think next, they will take the sea. It has its own darkness. Their spirits are so thin, I think they can live in the water. They do not breathe as people do."

They talked like this for some time. Baishan said he did not often speak of such things, as his men had little interest in the oldest stories and other worlds. They were young, had grown up in war and only knew war. He thanked her, and he and the others helped load Autie onto the horse. They bound his hands in horse-hair twine and lay his belly over the back of the mount, tied the other end to his remaining leg.

The air was cool, and the sun was well past its apex when she continued her way along the rocky trail. The old paths, they were the first serpents of the world, now slumbering but still perilous. It was impossible to tell if she were moving toward the head or the tail, to danger or deliverance.

43

A MOST UNUSUAL GLADE

Trixie had been withdrawn before. Now she was outright hostile.

Cecil couldn't reckon why. Of all the things they'd seen and done, putting down a monstrous toad -or whatever it was- seemed the least of it. Perhaps she was just tiring of the journey. He was sympathetic, but she should at least retain some gratitude for his vigilance, his regard. Instead, she seemed to hate the sight of him, for he caught her on more than one occasion looking at him, and frequently felt her eyes on him. She had fallen back to a consistent ten or twenty yards behind, and that look tapped a well of unknown guilt, like she was indicting him of a crime he could not discern. If this continued, Yuma might be the place they would part ways. At least she might be safe there. Safer than in this strange wilderness, anyway.

They had taken to walking farther from the river. After encountering more marshland and stretches of muddy clay, the terrain too near the water was delaying their progress. They walked within earshot of the water, continued to follow its course, but were no longer in sight of it.

The woods thinned forty or fifty yards from the Gila, where

the lush foliage gave way to a more arid climate. Mostly it was desert grass, woody bushes, and frail trees that were less closely clustered, and most of the low growth equipped with some manner of thorn or sticker. Cecil was grateful for his boots, but his pants were soon covered with a kind of foxtail, larger and darker than any he had seen before. They had to stop to remove them now and then, as they had a way of burrowing into clothing as you walked, then stabbing or scratching. The closest he and Trixie came to restoring their fraternity was that each pulled the foul things from the other's back side. But it was a matter of convenience - that or disrobe every time they stopped.

They made camp close to the water, but not proximal to any marshland. Cecil made a point of that, and Trixie didn't argue. He was still shaken by the incident the other night and knew he wouldn't be able to sleep if there were a risk of repeating it.

It was three or four days of this brushy trek, when Cecil came over the top of a small hill and was stopped dead in his tracks. He was still standing and staring when Trixie closed the distance between them. The hill spilled downward into a wide draw. It was bounded by more hills on either side, densely wooded with tall and thin trees, so the bottom had a bit of shade. To the limit of his vision, it was a meadow of bright orange flowers. Some grew on bushes or dwarf trees, but mostly it was a blanket of orange, nearly blinding to stare at too long.

"Wow, it's beautiful." Trixie had appeared at his side. Her pleasant comment came as more of a shock than her arrival.

"I don't like it. What the hell is it doing out here?"

"What do you mean? It's just some wildflowers. Maybe there's a trickle from the river that feeds it."

"Something's feeding it." Cecil would never trust a beautiful thing again, certainly not a wild thing. "I say we walk around."

"Look at how dense the wood is on the river side, and who knows how far afield we'd go to bypass the other side. We could lose the river. The way is obvious." And with that, Trixie bounded down the hill with Cecil following cautiously.

As the grade bottomed out, he felt his guard relaxing slightly. The smell of the meadow was intense, sweet, with an undertone that tickled his nostrils. A little like turpentine. His legs went soft. Soon it was an easy walk, no urgency. The ground had a give to it, like cotton batting.

He bent down, pressing some dense stems aside. A light green moss grew under the flowers. Where he touched it, it gave like a sponge, then parted where he lay his hand. He withdrew, stood back up, and watched as the flowers leaned back into place. It weren't right, not plant-like. Trixie was out of sight.

He walked the relative center of the draw, confident he would find her. Here, too, was a concern without urgency. It felt alien to him, a great weight softening. He'd been vigilant his whole life, but here, now, he could set that burden down. His gait was steady, slow, easy. He wanted to lie down, and it took effort to push the thought away. Silly.

The bushes, now that he was close to them, all looked like something other. One like a deer, lying in the flowers. It had thin branches that formed a rack off a thick branch that resembled a skull. Hollows where the eyes would be. He shivered.

A little further along, a bush was shaped vaguely like a dog, with a flowered snout and ears, woody paws.

Once when he was a young child, he had seen a topiary garden. It was a little like this, but that garden required meticulous work of an artist to maintain its delightful shapes. How could this happen by chance?

He decided to stop looking closely at the bushes, quickened his pace the best he could on the soft carpet. It reacted, softening further the faster he walked, like an invitation. The heavier his footfalls, the faster he tried to move, the harder it was to stay afoot. Finally, he had no choice but to slow.

When he found Trixie, she was squatting on her heels in the

midst of a large circle that was especially dense with bushes and little trees.

"What are you doing? I think we should keep moving."

She looked up at him, then back down. Cecil walked past her, into the circle.

At the center was the only piece of naked ground he'd seen since they wandered into the glade. Black soil, the moss retreated from it. He put the toe of his boot in it and when he withdrew it, a dusting of ash clung to it, and he agitated a little cloud.

"What the hell is this?" He heard a thump behind him. Trixie and fallen backward on her rump, or maybe just taken a more comfortable seat. She was ignoring him again, just stared at the ground, quiet.

He kicked at the ash and aroused another cloud of it. Exposed a few partially burned branches. Squatting down in the space was like being shaken from a daydream. He sat deep on his heels, breathed the ghost of long dead fire, and scanned the perimeter.

The largest specimens looked like men standing. Some had bifurcated trunks. Each had two main branches and a terminus just above those. The bushes were more of the same, but incomplete, like the remains of old statues. Here was a branch that resembled an arm, including five fingers at the end. And there was one that was like a leg, stems coming to a point on one side and thick knot of wood on the other, the heel and toe of a boot.

"Trixie!" He stood and rushed to her side. She did not look up, didn't make a sound.

"Trixie, we need to go!" He grabbed her arm, pulled. She tipped over on her side, softly. Her skin was cool.

Cecil lifted her by the armpits, brought her to a seat, but she wouldn't or couldn't support herself. Next, he tried to lift her to her feet, but her dead weight was very heavy, and he relented.

Sitting back for a moment, the sweetness again invaded his senses. Having been free of it a moment in the fire pit, the heaviness was much clearer, pleasant like a whiskey drunk. To sit beside Trixie and rest was a compulsion; it was a bitter fight resisting it.

He settled behind her, heels planted by her hips, to get the most leverage he could. Again, he tried to pull her to her feet, was met with even more resistance. He bent to check her hands, thought she might be clinging to the ground cover. What he saw was a gut punch, sucked the air right out of him. From the thigh down, stems of the orange flowers were woven around her legs. Moss crept around the underside of her feet and calves.

Cecil drew his knife, began furiously cutting at the plants. Invisible barbs stung his hand, and by the time he was done extricating one leg, he was bleeding from several small wounds. His fingertips were numbing. Moving to the other side, he began to free her right leg. It was hard work. The stems and the moss were more deeply affixed and denser on this side. Twice, he dropped the knife, and the second time he had to switch hands because he could no longer grip with his right, could no longer feel that hand at all.

Trixie began moaning. The sound was inhuman, like something thicker than air moved through her lungs and throat. Her closed eyes spasmed and her lips trembled.

Cecil could hardly get the knife back in the sheath, so numb had his hands become. And where he dripped blood on the ground, the flowers and moss shook softly.

He got his wrists under Trixie's armpits and finally got her standing, dropped low and brought her waist to his shoulder, lifting her completely off the ground. Then he ran as best he could over ground that gave way unnaturally. He hoped if he could just make it up the hill, that on the other side he would find the river.

The woods retreated before his eyes, each step bringing him no closer to what he prayed would be their salvation. The climb steepened too, so, soon he was no longer running, but leaning forward for leverage and taking small steps that half the time found no purchase, slowing his progress almost to a halt. Finally, he had to set Trixie down and drag her along behind him by looping his arms under her armpits. She was dead weight and more than that, the ground pulled at her whenever he paused.

He half fell backward, half sat, exhausted, defeated.

It occurred to him then that he should leave her, that his only chance for escape would be to make a run for it with all he had, unburdened. As the narcotic malaise crept on him, taking greater hold, his only clear thought was that Trixie gave him purpose. She would be the reason for him to continue to put one foot in front of the other. Without her, the call to lay down, to let sleep overtake him, would be irresistible.

Retrieving his canteen with his wrists -because his hands were still too numb to hold it- he brought it to his mouth and pulled the cork with his teeth. Even his wrists were beginning to numb, and as he took a drink, the canteen slipped. He watched in helpless agony as its contents gurgled out, taken up by the wretched flowers and moss. It immediately sunk an inch or so, and he was unable to pick it up again.

He wrestled with Trixie's body, resting her on the other shoulder this time, and surrendered to walking straight through the shallow valley. What followed was a blur. He walked until his feet were pulverized bone on bone. Until his knees creaked. Until his shoulder and his thighs burned with the effort, then went numb, then sang with pinprick shocks all over. Until he was bent over, and straightening felt like the muscles in his low back and buttocks tore free of their moorings.

When he was walking, the pain scattered all other thoughts, all other concerns, to the winds. Every bit of concentration was demanded for the next footfall, and the one after. Exhaustion was a sort of amnesia, erasing anything more than a minute past or hence.

Stopping to rest was much worse. One more minute became

just ten more minutes, and with no real sense of time, his heart raced in a panic that he might be dead or dying and his consciousness slipping away entirely. He stared at Trixie's limp body, and sometimes it took a moment to remember who she was, who she was to him. Even that was complicated, and his mind unfit for complicated thought.

Just rest, rest, rest. Let your eyes close just a moment. Let yourself forget completely. Surrender totally. Be free. These thoughts became more intense the less acute his pain. There was a time limit to how long he could stop and yet retain any hope of starting again. It was a line he could only know once he crossed it. That thought kindled terror, and when he first stood after a rest, the relief of standing tall without his burden brought fresh thoughts of abandoning the girl. Each time he had to fight these, tell himself he would never make it. If he left her, his next rest would be his last, his final resting place until some fresh victim wandered through the damned field and found a Cecil shaped bush. He pictured it. Crooked fingers of thin wood pointing in accusation at the sky, his leafy mouth agape in final, permanent, agony.

He shouldered Trixie and continued. Only aware of day and night, of the place of the sun and moon in the sky, by the shadow he cast that dulled the blazing orange or pallid yellow around him. It must have been cold at night because at times he could see the specter of his breath, like even his soul wanted to escape this unending torment. But no, that expectorated fog meant he still lived.

The glade unending, he walked for days. His tongue, dry and swollen in his mouth, reminded him how long he had gone without water, and the sucking hollow of his gut cried out for food. Beyond these immediate symptoms, his senses were untrustworthy. A dull electricity crept slowly back into his hands, but he still could not move his fingers. He thought he heard the river flowing loudly, but looking around it was still orange meadow as far as he could see, and the whooshing was only his heartbeat pounding in his ears.

Then he blinked and looked up to find himself in a river basin. The Gila -he assumed it must be- was to his right and only about twenty yards away. The ground felt hard again, the moss replaced with thin and yellow grass, and populated by the occasional squat sycamore. But when he blinked again -hard- it was gone. The flowers had returned, the ground softening. Not quite spongy though, and the smell was wrong. Where was the sweetness he remembered? This was his last thought as he pitched forward, Trixie spilling from his shoulder with a hard thud and then a groan, the first sound she had made since he had found her anchored to the ground.

He woke to a splash of water on his face and blinked hard at the man who crouched before him.

"You ok, pard?" He was a young man, sunburnt red at the cheeks and squinting in the bright sun. He handed Cecil a cup. "Here, I fetched y'all some water from the river."

Cecil took the cup, surprised to find his fingers, while stiff, were responsive. He sipped and sputtered.

"Slowly," the man steadied the cup for him. "The two of you is near dried up. Just take a little bit and wait a minute and take some more."

"What happened, where are we?" He spotted Trixie propped against a rock, shaded by a nearby bush. She caught his eye, made an effort at a little smile.

Someone took hold of his shoulder and he flinched.

"Easy, there, buddy. The two of you are safe." A low steady voice, he turned to look at the man behind it. He was older than the other one. Thick around the middle. Held his hat in the hand that wasn't on Cecil, and his hair was gray and thin on top. His features reminded Cecil a little of Red Club, and he winced at the recollection.

"In answer to your question, you're about ten miles from Yuma. The territorial prison is just the other side of yonder bluff. My son John and I were out here hunting up some quail when we found the two of you out cold, cooking in the sun here."

"That's impossible. We need to get out of here, get away from them flowers."

"Son," the old man looked puzzled, "Only flowers around here are desert wildflowers. They may not be pretty, but they won't hurt you none, neither."

Cecil pushed his hand away, got up on unsteady feet. A wave of nausea came over him and he flung out his arms. Both of the men helped steady him.

"You should probably sit a while longer."

"No, no. I need to look." He took a step, then another. Found his footing. The two stared at him as he walked further from the river. The whole landscape was alien. The meadow was nowhere to be seen. No moss, no flowers, just scrub and lonely trees.

He sat down hard. The feeling of relief almost put him on his back. A nagging sense of unreality tugged at him, and he wondered -after the last few days- if he would ever be sure of where he was again. He closed his eyes and saw the orange flowers, the endless meadow. How long would it be like this? How long until he were sure he had made it out, and wasn't being et, turnt to a bush somewhere?

44

YUCCA FLATS

Flowers for Hair had never seen a Joshua Tree, and what faint descriptions she could recall from a lifetime of collecting stories still did not prepare her for the reality. The larger specimens, especially, evoked awe. It was late in the day when she emerged onto the first great plain of them, and the hazy red skyline set fire to their great white blossoms. The effect was dazzling, utterly alien, and magical. The tallest were forty feet or more, arms all upraised in prayer or defiance. The energy of the place stoked the fire in her belly, and she could almost hear the regular drum in her breast over the lazy *clop clop clop* of the horse that followed behind her.

Autie had long passed the point of reliably discriminating between the real and the fevered reshaping of it in his mind. He was less surprised than she, mainly because his thoughts were in infinite regress, he could no more grasp them than river silt. Everything was soft and insubstantial.

His leg -what was left of it- had quit its throbbing and burning a day or two past. Time was as thin as everything else. Unsure whether this was a sign of healing or of moving into a further, irretrievable stage, and unsure what to think of that either way. If dying was a shutting down of the pain and a slow and quiet slipping, it might be a final mercy; there might even be some dignity to it.

The clopping of horse hoof, the accompanying *thump thump thump* of his belly on the animal's spine, with only a thick blanket to soften it. These were the most substantial anchors to time and space that were left to him. The tea, whatever potions the woman kept feeding him, twisted his eyes and ears constantly. Bands of color -the ground, the trees, the sky- wavered from some malformed version of themselves to a mixing of the three into one great canvas that spun and swirled and only occasionally resolved into distinct images. Images that once were meaningful, that had hinted at a fate yet spooled tight, only waiting for a push to unwind it. He must have misread them all, what other accounting could there be? His visions. A joke. They had always been the lie that hubris and ignorance had him telling himself.

What he saw most clearly -what seemed most real now- were giant figures conjured from myths he had read at West Point: gods and monsters. They must be pointing the way somewhere. But he could not steady his thoughts to recall the specifics of any single one, and so there was only vague recognition and the sting of tragedy. For he, like so many characters of myth, was being shown the signs and would only understand them when, on the precipice of the ending of him, he would alight on the fatal flaw they had laid bare and know in his soul that the divine spark at the center of the universe is ultimately unknowable, and only delights in the idiot blindness of men.

Even the trees were angry in this place, so he must be descending into ever lower pits of hell. Sounds that might be coyotes echoed at intervals, or was it the wild woman's cackling laugh, drinking deep of her perverse pleasure at his undoing?

Coyote sang his song of chaos, sang of the pleasures of madness, the invitation to loose oneself. It came at her from every side except the path in front. The world spoke only to itself. The story of people was of choosing to listen, to harvest what could be harvested, or to refuse. Here, the words were clearer. They would get ever clearer, she expected, until they reached the ocean. Until then, hers must be a great forgetting. Not of the stories told to her, but of the things she knew about the world. She must make room for the new, for the circle that would bring her back to the first, the before time.

Once she would have feared this. Coyotes do not travel in such groups, do not sing among themselves to shepherd a person along. But here, on this great artery of the dark maker, the one of many who dwell below, she must trust those who can smell blood at great distance, for blood was the guiding principle, the sand a restless and thirsty ghost.

She would not likely encounter a band of people again. They would steer clear of this carnivorous ground. The pilgrims she could avoid, if there were any, for she would smell them before they could see her.

It was a day or two later when the woman started letting him take a little water, and a little meat. His hands were still bound, and she fed him at first like a baby bird, chewing and spitting into his mouth. The color and the sound began to resolve themselves into something coherent, and every so often he felt thoughts resolve similarly, clouds parting for brief moments.

The landscape was no less strange the clearer it became. The trees were monstrous chimeras, as much cactus as anything else, great balls of spines like fists at the end of each branch that threatened him with quiet menace. They swayed sometimes in the breeze, a simmering mob.

His first clear thoughts were of escape -how to overpower the woman- but the cord that bound his wrists gave up nothing. It were a wonder he could feel his fingers at all. Palms pressed together, arms against his back, he could only slightly brush digits against one another.

By the time he was chewing his own food, he felt more of his strength returning. He had weathered the storm, and he buried those manic, terrified thoughts of the last several days in a deep place, somewhere he might hide it from himself forever. He remembered himself, how much he hated resignation, acquiescence, and like all the things he hated, he denied they could ever come from him. It was the fever, it was the drugs, never him. What more evidence did he need than how foreign those thoughts already seemed? He could scarcely imagine ever having conjured them. Had he asked the woman to kill him? No. No matter how low, how vulnerable he felt, such words would dissolve on his tongue before he could speak them. The drugs. The infection. Any memory of those days was suspect, could be dismissed as such.

He resolved to play possum, to hide his spirit from her until the right moment. He would know it when it came. When he was strong enough, the full light of his destiny would open the path to liberation. He clenched and unclenched his hands. It was agony at the bindings, but he did it as often and for as long as his strength would allow, and each day a little more. Tense, rest, tense again. He was the river that carved canyons. The rope would lose its resolve long before he did.

The woman was hardly aware of him. Everything she did now, she did with a quiet reverence. Deliberate and peaceful in her movements. She only burned what wood she could gather from the ground and whispered soft prayers while doing so. This was her church, the place where monsters bow to one another in feral recognition. Still, he wanted her. Her soft movements only magnified her beauty, and he fought the pull of it, told himself this were the last of her witchery working its way out of him.

"These gods of yours, what do they give you in exchange for your offerings and prayers?" He thought talking of spiritual matters might take his mind from base desire, and to provoke her might fortify him further.

She looked up from her gathering. Paused and stared. Perhaps she had never considered the question before.

"To be left alone."

"What?" Autie was mystified. "You don't expect so much as favorable wind, a good hunt? Protection? How on earth did you come to such an arrangement?" And it grieved him the more that a creature of such little ambition had got the better of him.

"Does your god meddle often in the affairs of men? If he does, of what good is it to those lying in shallow graves along the trail you yourself now travel? Of them that rode with you? Those broken by the path, were they less worthy than you, did they not pray as you?"

Autie stiffened. "It is not our right to question His will. He blesses those that please Him. And those He calls home will sit forever in His love and in His light. The perils of the world begin with our sin, not with his disregard."

"So, you submit yourself to the shifting moods of this god and ask nothing but his promise, whose truth you cannot know, and in exchange, you are to bend to his will all your life?" Flowers for Hair looked at him and smiled, cocked her head, like she were talking to a child.

"You're talking about a sacred covenant that goes back thousands of years. This is no simple promise." Autie was growing angry. Tensing where he sat, as her words sank hooks in him.

"Is this covenant like those your people have made with my people? It does not do man any good to invite the whims of gods into his world," she said.

"We are no more than sand to them, that sifts through the fingers and is lost to all reckoning. To be left alone is the greatest gift they can grant us. Your people think we don't understand property, the idea of owning the land on which we live. You misunderstand. We know that property is a tether. To own it is to lay claim to all that lives on it and all that moves underneath it. It is to bound yourself to that which we are not meant to under-stand. It is to be owned."

"And what of when you die, have you no recourse but to forfeit your soul." He looked up, regarded her coldly, tensed again at his bindings.

Flowers for Hair made a zig zag gesture upward with her right hand, looked to the sky.

"The life of a person is like a fire. All that remains after is the smoke. Smoke may linger for a time, longer if the weather is right, but it must fade and become part of the sky. To go on, without a heart, without hands, is to become nothing but maddening hunger. I suspect your heaven is full of such crea-tures, forever infecting you with their emptiness."

She brought a plate from the fire, began hand feeding him small pieces of meat, some kind of squirrel that ran along the ground here. Where her fingers alighted on his tongue, all thought of religion scattered.

Autie knew her sensuality must be cultivated. To soften him, to draw him to the damnation of her. Feeding him, she stood closer than was necessary, so her skirt and what lay under it was mere inches from his face, and unbidden thoughts of that sweet root swinging pendulous and free made him rigid.

She smiled broadly, reached down and squeezed him.

"Colonel. You lean and bend gentle, like a helpless pup. I think you deceive me. It seems your strength returns."

He strained at the bindings. They gave just a little, not nearly enough. Not yet. He spat half chewed meat at her. "Get away from me, you vile thing."

"Your body betrays you, Colonel," she laughed that tinkling laugh, and again he strained, until the pain made him go soft.

She pulled up her skirt and waggled her flaccid member at him. Kept laughing as she walked away.

She knew he would try to escape. Knew he had been working toward it since she stopped giving him the tea. Let him exhaust himself, it didn't matter any longer what he did. The course was set. He was gripped by an unbreakable tether just as she was. The bindings on his hands were redundant.

The next morning, she stripped a piece of yucca wood and fashioned him a crutch. The wider end she wrapped and tied with thickly layered strips of saddle blanket. When he leaned on it, it gave a little, but he soon found that this springiness aided him in his awkward walk.

"My turn to ride for a while." And she took the horse, walked it at a slow enough pace that he could stay just ahead. After all his efforts against the rope, unnecessary. It was anticlimactic. She had untied his hands to let him walk. But now she was mounted, with his smaller pistol in hand, resting heavy on the horse's withers.

45

FROM YUMA TO SAN DIEGO

The railroad in that part of the country was being built backwards from the west coast, so there was no train that went east further than Phoenix, but the route ran directly from Yuma to San Diego. Cecil and Trixie hid nearby and didn't sneak aboard the empty cattle car until the sun had set, and the steam began to pour steady into the twilight air from the engine far ahead of them. Even then, they were very cautious, though it appeared they needn't be. Either the railroad didn't expect stowaways or didn't care to prevent them.

The shushing of wheel on track was just beginning when they reached the car. Cecil threw himself in, and Trixie was walking an easy pace alongside when he reached out to pull her up. The car was empty, save a couple of half bales of hay that were dried to such an extent that the stray bits crunched underfoot. Cecil drug the two to one side of the car, leaving enough space for the both he and Trixie to hide behind. Then he stuffed some hay in his hat to fashion a sort of pillow, lay down his blanket, and rested. Weariness sucked at the marrow of his bones, and he felt his eyelids go near instantly heavy. Trixie sat against the wall opposite him, angled in the corner and staring out the void of the open door.

He thought about the last time he was on a train, how sleep was a haunting and restless thing then. This train rocked and shuddered much more than that had, and yet now it was a soothing motion. All the change in a life takes place in the heart and the mind, and the body is its text. For he was not the person who had boarded that train those many weeks ago, inside or out. He must be better, for having survived what he had and having hardened, so that he could take comfort in what once menaced him. He no longer felt eyes on him. There were enough real demons in the world that to conjure his own was a vanity. His crime was remote now, committed by someone else, and petty when held up to what transpired after. Whatever hunted him from that faraway place must have lost the trail or run out of steam. He would choose his destiny from now on. The ending and the beginning were so close, he could nearly taste the salt air of it, of amnesic rolling waves with the power to erase the past.

The train was in an agonal shushing when he woke, in the final effort of reaching full speed. He thought the stuttered movement or the sound must have woken him. That, or the first hints of morning light that forced their way into his sleepy eyes.

"Cecil. Cecil, wake up." It was Trixie, her voice cracked with distress.

He made as little noise as he could, still behind the cover of the bales. He clawed under the blanket and found his knife. Making himself small, he came to a crouch before rising completely, stepped over the hay and then froze.

"Drop the knife, kid. It's the end of the road for you."

The blade clattered from his hand on the wooden floor. The man had a grim look, his mouth a straight line under a thin mustache. He held Trixie tight to him, the crook of his right elbow around her neck. She strained at his arm with both hands, trying to make some space for herself. In his other hand was a pistol, hanging at his side.

"Who are you? What do you want?" The train was reaching full speed and the three of them all rocked slightly with the motion of it.

"I'm your reckoning. You've no idea what a terrible pain you've been to me, kid. The Branaghs don't want all of you, just enough to know they got their money's worth, but I've half a mind to drag you back to Ohio behind a horse until what's left of you won't fill a thimble. Maybe take your scalp first so's I have a receipt."

"You ok, Trixie?" She didn't look at him, just kept pulling at the man's arm.

"Cut it out you little cur," and he raised his pistol and rapped her on the forehead with the barrel. A little trickle of blood ran down her nose, but she didn't cry out, didn't make a sound.

Cecil took a step toward them.

"Ah, ah, ah. You just ease up son. Maybe you sit down, and we'll ride this train to the next stop and then be on our way. You almost made it. Guess that's something to be proud of. Better men than you haven't stayed ahead of me for half as long."

"I'm not going back with you."

"Not all of you, no."

Trixie went loose in the legs. It must have taken him off guard because his arm sagged a moment under her weight. Then she turned her head and bit into his forearm.

He cried out, loosened his grip a little, and for a moment it looked like she might get clear.

Cecil charged. Trixie still fought the man's arm, and his body was now mostly exposed. He looked up as Cecil planted both palms on his chest and shoved. Pulling his arms to his body as he fell back through the open door, he took Trixie with him.

Cecil rebounded and fell on his ass to the hard floor of the cattle car. The movement of the train was such that the two of them were there, suspended in midair for a moment, and then vanished. He flashed to that moment in the skeleton of a building, to his friend, lifeless and bloody on the ground. There was no ambiguity for him to hide in this time. He pictured Trixie bouncing along the hard packed earth, coming to a stop, twisted and broken. In the frozen moment, he felt the weight of all his compromises fall on him at once. A deluge, it ran over him, through him, went to ground and then kept going. In its wake, he felt relief, a numbness that was an answer to all the questions he had been asking since that day. And all he had to do was accept that answer, to make peace with it.

The train tracks were built on a little elevated berm, and Charlie knew he would clear that. It was a long fall, at high speed, so he did what needed doing. Turning in the air, he slipped his hands to the girl's shoulders, tucking his elbows. Her tiny body, the only cushion for his fall. The crunch he heard as they touched down was one of a handful of sounds that would at intervals be resurrected in his dreams. She let out a little squeak of a scream just before impact, but then there was no air to scream with, and no mouth to shape the sound.

She didn't fully break his fall, but took the brunt of it. He rolled and bounced in the dirt for a good five or ten yards before skidding to a halt. His left wrist was stiff and painful with a likely sprain, but otherwise it was scratches and bruises and friction rash. He sat on the ground, dusted himself off. The girl didn't move or make a sound, and he didn't want to look at her. Sparing a single glance, he saw her small body was face down, half buried. At least she didn't suffer. There are no mercies in this world but small mercies.

He thought of the old prospector and the shiver that rode up his spine was like lightning being drawn back to the cloud what made it. He was suddenly nauseous, told himself it was the kid's doing. He hadn't set out to hurt her. Anyway, what did he have to fear from a broken-down old man? He pushed the thought away, turned to consideration of the long walk back to the depot. The kid would pay a damned heavy price for this.

46

CUYAMACA AND THE SAN DIEGO RIVER

A few more days, and Autie was getting more comfortable on the crutch. A thick callous was forming under his arm, and his gate lengthened. With the quickening of his pace, progress along the plateau was less agonizing. Looking west, the outline of mountains was slowly taking shape, and he felt a shift in the air, like something had been gripping him in the chest and he only recognized it now, and only by its absence. For her part, Flowers for Hair seemed barely to notice him. Whether her vigilance was failing, or she didn't sense the growing threat of him, he could not tell.

She noticed everything. The confidence of his stride, the straightness of his back, the glimmer in his eye that betrayed all his plotting. He was not a man given to long planning, and it was apparent that it pained him to await the right moment. She didn't plan to shoot him unless he forced her hand. It was a novelty to stand back and see where this would go. The soil fairly churned beneath the horse's hooves, and she imagined their mirror image clopping underneath, dripping tar upward where it might seep through the soil in the softer, thinner places. The Colonel was at the mercy of its corruption now, and so was she.

The coyotes still bounded them, though their yips and howls became less frequent. The trees were beginning to thin, and the frosty tips of the mountains ahead promised water.

She still tied him up when they settled down for the night, but her heart was no longer in it. The only thing that kept him from running was the ruggedness of the terrain and his fear of trying to navigate it one legged in the dark. That and the howls. Wolves or coyotes. Maybe both. Their cries were more threatening in the dark.

"Why don't you just let me go. Make your way to some quiet place and live out your days. No one's going to look hard for you out here." He was walking beside her while she rode. She no longer kept him out front. So careless.

"There is no path left to me but forward. I'll see this to the end."

"The first white men we come across will skin you alive. If you're lucky. These old prospector types might do a lot worse to you first."

"Nothing can be taken from me that hasn't been. You know that better than anyone."

His intentions were louder than his words. She played her part, but she saw the river on the downward slope before he did, and saw the excitement course through him like a chill wind once he noticed it. The water must start somewhere higher up, and where it cut around the nearby peak and joined the gentle downward slope on which they walked, it was broad and restless. She knew mountain waterways, how deceptive they could be. Below the surface, that water was ice cold and moving at dangerous speed. She smiled.

Autie raised his crutch and shouted. The horse flinched but didn't buck. Rather, it turned away from him. Good enough. He stagger-ran to the river. A shot rang out, but found no purchase, and he didn't look back. When he reached the edge, he threw himself into the water headfirst, clutching his stick to his chest.

When the river took him, it was like being shot from a cannon, and it took all his strength to get face up and to stay that way. He heard another shot but knew he must be nearly out of pistol range already.

Flowers for Hair fired twice into the air. The horse whinnied and then stilled, and she laughed a deep-throated laugh. She would either find his broken body where the river bottomed out in the valley below, or she would track him to where he wound up. The coyotes yip-yipped and she joined in their chorus. The sky was an impossible blue, dotted by fluff as white as the snow caps behind and ahead of her. The faintest whiff of salt suffused the air. The water at the end of the world must taste like blood.

It was a mining camp that found him. They must have dragged him from the water unconscious because the next thing he knew he was on his back, sputtering. Someone turned him on his side, and he hacked and hacked. Water trickled down his cheek and a string of snot hung from his overgrown mustache.

When he regained his senses, an older man, red cheeked and clean shaven, with a broad brimmed hat folded up in the front, grabbed his lapels and pulled him up to a seat. Autie stared for a moment, still getting his bearings.

"Ye ain't a mermaid."

"What?"

"Ye ain't a mermaid. Nor a water sprite, I figger. River done spat you out right where we was panning. Queerest thing I ever saw. Sent a few of the young fellers running. Thought you might be a demon or something."

"I'm a colonel in the U.S. Army. Been held captive by… a band of Indians. A dozen or so braves it was. I need you to take me to the nearest outpost forthwith."

"Ain't none of us Army out here, I'm afraid. Lessen you got

some papers laying out your provenance, I don't know if we can help ye. You're welcome to wait until next we cash out. We usually go to town every few weeks."

Autie pawed at his clothes. He thought of Sheridan's letter. It was gone. Everything gone. He never wore the standard uniform, not that a uniform would convince anyone. Half the men in the camp probably still wore blue or grey trousers from the war. And he was reduced to his long underwear since the betrayal and butchery.

"Damn you. I'm injured, half starved, narrowly escaped captivity with my life."

"We go by dollars and cents here in the brambles. I don't mean to make offense, sir, but ye don't look like much. Lot of tramps come this way, it seems. Though not many float in on the river."

"Fine. Where's the nearest fort then?"

"San Diego has a garrison. That's where we generally do our trading, and like I said, we most likely be headin' that way the next week or so." The man scratched at his chin. A couple of others, younger men, had gathered behind him now.

"I can guarantee cash payment. A hundred dollars per man who accompanies me if we can take a wagon and leave immediately."

The old man's eyes lit up. "Let's talk about it over supper. You rest here and dry out a bit first."

They ate bacon and biscuits and ranch beans. The camp had an actual cook, and Autie cleaned his plate in a matter of a minute or so. Food had never tasted so good to him. They set him up with another portion, and he ate more slowly this time, told what parts of his story helped his cause. A half dozen men, no doubt starved for new stories, hung on his every word. There were audible gasps when he told of his betrayal by his own men, about the amputation and being left for dead, and then his captivity, the conditions of which he greatly exaggerated.

When he was done, the old timer and a few others went off ten paces or so, and huddled. When they came back, he knew the decision before the old man said a word.

"We'll take ye, first light tomorrow. If you're who you say you are, we'll take the hunderd, but we also want a picture with ye, and our names in the paper next to yours as them that brung you home."

Autie smiled. "Of course."

————————

Flowers for Hair watched from the rocks above. She stripped the saddle blanket and slapped the animal on the rump. It would find its way home. She must move quietly now.

47

THE CALIFORNIA COAST, FIRE AND EARTH AND WATER

Cecil had plenty of time to think on what he'd done. Whenever he closed his eyes, it was the look of surprise on Trixie's face he saw, and each time some new subtlety that screamed at him of betrayal. Each time putting a fresh ten penny nail in his chest. But since the train, every pang of guilt was an echo, more removed from the origin. Fading. He was clinging to the pain because the alternative was a sort of free fall. Who would he be without it? Closing his eyes, the events on the train and those in Columbus and every horror in between mingled in endless variation. The head and tail of a hoop snake, running ever into one another. To be free was simply to exit the circle. The numbness he had felt for a moment on the train, to surrender to that was like walking the downslope of a gentle hill. It only asked him to let go.

He couldn't be sure the man was dead. The more he thought about it, the more certain he became that the mercenary still lived. And what if there were others? He wondered if he should turn himself in, take his chances with the law. Did he deserve hanging? Deserve was a concept irreconcilable to what he had seen. No, it would be the rope for him if he surrendered. At least with the hired guns he had a chance, small though it might be.

He slipped off his boot. Removed the paper secreted there. Of all the things, it was astonishing it had survived the journey. Unfolding it, he read it in its entirety again. It was a deed of partial ownership in a plot here in San Diego.

Twenty five percent. 355 Market Street.
Benjamin Gielgud.

He could be anyone out here. People of the west had no history. Benjamin was as good a name as any.

He shook his boot and a few loose coins and bills fell out. Everything he had. Seven dollars, thirty-five cents.

Charlie had underestimated his injuries. A mile or so into his walk, once the initial stiffness of the fall let up, his right knee began to click and pop painfully. He pulled down his pants to examine it and the kneecap had shifted and something was protruding on the outside. Sitting down, he probed at it, tried to push things back into place. When he pressed firmly, a shock of pain ran up his leg and down to his foot. The intensity left him momentarily dizzy. He removed his shirt, carefully cut off the sleeves. It killed him to do it. He would stumble back to the stop where he had boarded the cattle car looking like a rube, some poor soul who got taken advantage of or tossed off the train by the Pinkertons.

He bound his knee with the two shirtsleeves, gritting his teeth as he cinched the knots hard. It left him walking nearly straight legged on the right side, but the popping and clicking eased considerably and progress became easier. The ledger against the kid grew substantially. He wasn't generally one to cause hurt where there was no profit to be made, but he sure as shit would savor every dollar's worth of flesh he took out of the boy's hide. He pictured a canvas sack, opening it for the Branaghs and sprinkling fingers and toes from it like pea gravel. Each joint separate, cut neatly, falling in a tidy pile. The thought brought a whisper of a smile.

Sometimes, letting the rage burn itself out was profit enough.

The little whistle stop was no more than a general store and a few one room shacks. He found his horse where he had left her, munching on hay behind the store. He paid the shopkeep in silence, and his face must have spoke volumes because the man didn't so much as make eye contact, but simply nodded and accepted his payment with an affirmative grunt.

Two others browsed nearby, a young woman dangling a basket at the crook of her elbow, and a greasy prospector type. Both glanced in his direction. The woman quickly cast her eyes downward. The man stared a second longer and then shifted his attention back to the canned goods. Charlie was in a killing mood, his temper like old dynamite, sweating nitro. At that moment, he wanted the spark -the excuse. None here were ill tempered or ignorant enough to give it to him.

He mounted up and rode for the tracks, for San Diego, and a reckoning.

Autie felt like a new man. Freshly bathed, new clothes, wound cleaned and attended to. The enlisted men fawned over him, brought him whatever he asked for. There were two newspapers with offices here. The San Diego County Star was local, and the San Francisco Chronicle had a few people stationed in a small office near the docks. Both had interviewed him extensively. News of his arrival was wired across the country. It would be headlines in every continental paper for the next few days.

He sent a discreet message to Sheridan about the betrayal. Sullivan would run if he had any sense. Otherwise, he would find himself in shackles in a week's time and at the end of a rope not long after.

The garrison in San Diego was thin, and they could only spare a unit to backtrack his path and search for the woman. But there would be hundreds more to search for her in the coming weeks. As much as he would have liked her alive, what she might confess was too great a risk, so he gave the order she was to be shot on sight. The man with a confirmed kill would be bonused a month's salary. They would be falling over one another to murder the bitch.

He would ride out with them himself once he got another day or two of rest.

———

Flowers for Hair crept into the town in the chill of evening. It wasn't difficult to find the place where few white men wandered. The rail workers had their own neighborhood, were relegated to a place peripheral and undeveloped. Adjacent to the docks, their buildings were tightly packed together, shacks mostly. Many had no doors, and the windows were simply smaller holes they shuttered closed when the air got too cold.

The breeze off the ocean was salty and sweet. A comfortable cool, and it mixed with smells of cooking meat and spices. People shuffled all around her, whispered to one another when she passed.

In an apothecary, she was able -through a clumsy language of simple gestures and a few common words of English- to barter. The flowers that she so carefully wove through her braids and the remnants of the pouch that dangled from her neck. Medicinal herbs. These people knew their value.

She left the place with a little money and a new set of

clothes, the simple dress of the local workers, which would allow her to move more easily in the town. The Colonel's pistol hung under her shirt by a leather cord, slapping gently against her as she moved, the pendulous yoke of fate. Four bullets remained, like the four winds.

Cecil asked directions three times before finding his way to the address. Steinbeck's was a dry goods and general store. A silhouette of a wolf's head hung over the door. He watched for a while. Around midday, a man came out and swept the steps. He was fairly young, maybe in his twenties. Bespectacled, thick around the middle. He moved with an ease that said any hard times were a remote memory. His pale features stood testament to a life indoors. It made Cecil's heart light. Everything he wanted. Everything he felt he had earned.

At a tiny blacksmith's shop, Cecil found a used pepper box .38 that was similar to the one he took from his father. It was a bit larger and heavier, as the barrels weren't chopped. The man included twenty-five shells for an even four dollars. He bought a small chisel and a hammer for another dollar, which left him just enough for the night's lodging. It must happen tonight.

The woman at the rooming house looked at him funny when he requested two adjacent rooms in two different names. He explained that his sister would be arriving and would be expecting her own space. She stared for a moment, then took his money and handed him a pair of keys.

He took the bedding from "Trixie's" room and rolled it up, put it under the blanket in his own. After a half hour of rearranging, stepping back, looking, rearranging again, he was satisfied that the lump was a close enough approximation of his sleeping form.

Returning to the other room, he began working as quietly as

he could manage with the hammer and chisel. The wood was fairly soft, cheap, and soon he had worked a good-sized slit at shoulder level. He maneuvered the pistol barrel around it, found he was able to cover the whole space. He pulled a wooden stool over to the wall, sat, and waited. The ocean murmured in the distance, a soft susurrus.

Charlie rode into town around sunset. There were no vacancies at the good hotel, and he found a passable one nearby. The second-best hotel in San Diego was the best deal he'd had in a long time. He wired the Branaghs, a stilted and brief missive that teased them with how close he was to completing his task. He bought two new shirts and a clean pair of pants. They needed a bit of tailoring, and the man would bring them to the hotel the next morning.

The Sunset had two stories of rooms, and a copper bath on the roof top. Lady Eveline, who ran the place, wore her dark hair short, and wrapped it in a silk scarf. Her brown eyes teased at mischief, with a sort of predatory edge, and she moved with a quiet confidence.

Charlie luxuriated in the hot bath. Eveline brought him a pitcher of chilled tea with a healthy pour of whiskey. Lemon slices bobbed and floated in the glass, and he got drunk watching the sun set over the Pacific.

Autie had taken to walking the beach in the morning. The early sun would set the horizon ablaze, and he watched the bright disc crawl out of that fire, watched seals flop clumsily in the shallows and on the nearby rocks. His new crutches sunk into the sand, so his movements were awkward, but the only one around to witness were the railroad and dock workers, who paid him no mind, washing their dishes in knee deep water.

He had a new Peacemaker, and he absently massaged the back strap and fingered the polished bison horn of the grips. He wandered toward a washed-out dock, where an assortment of bottles spoke to its status as a gathering place for sailors. He gathered a few of the larger and more intact specimens and hobbled onto the creaking platform. It ended abruptly just over the water, looked like something had smashed it. He glanced around for a stretch of sand where he might do some target practice. It was a new pistol after all, and he didn't want too many witnesses or distractions as he learned his way around it.

A rocky outcropping stretched a ways distant down the shore, flat enough that he might make his way on crutches more easily than on the sand. He didn't notice the woman who lingered fifty yards behind. Didn't feel her eyes on him. She was dressed in the style of the Chinese workers, simple shirt, skirt, trousers. She didn't stand out, and he didn't notice her even as she began following him.

The rocky path wound around to a small tidal pool, where water sloshed at toothy rocks and drifted in and out of a dark and narrow throat. He might be able to crawl through it if he had two intact legs, but the air that wafted from it was sickly sweet with rot and he imagined it must be some natural depository of dead fish.

He carefully placed the bottles atop the tallest rocks and made his way back about thirty paces.

He was used to a heavier pistol, and his first shots ricocheted off the rocky wall with loud pings that roused dust and debris. He ran the gun dry, hitting just one of the bottles. He reloaded and went again, and did a little better. Two of three hits, clean and dead center as far as he could tell. He spent the next three shots clearing the pointed bits from three of the cavern's teeth.

Holstering his weapon, he made his way to more closely examine the fruits of his efforts.

The bottles were shattered completely. He threw the larger bits into the cave. Then he heard a trilling sound. Wind from out the cave? No, he would have heard that before. And even now, it was shifting in pitch, had the character of a song.

The music moved through him, a tickle of a breeze on the inside, like his blood danced in rhythm with it. A wave of dizziness struck, and he leaned heavily on his weak side crutch.

Turning, he saw a glimmer of white twinkling in what scant light penetrated the tunnel. It moved closer. Eyes. Then the mouth opened, full lips, glistening red, and then there was a wall of sound. The song was blinding, scaring loose all his senses but hearing, and even that was fractured. His mind could not decipher, could not grasp what moved through his ears, through his body. He swooned, dizzy, like his head had been thrust below the pounding waves that broke on the rocks nearby. But it was his mind and not the rocks that was being dashed.

"NO!" He screamed and staggered backward, barely caught himself before pitching off the rock. He drew his pistol, pulling the trigger on three dead chambers before he realized it was unloaded.

It was the body of a woman he saw, long, dark hair obscuring her face. She moved over the rocks. Bare breasted, strings of green clung to her body, she pulled herself toward him with her hands. A long tail, iridescent green, covered in fins, dragged behind her, carving a furrow in the sand.

She paused, opened her mouth, and before the next note turned out his lights, he saw two more sets of eyes emerging behind her.

He dropped the pistol, and it skittered on the rock. He brought up his crutch and swung wide. The hickory landed with a loud crack, and the song stopped.

Opening his eyes, the thing was trembling on the rock before him, a black trickle running through the dark hair that framed her face.

Then there was another *crack*. Familiar. He recognized the sound of his old pistol as the bullet chipped the rock in front of him. Turning, he saw her. Flowers for Hair looked different without the flowers. She was more menacing, even if she hadn't been holding a gun, hadn't been adjusting her aim for the next shot -the one that would surely hit him. She was no more than ten paces from him, steady hand, moving slowly closer.

He pivoted, ready to charge her, then froze at the impossibility of it on this terrain, and with just one leg.

The creatures had withdrawn to the mouth of the cave, pulling their dazed companion to safety, where she stared at him with palpable contempt.

Flowers for Hair was five paces away now. "For the great family, the Lakota, and my part of it, the Oglala." She was yelling the words, each syllable hard as tempered steel.

Crack. Like an exclamation point that plunged the words into his heart. But it was his good leg that flew from under him as he crashed into the rock. It burned at the knee, and he could feel nothing below it.

Three paces. Practically standing over him. He could now see her cheeks, and they shone like crystal where the tears nearly covered them. Even now she was beautiful. Damn her. The more so in her incandescence, in her grief.

"Stop." He screamed. "Stop. Talk to me. We've been through so much, you and me. You don't have to do this."

"For the Oyuhpe." She showed no sign of hearing him. "For the band. The hearts that beat in mine when my heart still beat with love and life."

Crack.

This one went into his shoulder, and he felt it ping on the rock on the other side. His hand went loose on the crutch, and he found he could not again close it.

"Please. Please. Please." He was crying, and found he would give anything for the next breath. For just one more moment. The truth of it burned in tandem with his wounds. All his lies, his pretensions, crumpling.

"For the Maka. For my mother, for the first mother, for all the mothers, the makers, the things you will never understand, you who only destroy."

Crack.

This one went into his gut, and now he could feel nothing below his waist. He was shaking now, teeth chattering. He felt cold. He tried to steady himself, but he only trembled more at the effort.

Flowers for Hair took a last look at the Colonel's gun, spat on it. Her spit sizzled on the hot barrel. It was a thing of hell and damnation just like the man. She threw it to the sea. She backed off to a flat rock a few yards away and sat down to watch the devil die.

Autie stared at her, tried to summon indignation, defiance, but he could scarcely chase the terror from his eyes. Movement to his left turned his attention from Flowers for Hair. The things from the cave were crawling toward him now. No more song to pacify him, their casual predation was the last insult.

Claws raked his arms, and he was being dragged toward that wretched throat of water and rock. The smell was overpowering, and he realized it was coming off the two who dragged him. The other had recovered her senses and pulled herself ahead. He screamed, and the echo of it mocked him from the narrow walls. His last look before there was no light by which to see, was of the two pulling him, mouths wide to draw air for the effort, their white teeth glittering, pointed, carnivorous.

His leg caught on some rocks and when they yanked at him, the part below the knee came loose. His consciousness was slipping, and he fought to hold on. He'd never considered he could die, not even when he had prayed for it. That the world would go on without him, ignorant of his last moments. He flashed on Aurelius. 'To bear misfortune worthily is good fortune.' *Fuck Aurelius*. It was his last thought before the darkness closed on him.

The boy was not hard to find. Charlie laughed at the ease of it, that after all he'd been through it should end like this. The fool hadn't even bothered to use an alias. Char, the woman running the desk, said he had checked in the night before and had not left, could not leave without her seeing him.

The man didn't ask about a girl, and his tone left Char disinclined to provide what wasn't prompted explicitly. She didn't like the look of him, and didn't like his arrogance. Was fear alone that moved her to cooperate, though the bribe didn't hurt none.

Removing his boots in the parlor, he crept along the dim hallway in sock feet, sure that he was giving the kid more credit than he deserved. The spare key had cost him a twenty-dollar gold piece, and he turned it in the lock like it were made of soft clay that might come apart if he so much as looked at it wrong. It was an old lock, though, and the slow turning only magnified the agony of its squeaking and the *clack clack clack* of tumblers falling into place.

He eased the door to; took slow and gentle steps. His prize was stock still, apparently unroused by all the racket, blankets pulled over his head. Charlie wasn't taking any chances this time. He reached for his Bowie and winced afresh at its loss. Then he drew his smaller dagger, and hammer fisted the blade on the leg closest to him -right in the meaty part of the thigh. It sunk to the hilt, and he felt the tip go through to the mattress.

"What the fuck?" He had to steady himself to keep from falling atop the knife. Withdrawing it, he probed where it had been. "Sum bitch," he turned toward the door. But his injured leg -stiff with a proper bandage now- slowed him.

Cecil had dozed a few times in the night, and was only half awake when he heard the key fighting the lock; he hadn't heard a thing before that. He watched Charlie, took careful aim, waited for his moment. He wanted the man either fully facing him or fully facing away, so he had the largest target to hit. When the man recoiled from his discovery of Cecil's ruse, he thought he had missed his chance. But when Charlie pivoted away from the bed, his right leg dragged behind him and he slowed. Cecil flinched. He didn't squeeze the trigger so much as wrench it.

Instead of a pop, it was a series of five, close together, distorted and elongated into one long *brraappp*. He tensed, eyes closed and turning away and felt something hot tear into his right cheek. His hand was numb for a second and then felt like someone had peeled the skin off. It was an agony so great he feared to look.

When he finally opened his eyes, the pistol was in pieces on the floor. Chain fire, he thought they called it, when one cartridge sets off all the others. His right hand was a bloody mess. The tips of his index finger and thumb were missing and his middle finger was bent back. He looked through the slit, and Charlie was on his back, groaning and shaking. Cecil wrapped the rag from his washbasin around his hand and fled.

Charlie spat blood. He couldn't feel his left arm from the elbow down, nor could he move it. The left side of his face stung sharply, and his ears rung so loud it made him dizzy. He was losing blood, felt warm and wet all down his left side. His chest hurt something fierce as well. He couldn't draw a full breath and when he tried, he wheezed and hurt even worse. He pulled himself to the wall with his good hand and leaned there waiting for the crowd that inevitably followed gunfire.

He was a month convalescing. He lost the left arm and most of his left ear; was told he would get used to the wheezing and the cough.

"Good thing God give us two lungs," the surgeon said, "So's you had the spare."

Charlie looked at him. Men had wilted under that gaze before, but it didn't move the surgeon. He turned to the whiskey bottle at his bedside and the man took the hint finally, and withdrew.

A few days into his recovery, he received a letter from the Branaghs.

Dear Sir,

I trust that you are being well cared for, and have been assured that you will continue to receive all that you need until you reach whatever optimal recovery the Lord wills. You came highly recommended, and I believed you capable of the modest task to which you were appointed. It was with great disappointment that I received news of your rather abhorrent performance. In light of your failure, I have little faith that you are anything but a sort of snake oil salesman, who has been exploiting my family's grief to fund his western adventure.

Please consider the funds you have received already, as well as those expenses being paid for your care, to be the final settlement of our contract. Do not attempt to contact us. These terms are non-negotiable.

Sincerely,
The Branaghs

P.S. I am aware of your history of resolving contractual disputes, and any moves of this kind will result in the severest of repercussions. See below.

Abhorrent. That mother fucker. The stingy fuck. Repercussions. It was his mother's address that was stenciled at the bottom of the letter in red ink.

"You've got no idea about repercussions." He ripped the letter apart with his teeth.

Cecil took one last look at himself, at his reflection in the storefront glass. He had nothing but the paper. Less than nothing. His right hand dripped blood through the soaked rag that he gripped with the two fingers that remained intact. He had bent the middle finger forward again but something were broke inside it. His transformation was complete. Even before the incident with the exploding gun, he scarcely looked like the boy who left Ohio. With the mangled hand and the wound on his cheek and neck, he would be unrecognizable now.

He no longer cared about some broken down bounty hunter coming for him, decided he was a match for any of them. The broken places in him pressed together now, and it was like the rest of him was wet wood, swelling and closing all the gaps. It would keep everything out.

When the pudgy man at Steinbeck's met him, he looked hard at the deed, then at Cecil. Daniel Peck was probably twice his age, but would only make fleeting eye contact. He flipped the sign on the door to closed, pulled the blind, then disappeared into the back.

He emerged with two others, a tall and lean man named

Gutierrez, who had come up from old Mexico, working cattle and panning gold, until he saved enough for a more sedentary life. And there was another heavy-set fellow: Daniel had a twin named David. It took a little convincing. None of them had known Benjamin particularly well, and had liked him even less. He had bullied his way into partial ownership in exchange for guiding the Peck brothers across the Santa Fe and protecting them from worse outlaws than him. Cecil told them he won the deed in a game of cards. They appeared skeptical; to be fair, there were holes in the story big enough for half the world to pass through. "Did you win his name in the same pot?" David had asked. But in the end, the three were already floundering and in need of what help they could get. They didn't have five years of formal schooling among them, and when they found Cecil, or rather Benjamin, could count without the use of fingers and toes –good thing, given his lack of some of these- it was all but settled. That he had in some way overcome the man they had feared surely worked its way into the calculation as well.

By the time he was eighteen, he had bought the other three out. The hunger in him was too great, too all consuming, to have room for partners. A vacuum that never let him feel secure or settled. He must always be grasping, must never let go, lest it all be taken away and he be that boy again, frightened beyond reckoning, at the mercy of the merciless.

48

ENDINGS

Benjamin's sleep, when it comes, is restless. Rarely haunted by the things he has done, which now seem remote to him as the name Cecil; to them who named him and them he knew. No, his dreams mostly reach forward, not past, and are filled with unsettling visions of things to come. When he lays down, sometimes he feels the ground shifting under him, and senses that some dark thing moves below in unseen ways, pushing and pulling men into its designs. But he's decided it's a fancy. People don't need a devil to foster their undoing. They never did.

Waking, he is often plagued by the emptiness of acquisition. He reaches for the stray threads of those he lost, and even his betrayal, his many compromises that made him complicit in their endings has grown dull. Numbness is its own sort of comfort when compared to the alternative, to what came before. Now there is no one to fully trust, only rivals and con men. Every promise is impregnated with the seed of its undoing. It is a hope for change in a world where nothing ever changes. Handshakes mean nothing, contracts only a little more. The magic of words and paper a pretense at a greater reality.

In sleep, in those wavering moments when the veil thins until

310

he shudders awake in discomfort or discomforting truth, he sees the whole of it, in fleeting glimpses, revealed. The torment that lays bare the game only after the final die has already been cast.

We are alone in our grievances and imagine the trauma the world has wrought on us incurs a debit, that cashed out might be exchanged for some measure of innocence. But the past is immutable, and nothing permanent can be bought or sold. Rather, it mocks us in our transience.

They call him The One-Armed Gentleman now. Not to his face, at least not yet, but the respect, so hard earned, is diminished, is all but gone. Charlie lived with his mother at first, but she quickly grew tired of him. "Your face makes me sad," she said, "and none of my friends want to come around with you puttering and moping all goddamn day."

If only she knew that he might be her only protection. The Branaghs died in a house fire, the paper said, common enough that it didn't arouse suspicion. Bodies burnt so that the great gashes in their throats were no longer distinguishable. He worried for a time that some assassin might do likewise to his mother, but by the time he moved out, was fairly confident their threats had died with the wealthy couple.

He bought a cottage a quarter mile down the road, but he spends his time making what repairs he can on his mother's place, them that can be done one armed. She cooks most of his meals and he's grown accustomed to her coffee. When he gets lonely, he goes to the Three Cocks, the only saloon where no one knows his mother, and where he can buy some company when it suits him. It rarely does. Most nights, he finds a black smudge of sky to stare at and drinks hot tea with whiskey.

The only ones who seek him out are the young men with wide-eyed longing. To them, his injuries and complaints are sublime, his stories and warnings a poetry to build a religion on. He realizes that the west is a will o' the wisp, that will forever draw young men seeking adventure to their doom. All of them, like pilgrims seeking God in each place they look, so convinced he must be there that each failed attempt only heightens their resolve.

They mistake his silence for strength, projecting their dreams onto his broken body. Their questions are a closed fist on a ripe piece of fruit, and they greedily slurp every drop of its sickly-sweet nectar. Their eyes tell him they cannot be saved. Each must first grieve for a world that is lost to them, that never was, and then be broken by the world that is. And if it must be so, let them hold onto the fantasy for as long as they can.

He has all but forgotten the man he once was, the things that once were important to him, when a small parcel arrives in the mail. It has no return address, but the postmark is Santa Fe. Neatly tied with twine and wrapped in brown paper. He takes great care opening it, as though it might contain an answer to a riddle, some forgotten thing that could restore him. Inside is a small cedar cigar box. Under the hinged lid is a scroll of paper sealed in wax. Breaking the seal, gently unrolling, reveals a small piece of blood red garnet. He holds it between thumb and forefinger, and steps outside to get a clearer look. It's carved in the shape of a beetle. When the light catches it, there is the impression of a skull on its back, which, looking closer, more accurately appears to be etched inside the stone.

Walking back inside, he retrieves the bit of scroll. Pressing it flat, there is just one word, written in shaky script. "Trixie." He hurls the stone against the wall and crumbles the paper, shoves it in his wood stove and slams the door.

He sits down and laughs a moment, but it is a hollow kind of laughter, trying to talk himself out of how shaken he feels. It doesn't work. That day and in those that follow, he drinks less and less tea, more and more whiskey.

At first, he thinks he has mice. The scratching is soft. At times, it's more of a feeling than a sound. Impossible to pinpoint in space. But each day, there is more of it, growing louder, more insistent. No longer limited to his home, everywhere he goes he hears it. When he tells his mother, she looks at him like he's lost his mind.

"Maybe you should take a little break from the sauce," she says with a concerned smile.

"You're one to talk." And he's said the wrong thing, because her smile fades and she goes cold, and he wants only to be told he'll be ok, but she is closed to him now, if ever it were otherwise.

At the saloon, with his sometime girl, the scratching in the walls is so loud he can't finish the act.

"You need to do something about the mice in this place. It's filthy." She looks at him when he says this, and it's like how Mabel looked at him, only with a greater measure of pity.

At home, he can't drink himself to sleep because the scratching only gets louder the drunker he gets. The next morning, his skin starts to itch, and he can hear the same scratching coming from just below the surface. He digs his nails into his arms with no relief. He pours a hot bath -so hot it pinks his skin- and still he itches.

The next day he visits the doctor. The man examines him. Offers him a sedative. He storms out.

That night, he can feel things crawling around inside him. In his guts, under his scalp. Tickling his eyeballs like a stray lash.

Strange thoughts. Alien. His ideas seem crazy even to him, like maybe something is crawling and scratching inside his skull now. By the time he is standing by the creek, having doused himself in kerosene -match in hand- it is the most obvious thing in the world. Just burn until the itching and the crawling stops, then fall into the creek. It doesn't stop. He doesn't make it to the creek.

Flowers for Hair was never seen again, but a woman with a fondness for wildflower garlands worn like a tiara was known to live among the rail workers in San Diego for a time. She spoke their language awkwardly at first, but soon developed a fair mastery of it, and ran a successful apothecary, making remedies from local plants and sharing stories of the wild places that once were. It is said she later made her way to San Francisco, where people from all walks of life, some traveling great distances, sought her counsel and her cures. She took many lovers, but none could cleave the stony center of her.

None who shared her company spoke ill of it. Most would not speak of it at all. For they saw in her eyes the pinpoint lights of distant stars, her pupils the great void that is fit to bust with its potential energy – likened to the birthplace of the universe itself. Her words were whispered prayers of ineffable promise, of that greater other of which we are all but a piece, and that someday we might all be home together, again.

No, most of those who shared moments with her knew that they had but touched the edge of some language beyond their ken, and the more beautiful for it, and they knew their tongues could not find words to describe it to them who were not similarly moved. They scarcely understood it themselves

After the great earthquake of 1906, she sold her shop and set out for the Great Plains. Those who remember her at the time say she had a shadow of guilt about her, like a great weight hung from her neck. Like she fancied the quake was her fault. When asked why she would abandon her life, at her age, to head out to such an inhospitable place, she said simply, "I dreamed that the land might sleep, but it is yet restless, and it never forgets."

49

THE DRAW

There will be no final battle, no showdown. The imagination of these creatures is impoverished. Them that finally sense its presence rarely do so when they have enough meat on their bones to be worthy to see it.

Its way is the winnowing way, the shedding of the chaff until all that is left is the pure grain of man, which is meanness and fear, the things that keep them forever alone.

Every compromise, every bit of noble pretension it strips from them, makes the next that much easier. Until, like the boy, there is nothing left to compromise, only a hollow shell. Its fangs invisible, not a mark where it drained from each of them their marrow.

It finds pleasure in leaving them here, at the edge of the world, staring at the open sea whose empty promise to wash away their sins is but one final sting. The boy will watch the tide come in, the tide roll out, and like a forgotten dream -an itching sense of absence- he will scrape and claw at what he could give up to buy back that lost thing, how he might atone. Its final gift to him, its final meal, that he no longer has the means to understand that his only hope for liberation is in surrender.

50

BENJAMIN

"You were dreaming again."

"I'm always dreaming. I told you not to wake me." Henry was blonde and beautiful in the early morning light, his muscle something real, something to hold onto. The cleft of his chin reminded Benjamin of something lost.

"You were kicking me, you beast," and Henry pulled the covers from him, dragged them from the bed as he walked to the bathroom.

"You're lucky you're so beautiful."

"You can talk to me, you know. Like, really talk to me about real stuff." Henry yelled above his pattering stream.

He was too pure, not in the way of the things they did together. Benjamin smiled a little. Nothing pure about that. No, Henry had the quality of the sand below. Bleached and washed clean. He had been born here, didn't claw through the muck to reach California, didn't have the regret, the ghosts that haunted the prairies and the old places.

He wished there were a way to extract it, or he had the courage to make a home for himself there. Instead, he could only borrow a little warmth and pretend – for minutes, for hours.

316

Henry tossed the blanket at him, sat on the edge of the bed, still glistening with a sheen of sweat. Innocent, yes, in a way Benjamin was sure he had never been.

Taking his hand – the bad one – and capturing his eyes with his own limpid blues, holding him there. Benjamin tried to pull away, but Henry was strong, held fast.

"Why don't you tell me about this, for a start?" And he squeezed Benjamin's hand.

"Because it's ugly, as I am ugly."

"You're scarred. I love your scars." And he held Benjamin's hand to his lips; breathed his warmth on it; took the ache away, if only for a moment.

Benjamin, the desiccated thing inside him that was Cecil, wanted to believe in the magic of that.

"It's the end of a long story. I don't know if I believe the story myself anymore."

"Maybe you can figure it out in the telling of it."

But he knew he could not. The reckoning of it was as much a phantom as his aching fingertips.

ACKNOWLEDGMENTS

This book is for Geronimo, Crazy Horse, and the countless others who have demonstrated and continue to demonstrate unimaginable courage in the face of empire. We live in dark times. May we never forget the power of saying no.

Thanks to my wife Amy for her unwavering love and support. Thanks to Sabrina and Sunny for all the walks.

Thanks to Kerry St. Laurent for another great cover and for investing the time and energy to get to know me and my words, and making Flowers for Hair come to life.

Thanks to Jerad Shealey for the interior art, for his generosity, and being one of the best humans I know.

Thanks also to Toby Gehrlich and Andrew Tresler for interior art. You guys are awesome.

Thanks to Mae Murray for your care and attention as a sensitivity reader.

Thanks to Barbara Castro-Rojas for being the most brilliant beta reader I could ever hope for, your friendship means the world to me.

Thanks to the Void Crew for the feedback and just for being a rad family.

Thanks to Joe Koch for being the closest thing to a mentor I've ever had. Wound of the West would not exist if not for you.

Thanks to L.A. Witch, John Garcia/Hermano, Mazzy Star, Dark Watcher, Orville Peck, and Grails for the music.

Thanks to Castaigne for continuing to believe in my work.

Thanks to Jodi Byrd, Roxanne Dunbar-Ortiz, Gloria Anzaldua, and Kimberly B. George for their scholarship and insight.

Thank you, reader, for your time and attention. I hope the work was worthy of it.

ABOUT THE AUTHOR

Michael Tichy is the author of Behind Every Tree, Beneath Every Rock and Wound of the West (Castaigne). His stories have appeared in the anthologies Shredded, Into the Crypts of Rays, and Shiver. This is his first novel.

www.ingramcontent.com/pod-product-compliance
Lightning Source LLC
Chambersburg PA
CBHW021802130726
47987CB00008B/2977